A MAN COULD STAND UP —

Surrounded by the jubilation of Armistice Day, Valentine Wannop receives a telephone call which brings alarming news of her dear friend Christopher Tietjens. For whilst she strains to hear against the racket of celebratory firecrackers, Christopher's mind still echoes with the bombardments and horrors he endured in the hell of the Front. With trepidation, harbouring deep concerns over his mental equilibrium, the pacifist Valentine must seek out Christopher once more — but what will come of their reunion?

Books by Ford Madox Ford
Published by The House of Ulverscroft:

SOME DO NOT . . .
(*Parade's End* Part 1)

NO MORE PARADES —
(*Parade's End* Part 2)

THE LAST POST
(*Parade's End* Part 4)

FORD MADOX FORD

A MAN COULD STAND UP —

PARADE'S END PART 3

Complete and Unabridged

ULVERSCROFT
Leicester

First published in Great Britain in 1926

This Large Print Edition
published 2013

A catalogue record for this book is available
from the British Library

ISBN 978–1–4448–1677–8

Published by
F. A. Thorpe (Publishing)
Anstey, Leicestershire

Set by Words & Graphics Ltd.
Anstey, Leicestershire
Printed and bound in Great Britain by
T. J. International Ltd., Padstow, Cornwall

This book is printed on acid-free paper

Part One

1

Slowly, amidst intolerable noises from, on the one hand the street and, on the other, from the large and voluminously echoing playground, the depths of the telephone began, for Valentine, to assume an aspect that, years ago it had used to have — of being a part of the supernatural paraphernalia of inscrutable Destiny.

The telephone, for some ingeniously torturing reason, was in a corner of the great schoolroom without any protection and, called imperatively, at a moment of considerable suspense, out of the asphalt playground where, under her command ranks of girls had stood electrically only just within the margin of control, Valentine with the receiver at her ear was plunged immediately into incomprehensible news uttered by a voice that she seemed half to remember. Right in the middle of a sentence it hit her:

'. . . . that he ought presumably to be under control, which you mightn't like!'; after that the noise burst out again and rendered the voice inaudible.

It occurred to her that probably at that

3

minute the whole population of the world needed to be under control; she knew she herself did. But she had no male relative that the verdict could apply to in especial. Her brother? But he was on a mine-sweeper. In dock at the moment. And now . . . safe for good! There was also an aged great-uncle that she had never seen. Dean of somewhere . . . Hereford? Exeter? . . . Somewhere . . . Had she just said *safe? She* was shaken with joy!

She said into the mouthpiece:

'Valentine Wannop speaking . . . Physical Instructress at this school, you know!'

She had to present an appearance of sanity . . . a sane voice at the very least!

The tantalisingly half-remembered voice in the telephone now got in some more incomprehensibilities. It came as if from caverns and as if with exasperated rapidity it exaggerated its 's's with an effect of spitting vehemence.

'His brothers.s.s got pneumonia, so his mistress.ss.ss even is unavailable to look after . . .'

The voice disappeared; then it emerged again with:

'They're said to be friends now!'

It was drowned then, for a long period in a sea of shrill girls' voices from the playground, in an ocean of factory-hooter's ululations,

4

amongst innumerable explosions that trod upon one another's heels. From where on earth did they get explosives, the population of squalid suburban streets amidst which the school lay? For the matter of that where did they get the spirits to make such an appalling row? Pretty drab people! Inhabiting liver-coloured boxes. Not on the face of it an imperial race.

The sibillating voice in the telephone went on spitting out spitefully that the porter said he had no furniture at all; that he did not appear to recognise the porter ... Improbable-sounding pieces of information half-extinguished by the external sounds, but uttered in a voice that seemed to mean to give pain by what it said.

Nevertheless it was impossible not to take it gaily. The thing, out there, miles and miles away must have been signed — a few minutes ago. She imagined along an immense line sullen and disgruntled cannon sounding for a last time.

'I haven't,' Valentine Wannop shouted into the mouthpiece, 'the least idea of what you want or who you are.'

She got back a title ... Lady someone or other ... It might have been Blastus. She imagined that one of the lady governoresses of the school must be wanting to order something in the way of school sports organised to celebrate the auspicious day. A lady governoress or other was always wanting something done by the School to celebrate something. No doubt the Head who was not wanting in a sense of humour — not *absolutely* wanting! — had turned this lady of title onto Valentine Wannop after having listened with patience to her for half an hour. The Head had certainly sent out to where in the playground they all had stood breathless, to tell Valentine Wannop that there was someone on the telephone that she — Miss Wanostrocht, the said Head — thought that she, Miss Wannop, ought to listen to . . . Then: Miss Wanostrocht must have been able to distinguish what had been said by the now indistinguishable lady of title. But of course that had been ten minutes ago . . . Before the maroons or the sirens, whichever it had been, had sounded . . . 'The porter said he had no furniture at all . . . He did not appear to recognise the porter . . . Ought presumably to be under control!' Valentine's mind thus recapitulated the information that she had from Lady (provisionally) Blastus. She imagined now that the Lady must be concerned for the superannuated drill-sergeant the school had had before it had acquired her, Valentine, as physical instructor.

She figured to herself the venerable, mumbling gentleman, with several ribbons on a black commissionaire's tunic. In an alm-house, probably. Placed there by the Governors of the school. Had pawned his furniture no doubt . . .

Intense heat possessed Valentine Wannop. She imagined indeed her eyes flashing. Was this the moment?

She didn't even know whether what they had let off had been maroons or aircraft guns or sirens. It had happened — the noise, whatever it was — whilst she had been coming through the underground passage from the playground to the schoolroom to answer this wicked telephone. So she had not heard the sound. She had missed the sound for which the ears of a world had waited for years, for a generation. For an eternity. No sound. When she had left the playground there had been dead silence. All waiting: girls rubbing one ankle with the other rubber sole . . .

Then . . . For the rest of her life she was never to be able to remember the greatest stab of joy that had ever been known by waiting millions. There would be no one but she who would not be able to remember that . . . Probably a stirring of the heart that was like a stab; probably a catching of the breath that was like the inhalation of flame! It was over now; they were by now in a situation; a condition, something that would affect certain things in certain ways . . .

She remembered that the putative ex-drill sergeant had a brother who had pneumonia and thus an unavailable mistress . . .

She was about to say to herself:

'That's just my luck!' When she remembered good-humouredly that her luck was not like that at all. On the whole she had had good luck — ups and downs. A good deal of anxiety at one time — but who hadn't had! But good health; a mother with good health; a brother safe . . . Anxieties, yes! But nothing that had gone so very wrong . . .

This then was an exceptional stroke of bad luck! Might it be an omen — to the effect that things in future *would* go wrong: to the effect that she would miss other universal experiences. Never marry, say; or never know the joy of childbearing, if it was a joy! Perhaps it was; perhaps it wasn't. One said one thing, one another. At any rate might it not be an omen that she would miss some universal and necessary experience! . . . Never see Carcassonne, the French said . . . Perhaps she would never see the Mediterranean. You could not be a proper man if you had never seen the Mediterranean; the sea of Tibullus, of the Anthologists, of Sappho, even . . . Blue: incredibly blue!

People would be able to travel now. It was incredible! Incredible! Incredible! But you *could*. Next week you would be able to! You could call a taxi! And go to Charing Cross! And have a porter! A whole porter! . . . The wings, the wings of a dove; then would I flee away, flee away and eat pomegranates beside an infinite washtub of Reckitt's blue. Incredible, but you *could*!

She felt eighteen again. Cocky! She said, using the good, metallic. Cockney bottoms of her lungs that she had used for shouting back at interrupters at Suffrage meetings before . . . before this . . . she shouted blatantly into the telephone:

'I say, whoever you are! I suppose they have *done* it; did they announce it in your parts by maroons or sirens?' She repeated it three times, she did not care for Lady Blastus or Lady Blast Anybody else. She was going to leave that old school and eat pomegranates in the shadow of the rock where Penelope, wife of Ulysses, did her washing. With lashings of blue in the water! Was all your underlinen bluish in those parts owing to the colour of the sea? She could! She could! She *could*! Go with her mother and brother and all to where you could eat . . . Oh, new potatoes! In

December, the sea being blue . . . *What songs the sirens sang and whether . . .*

She was not going to show respect for any Lady anything ever again. She had had to hitherto, independent young woman of means though she were, so as not to damage the school and Miss Wanostrocht with the Governoresses. Now . . . She was never going to show respect for anyone ever again. She had been through the mill: the whole world had been through the mill! No more respect!

As she might have expected she got it in the neck immediately afterwards — for overcockiness!

The hissing, bitter voice from the telephone enunciated the one address she did not want to hear:

'Lincolnss.s.s . . . Inn!'

Sin! . . . Like the Devil!

It hurt.

The cruel voice said:

'I'm s.s.peaking from there!'

Valentine said courageously:

'Well; it's a great day. I suppose you're bothered by the cheering like me. I can't hear what you want. I don't care. Let 'em cheer!'

She felt like that. She should not have.

The voice said:

'You remember your Carlyle . . . '

It was exactly what she did not want to

10

hear. With the receiver hard at her ear she looked round at the great schoolroom — the Hall, made to let a thousand girls sit silent while the Head made the speeches that were the note of the school. Repressive! . . . The place was like a nonconformist chapel, high, bare walls with Gothic windows running up to a pitch-pine varnished roof. Repression, the note of the place; the place, the very place not to be in to-day . . . You *ought* to be in the streets, hitting policemen's helmets with bladders. This was Cockney London: that was how Cockney London expressed itself. Hit policeman innocuously because policemen were stiff, embarrassed at these tributes of affection, swayed in rejoicing mobs over whose heads they looked remotely, like poplar trees jostled by vulgarer vegetables!

But she was there, being reminded of the dyspepsia of Thomas Carlyle!

'*Oh!*' she exclaimed into the instrument, 'You're Edith Ethel!' Edith Ethel Duchemin, now of course Lady Macmaster! But you weren't used to thinking of her as Lady Somebody.

The last person in the world, the very last! Because, long ago she had made up her mind that it was all over between herself and Edith Ethel. She certainly could not make any advance to the ennobled personage who

11

vindictively disapproved of all things made — with a black thought in a black shade, as you might say. Of all things that were not being immediately useful to Edith Ethel!

And, æsthetically draped and meagre, she had sets of quotations for appropriate occasions. Rossetti for Love; Browning for optimism — not frequent that; Walter Savage Landor to show acquaintance with more esoteric prose. And the unfailing quotation from Carlyle for damping off saturnalia: for New Year's Day, Te Deums, Victories, anniversaries, celebrations . . . It was coming over the wire now, that quotation:

' . . . And then I remembered that it was the birthday of their Redeemer!'

How well Valentine knew it: how often with spiteful conceit had not Edith Ethel intoned that. A passage from the diary of the Sage of Chelsea who lived near the Barracks.

'To-day,' the quotation ran, 'I saw that the soldiers by the public house at the corner were more than usually drunk. And then I remembered that it was the birthday of their Redeemer!'

How superior of the Sage of Chelsea not to remember till then that that had been Christmas Day! Edith Ethel, too, was trying to show how superior she was. She wanted to prove that until she, Valentine Wannop, had

12

reminded her, Lady Macmaster, that that day had about it something of the popularly festival she, Lady Mac, had been unaware of the fact. Really quite unaware, you know. She lived in her rapt seclusion along with Sir Vincent — the critic, you know; their eyes fixed on the higher things, they disregarded maroons and had really a quite remarkable collection, by now, of first editions, official-titled friends and At Homes to their credit.

Yet Valentine remembered that once she had sat at the feet of the darkly mysterious Edith Ethel Duchemin — where had *that* all gone? — and had sympathised with her marital martyrdoms, her impressive taste in furniture, her large rooms, and her spiritual adulteries. So she said good-humouredly to the instrument:

'Aren't you just the same, Edith Ethel? And what can I do for you?'

The good-natured patronage in her tone astonished her, and she was astonished, too, at the ease with which she spoke. Then she realised that the noises had been going away, silence was falling, the cries receded. They were going towards a cumulation at a distance. The girls' voices in the playground no longer existed: the Head must have let them go. Naturally, too, the local population wasn't going to go on letting off crackers in

13

side streets . . . She was alone, cloistered with the utterly improbable!

Lady Macmaster had sought her out and here was she, Valentine Wannop, patronising Lady Macmaster! Why? What could Lady Macmaster want her to do? She *couldn't* — but of course she jolly well could! — be thinking of being unfaithful to Macmaster and be wanting her, Valentine Wannop, to play the innocent, the virginal gooseberry or Disciple. Or alibi. Whatever it was. Goose was the most appropriate word . . . Obviously Macmaster was the sort of person to whom any Lady Macmaster would want — would have — to be unfaithful. A little, dark-bearded, drooping, deprecatory fellow. A typical Critic! All Critics' wives were probably unfaithful to them. They lacked the creative gift. What did you call it? A word unfit for a young lady to use!

Her mind ran about in this unbridled Cockney school-girl's vein. There was no stopping it. It was in honour of the DAY! She was temporarily inhibited from bashing policemen on the head, so she was mentally disrespectful to constituted authority — to Sir Vincent Macmaster, Principal Secretary to H.M. Department of Statistics, author of Walter Savage Landor, a Critical Monograph, and of twenty-two other Critical Monographs

14

in the Eminent Bores' Series ... *Such* books! And she was being disrespectful and patronising to Lady Macmaster, Egeria to innumerable Scottish Men of Letters! No more respect! Was that to be a lasting effect of the cataclysm that had involved the world? The *late* cataclysm! Thank God, since ten minutes ago they could call it the late cataclysm!

She was positively tittering in front of the telephone from which Lady Macmaster's voice was now coming in earnest, cajoling tones — as if she knew that Valentine was not paying very much attention, saying:

'Valentine! Valentine! *Valentine!*'

Valentine said negligently:

'I'm listening!'

She wasn't really. She was really reflecting on whether there had not been more sense in the Mistress's Conference that that morning, solemnly, had taken place in the Head's private room. Undoubtedly what the Mistresses with the Head at their head had feared was that if they, Headmistresses, Mistresses, Masters, Pastors — by whom I was made etcetera! — should cease to be respected because saturnalia broke out on the sounding of a maroon the world would go to pieces! An awful thought! The Girls no longer sitting silent in the nonconformist hall while the

Head addressed repressive speeches to them . . .

She had addressed a speech, containing the phrase: 'the credit of a Great Public School,' in that Hall only last afternoon in which, fair, thin woman, square-elbowed, with a little of sunlight really still in her coiled fair hair, she had seriously requested the Girls not again to repeat the manifestations of joy of the day before. The day before there had been a false alarm and the School — horribly — had sung:

'Hang Kaiser Bill from the hoar apple tree
And Glory, Glory, Glory till it's tea-time!'

The Head, now, making her speech was certain that she had now before her a chastened School, a School that anyhow felt foolish because the rumour of the day before had turned out to be a canard. So she impressed on the Girls the nature of the joy they ought to feel, a joy repressed that should send them silent home. Blood was to cease to be shed: a fitting cause for home-joy — as it were a home-lesson. But there was to be no triumph. The very fact that you had ceased hostilities precluded triumph . . .

Valentine, to her surprise, had found herself wondering when you *might* feel

16

triumph? . . . You couldn't whilst you were still contending; you must not when you had won! Then when? The Head told the girls that it was their province as the future mothers of England — nay, of reunited Europe! — to — well, in fact, to go on with their home-lessons and not run about the streets with effigies of the Great Defeated! She put it that it was their function to shed further light of womanly culture — that there, Thank Heaven, they had never been allowed to forget! — athwart a re-illumined Continent . . . As if you could light up now there was no fear of submarines or raids!

And Valentine wondered why, for a mutinous moment, she had wanted to feel triumph . . . had wanted *someone* to feel triumph. Well, he . . . they . . . had wanted it so much. Couldn't they have it just for a moment — for the space of one Benkollerdy! Even if it were wrong? or vulgar? something human, someone had once said is dearer than a wilderness of decalogues!

But at the Mistress's Conference that morning Valentine had realised that what was really frightening them was the other note. A quite definite fear. If, at this parting of the ways, at this crack across the table of History, the School — the World, the future mothers of Europe — got out of hand, would they ever come back? The Authorities — Authority all over the world — was afraid of that; more afraid of that than of any other thing. Wasn't it a possibility that there was to be no more Respect? None for constituted Authority and consecrated Experience?

And, listening to the fears of those careworn, faded, ill-nourished gentlewomen, Valentine Wannop had found herself speculating.

'No more respect . . . For the Equator! For the Metric system. For Sir Walter Scott! Or George Washington! Or Abraham Lincoln! Or the Seventh Commandment!'

And she had a blushing vision of fair, shy, square-elbowed Miss Wanostrocht — the head! — succumbing to some specious-tongued beguiler! . . . That was where the shoe really pinched! You had to keep them — the Girls, the Populace, everybody! — in hand now, for once you let go there was no knowing where They, like waters parted from the seas, mightn't carry You. Goodness knew! You might arrive anywhere — at county families taking to trade; gentlefolk selling for profit! All the unthinkable sorts of things!

And with a little inward smirk of pleasure Valentine realised that that Conference was deciding that the Girls were to be kept in the playground that morning — at Physical Jerks.

She hadn't ever put up with *much* in the way of patronage from the rather untidy-haired bookish branch of the establishment. Still, accomplished Classicist as she once had been, she had had to acknowledge that the bookish branch of a School was what you might call the Senior Service. She was there only to oblige — because her distinguished father had insisted on paying minute attention to her physique which was vital and admirable. She had been there, for some time past only to oblige — War Work and all that — but still she had always kept her place and had never hitherto raised her voice at a Mistress's Conference. So it was indeed the World Turned Upside Down — already! — when Miss Wanostrocht hopefully from behind her desk decorated with two pale pink carnations said:

'The idea is, Miss Wannop, that They should be kept — that you should keep them, please — as nearly as possible — isn't it called? — at attention until the — eh — noises . . . announce the . . . well, *you* know. Then we suppose they will have to give, say, three cheers. And then perhaps you could get them — in an orderly way — back to their classrooms . . . '

Valentine felt that she was by no means certain that she *could*. It was not really practicable to keep every one of six hundred aligned girls under your eye. Still she was ready to have a shot. She was ready to concede that it might not be altogether — oh, expedient! — to turn six hundred girls stark mad with excitement into the streets already filled with populations that would no doubt be also stark mad with excitement. You had better keep them in if you could. She would have a shot. And she was pleased. She felt fit: amazingly fit! Fit to do the quarter in . . . oh, in any time? And to give a clump on the jaw to any large, troublesome Jewish type of maiden — or Anglo-Teutonic — who should try to break ranks. Which was more than the Head or any one of the other worried and underfed ones could do. She was pleased that they recognised it. Still she was also generous and recognising that the world ought not really to be turned upside down at any rate until the maroons went, she said:

'Of course I will have a shot at it. But it would be a reinforcement, in the way of keeping order, if the Head — you Miss Wanostrocht — and one or two others of the Mistresses would be strolling about. In relays, of course; not all of the staff all the morning . . .'

That had been two and a half hours or so ago: before the world changed, the Conference having taken place at eight-thirty. Now here she was, after having kept those girls pretty exhaustingly jumping about for most of the intervening time — here she was treating with disrespect obviously constituted Authority. For whom *ought* you to respect if not the wife of the Head of a Department, with a title, a country place, and most highly attended Thursday afternoons?

She was not really listening to the telephone because Edith Ethel was telling her about the condition of Sir Vincent: so overworked, poor man, over Statistics that a nervous breakdown was imminently to be expected. Worried over money, too. Those dreadful taxes for this iniquitous affair . . .

Valentine took leisure to wonder why — why in the world! — Miss Wanostrocht who must know at the least the burden of Edith Ethel's story had sent for her to hear this farrago? Miss Wanostrocht must know: she had obviously been talked to by Edith Ethel for long enough to form a judgment. Then the matter must be of importance. Urgent even, since the keeping of discipline in the playground was of such utter importance to Miss Wanostrocht; a crucial point in the history of the School and the mothers of Europe.

But to whom, then, could Lady Macmaster's communication be of life and death importance? To her, Valentine Wannop? It could not be: there were no events of importance that could affect her life outside the playground, her mother safe at home and her brother safe on a mine-sweeper in Pembroke Dock . . .

Then . . . of importance to Lady Macmaster herself? But how? What could she do for Lady Macmaster? Was she wanted to teach Sir Vincent to perform physical exercises so that he might avoid his nervous breakdown and, in excess of physical health, get the mortgage taken off his country place which she gathered was proving an overwhelming burden on account of iniquitous taxes the result of a war that ought never to have been waged?

It was absurd to think that she could be wanted for that? An absurd business . . . There she was, bursting with health, strength, good-humour, perfectly *full* of beans — there she was, ready in the cause of order to give Leah Heldenstamm, the large girl, no end of a clump on the side of the jaw or, alternatively, for the sake of all the beanfeast-ishnesses in the world to assist in the amiable discomfiture of the police. There she was in a sort of nonconformist cloister. Nunlike! Positively nunlike! At the parting of the ways of the universe!

She whistled slightly to herself.

'By Jove,' she exclaimed coolly, 'I hope it does not mean an omen that I'm to be — oh, nunlike — for the rest of my career in the reconstructed world!'

She began for a moment seriously to take stock of her position — of her whole position in life. It had certainly been hitherto rather nunlike. She was twenty-threeish, rising twenty-four. As fit as a fiddle; as clean as a whistle. Five foot in her gym shoes. And no one had ever wanted to marry her. No doubt that was because she was so clean and fit. No one even had ever tried to seduce her. That was *certainly* because she was so clean-run. She didn't obviously offer — what was it the fellow called it? — promise of pneumatic bliss to the gentlemen with sergeant-majors' horse-shoe moustaches and gurglish voices! She never would. Then perhaps she would never marry. And never be seduced!

Nunlike! She would have to stand at an attitude of attention besides a telephone all her life; in an empty schoolroom with the world shouting from the playground. Or not even shouting from the playground any more. Gone to Piccadilly!

But, hang it all, she wanted some fun! Now!

For years now she had been — oh, yes, nunlike! — looking after the lungs and limbs of the girls of the adenoidy, nonconformitish — really undenominational or so little Established as made no difference! — Great Public Girl's School. She had had to worry about impossible but not repulsive little Cockney creatures' breathing when they had their arms extended . . . You *mustn't* breathe rhythmically with your movements. No. No. No! . . . *Don't* breathe out with the first movement and in with the second! Breathe naturally! Look at me! . . . She breathed perfectly!

Well, for years, that! War-work for a b—y Pro-German. Or Pacifist. Yes, that too she had been for years. She hadn't liked being it because it was the attitude of the superior and she did not like being superior. Like Edith Ethel!

But now! Wasn't it manifest? She could put her hand whole-heartedly into the hand of any Tom, Dick or Harry. And wish him luck! Whole-heartedly! Luck for himself and for his enterprise. She came back, into the fold, into the Nation even. She could open her mouth! She could let out the good little Cockney yelps that were her birthright. She could be free, independent!

Even her dear, blessed, muddle-headed, tremendously eminent mother by now had a depressed-looking Secretary. She, Valentine Wannop, didn't have to sit up all night typing after all day enjoining perfection of breathing in the playground . . . By Jove they could go all, brother, mother in untidy black and mauve, secretary in untidy black without mauve, and she, Valentine, out of her imitation Girl Scout's uniform and in — oh, white muslin or Harris tweeds — and with Cockney yawps discuss the cooking under the stone-pines of Amalfi. By the Mediterranean . . . No one, then, would be able to say that she had never seen the sea of Penelope, the Mother of the Gracchi, Delia, Lesbia, Nausicaä, Sappho . . .

'*Saepe te in somnis vidi!*'

She said:

'Good . . . God!'

Not in the least with a Cockney intonation but like a good Tory English gentleman confronted by an unspeakable proposition. Well, it was an unspeakable proposition. For the voice from the telephone had been saying to her inattention, rather crawlingly, after no end of details as to the financial position of the house of Macmaster:

'So I thought, my dear Val, in remembrance

25

of old times, that . . . If in short I were the means of bringing you together again . . . For I believe you have not been corresponding . . . You might in return . . . You can see for yourself that at this moment the sum would be absolutely *crushing* . . . '

2

Ten minutes later she was putting to Miss Wanostrocht, firmly if without ferocity, the question:

'Look here, Head, what did that woman say to you. I don't like her; I don't approve of her and I didn't really listen to her. But I want to hear!'

Miss Wanostrocht, who had been taking her thin, black cloth coat from its peg behind the highly varnished pitch-pine door of her own private cell, flushed, hung up her garment again and turned from the door. She stood, thin, a little rigid, a little flushed, faded, and a little as it were at bay.

'You must remember,' she began, 'that I am a schoolmistress.' She pressed, with a gesture she constantly had, the noticeably golden plait of her dun-coloured hair with the palm of her thin left hand. None of the gentlewomen of that school had had quite enough to eat — for years now. 'It's,' she continued, 'an instinct to accept any means of knowledge. I like you so much, Valentine — if in private you'll let me call you that.

27

And it seemed to me that if you were in . . . '

'In what?' Valentine asked, 'Danger? . . . Trouble?'

'You understand,' Miss Wanostrocht replied, 'That . . . person seemed as anxious to communicate to me facts about yourself as to give you — that was her ostensible reason for ringing you up — news about a . . . another person. With whom you once had . . . relations. And who has reappeared.'

'Ah,' Valentine heard herself exclaim. 'He has reappeared, has he? I gathered as much.' She was glad to be able to keep herself under control to that extent.

Perhaps she did not have to trouble. She could not say that she felt changed from what she had been — just before ten minutes ago, by the reappearance of a man she hoped she had put out of her mind. A man who had 'insulted' her. In one way or the other he had insulted her!

But probably all her circumstances had changed. Before Edith Ethel had uttered her impossible sentence in that instrument her complete prospects had consisted of no more than the family picnic, under fig-trees, beside an unusually blue sea — and the prospect had seemed as near — as near as kiss your finger! Mother in black and purple; mother's secretary in black without adornments. Brother? Oh, a romantic figure; slight, muscular, in white flannels with a Leghorn hat and — well, why *not* be romantic over one's brother — with a broad scarlet sash. One foot on shore and one . . . in a light skiff that gently bobbed in the lapping tide. Nice boy; nice little brother. Lately employed nautically, so up to managing a light skiff. They were going tomorrow . . . but why not that very afternoon by the 4.20?

'They'd got the ships, they'd got the men,
They'd got the money too!'

Thank goodness they'd got the money!
The ships, Charing Cross to Vallambrosa, would no doubt run in a fortnight. The men — the porters — would also be released. You can't travel in any comfort with mother, mother's secretary, and brother — with your whole world and its baggage — without lots of porters . . . Talk about rationed butter! What was that to trying to get on without porters?
Once having begun it her mind went on singing the old eighteen-fiftyish, or seventyish, martial, British, and anti-Russian patriotic song that one of her little friends had unearthed lately — to prove the historic ferocity of his countrymen:

29

'We've fought the Bear before,
And so we will again!
The Russians shall not have Constan-
    tino . . .'

She exclaimed suddenly: '*Oh!*'

She had been about to say: 'Oh, *Hell!*' but the sudden recollection that the War had been over a quarter of an hour made her leave it at '*Oh!*' You would have to drop war-time phraseology! You became again a Young Lady. Peace, too, has its Defence of the Realm Acts. Nevertheless, she had been thinking of the man who had once insulted her as the Bear, whom she would have to fight again! But with warm generosity she said:

'It's a shame to call him the Bear!' Nevertheless he was — the man who was said to have 'reappeared' — with his problems and all, something devouring . . . Overwhelming, with rolling grey shoulders that with their intolerable problems pushed you and your own problems out of the road . . .

She had been thinking all that whilst still in the School Hall, before she had gone to see the Head, immediately after Edith Ethel, Lady Macmaster had uttered the *intolerable* sentence.

She had gone on thinking there for a long time . . . Ten minutes!

She formulated for herself summarily the first item of a period of nasty worries of a time she flattered herself she had nearly forgotten. Years ago, Edith Ethel, out of a clear sky, had accused her of having had a child by that man. But she hardly thought of him as a man. She thought of him as a ponderous, grey, intellectual mass who now, presumably, was mooning, obviously dotty, since he did not recognise the porter, behind the closed shutters of an empty house in Lincoln's Inn ... Nothing less, I assure you! She had never been in that house, but she figured him, with cracks of light coming between the shutters, looking back over his shoulder at you in the doorway, grey, super-ursine ... Ready to envelop you in suffocating bothers!

She wondered how long it had been since the egregious Edith Ethel had made that assertion ... with, naturally, every appearance of indignation for the sake of the man's Wife with whom, equally naturally, Edith Ethel had 'sided.' (Now she was trying to 'bring you together again.' ... The Wife, presumably, did not go to Edith Ethel's tea-parties often enough, or was too brilliantly conspicuous when there. Probably the latter!). How many years ago? Two? Not so much! Eighteen months, then?

Surely more! ... surely, surely more! ... When you thought of Time in those days your mind wavered impotently like eyes tired by reading too small print ... He went out surely in the autumn of ... No, it had been the first time he went that he went in the autumn. It was her brother's friend, Ted, that went in '16. Or the other ... Malachi. So many going out and returning, and going out and perhaps not returning. Or only bits: the nose gone ... or both eyes. Or — or Hell! oh, Hell! and she clenched her fists, her nails into her palms — no mind!

You'd think it must be that from what Edith Ethel had said. He hadn't recognised the porter; he was reported to have no furniture. Then ... She remembered ...

She was then — ten minutes before she interviewed Miss Wanostrocht, ten seconds after she had been blown out of the mouth of the telephone — sitting on a varnished pitch-pine bench that had black iron, clamped legs against the plaster wall, nonconformish-istically distempered in torpedo-grey; and she had thought all that in ten seconds ... But that had been *really* how it had been!

The minute Edith Ethel had finished saying the words:

'The sum would be absolutely *crushing* . . . .' Valentine had realised that she had been talking about a debt owed by her miserable husband to the one human being she, Valentine, could not bear to think about. It had naturally at the same moment flashed upon her that Edith Ethel had been giving her his news: He was in new troubles; broken down, broken up, broke to the wide . . . Anything in the world but broken in . . . But broken . . . And alone. And calling for her!

She could not afford — she could not bear! — to recall even his name or to so much as bring up before her mind, into which, nevertheless, they were continually forcing themselves, his grey-blond face, his clumsy, square, reliable feet; his humpish bulk; his calculatedly wooden expression; his perfectly overwhelming, but authentic omniscience . . . His masculinity. His . . . his Frightfulness!

Now, through Edith Ethel — you would have thought that even *he* would have found someone more appropriate — he was calling to her again to enter into the suffocating web of his imbroglios. Not even Edith Ethel would have dared to speak to her again of him without his having taken the first step . . .

It was unthinkable; it was intolerable; and it had been as if she had been lifted off her feet and deposited on that bench against the wall by the mere sound of the offer . . . What was the offer?

'I thought that you might, if I were the means of bringing you together . . . ' She might . . . what?

Intercede with that man, that grey mass not to enforce the pecuniary claim that it had against Sir Vincent Macmaster. No doubt she and . . . the grey mass! . . . would then be allowed the Macmaster drawing-room to . . . to discuss the ethics of the day in! Just like that!

She was still breathless; the telephone continued to quack. She wished it would stop, but she felt too weak to get up and hang the receiver on its hook. She wished it would stop; it gave her the feeling that a strand of Edith Ethel's hair, say, was penetrating nauseously to her torpedo-grey cloister. Something like that!

The grey mass never would enforce its pecuniary claim . . . Those people had sponged mercilessly on him for years and years without ever knowing the kind of object upon which they sponged. It made them the more pitiful. For it *was* pitiful to clamour to be allowed to become a pimp in order to evade debts that would never be reclaimed . . .

Now, in the empty rooms at Lincoln's Inn

— for that was probably what it came to! — that man was a grey ball of mist! a grey bear rolling tenebrously about an empty room with closed shutters. A grey problem, calling to *her*!

A hell of a lot . . . Beg pardon, she meant a remarkably great deal! . . . to have thought of in ten minutes! Eleven, by now, probably. Later she realised that that was what thought was. In ten minutes after large, impressive arms had carried you away from a telephone and deposited you on a clamped bench against a wall of the peculiar coldness of torpedo-grey distempered plaster, the sort of thing rejoiced in by Great Public (Girls') Schools . . . in those ten minutes you found you thought out more than in two years. Or it was not as long ago as that.

Perhaps that was not astonishing. If you had not thought about, say, washable distemper for two years and then thought about it for ten minutes you could think a hell of a lot about it in those ten minutes. Probably all there was to think. Still, of course, washable distemper was not like the poor — always with you. At least it always was in those cloisters, but not spiritually. On the other hand you always *were* with yourself.

But perhaps you were not always with yourself spiritually; you went on explaining

how to breathe without thinking of how the
life you were leading was influencing your
. . . What? Immortal soul? Aura? Personality?
. . . Something!

Well, for two years . . . Oh, *call* it two
years, for goodness' sake, and get it over!
. . . she must have been in . . . well, call *that* a
'state of suspended animation' and get that
over too! A sort of what they called
inhibition. She had been inhibiting — *prohib-
iting* — herself from thinking about herself.
Well, hadn't she been right? What had a b—y
Pro-German to think about in an embattled,
engrossed, clamouring nation, especially
when she had not much liked her brother-
Pro's! A solitary state, only to be dissolved by
. . . maroons! In suspension!

But . . . Be conscientious with yourself, my
good girl! *When that telephone blew you out
of its mouth you knew really that for two
years you had been avoiding wondering
whether you had not been insulted!* Avoiding
wondering that. And nothing else! No other
qualified thing!

She had, of course, been, not in suspension,
but in suspense. Because, if he made a sign
— 'I understand,' Edith Ethel had said, 'that
you have not been in correspondence' . . . or
had it been 'in communication' that she had
said? . . . Well, they hadn't been either . . .

Anyhow, if that grey Problem, that ravelled ball of grey knitting worsted, had made a sign she would have known that she had not been insulted. Or was there any sense in that?

Was it really true that if a male and female of the same species were alone in a room together and the male didn't . . . then it was an insult? That was an idea that did not exist in a girl's head without someone to put it there, but once it had been put there it became a luminous veracity! It had been put into her, Valentine Wannop's head, naturally by Edith Ethel, who equally naturally said that she did not believe it, but that it was a tenet of . . . oh, the man's wife! Of the idle, surpassing-the-Lily-and-Solomon-too, surprisingly svelte, tall, clean-run creature who for ever on the shining paper of illustrated journals advanced towards you with improbable strides along the railings of the Row, laughing, in company with the Honourable Somebody, second son of Lord Some-one-or-other . . . Edith Ethel was more refined. She had a title, whereas the other hadn't, but she was pensive. She showed you that she had read Walter Savage Landor, and had only very lately given up wearing opaque amber beads, as affected by the later pre-Raphaelites. She was practically never in the illustrated papers, but she held more refined views. She held that there were some men who were not like that — and those, all of them, were the men to whom Edith Ethel accorded the *entrée* to her Afternoons. She was their Egeria! A refining influence!

The Husband of the Wife, then? Once he had been allowed in Edith Ethel's drawing-room: now he wasn't! . . . Must have deteriorated!

She said to herself sharply, in her 'No nonsense, there' mood:

'Chuck it. You're in love with a married man who's a Society wife and you're upset because the Titled Lady has put into your head the idea that you might 'come together again.' After ten years!'

But immediately she protested:

'No. NO. No! It isn't that. It's all right the habit of putting things incisively, but it's misleading to put things too crudely.'

What was the coming together that was offered her? Nothing, on the face of it, but being dragged again into that man's intolerable worries as unfortunate machinists are dragged into wheels by belts — and all the flesh torn off their bones! Upon her word that had been her first thought. She was afraid, afraid, afraid! She suddenly appreciated the advantages of nunlike seclusion. Besides she wanted to be bashing policemen with bladders in celebration of Eleven Eleven!

That fellow — he had no furniture; he did not appear to recognise the hall porter . . . Dotty. Dotty and too morally deteriorated to be admitted to drawing-room of titled lady, the frequenters of which could be trusted not to make love to you on insufficient provocation, if left alone with you . . .

Her generous mind reacted painfully.

'Oh, that's not *fair*!' she said.

There were all sorts of sides to the unfairness. Before this War, and, of course, before he had lent all his money to Vincent Macmaster that — that grey grizzly had been perfectly fit for the country-parsonage drawing-room of Edith Ethel Duchemin: he had been welcomed there with effusion! . . . After the War and when his money was — presumably — exhausted, and his mind exhausted, for he had no furniture and did not know the porter . . . After the War, then, and when his money was exhausted he was not fit for the Salon of Lady Macmaster — the only Lady to have a Salon in London.

It was what you called kicking down your ladder!

Obviously it had to be done. There were such a lot of these bothering War heroes that if you let them all into your Salon it would cease to be a Salon, particularly if you were under obligations to them! . . . That was already a pressing national problem; it was going to become an overwhelming one now — in twenty minutes' time; after those maroons. The impoverished War Heroes would all be coming back. Innumerable. You would have to tell your parlourmaid that you weren't at home to . . . about seven million!

But wait a minute . . . Where did they just stand?

He . . . But she could not go on calling him just 'he' like a school-girl of eighteen, thinking of her favourite actor . . . in the purity of her young thoughts. What was she to call him? She had never — even when they had known each other — called him anything other than Mr. So and So . . . She could not bring herself to let her mental lips frame his name . . . She had never used anything but his surname to this grey thing, familiar object of her mother's study, seen frequently at tea-parties . . . Once she had been out with it for a whole night in a dog cart! Think of that! . . . And they had spouted Tibullus one to another in moon-lit mist. And she had certainly wanted it to kiss her — in the moon-lit mists a practically, a really completely strange bear!

It couldn't be done, of course, but she

remembered still how she had shivered . . .
Ph . . . Ph . . . Ph . . . Shivering.

She shivered.

Afterwards they had been run into by the car of General Lord Edward Campion, V. C., P. G. Heaven knows what! Godfather of the man's Society Wife, then taking the waters in Germany . . . Or perhaps not *her* Godfather. The man's rather; but her especial champion, in shining armour. In these days they had worn broad red stripes down the outsides of their trousers, Generals. What a change! *How* significant of the times!

That had been in 1912 . . . Say the first of July; she could not remember exactly. Summer weather, anyhow, before haymaking or just about. The grass had been long in Hogg's Forty Acre, when they had walked through it, discussing Woman's Suffrage. She had brushed the seed-tops of the heavy grass with her hands as they walked . . . Say the 1/7/12.

Now it was Eleven Eleven . . . What? Oh, Eighteen, of course!

Six years ago! What changes in the world! What cataclysms! What Revolutions! . . . She heard all the newspapers, all the halfpenny paper journalists in creation crying in chorus!

But hang it, it was true! If, six years ago she had kissed the . . . the greyish lacuna of her

41

mind then sitting beside her on the dogcart
seat it would have been the larkish freak of a
school-girl; if she did it to-day — as per
invitation presumably of Lady Macmaster,
bringing them together, for, of course, it
could not be performed from a distance or
without correspondence — no, communication! . . . If, then, she did it to-day . . . to-day
. . . to-day — the Eleven Eleven! Oh, what a
day to-day would be . . . Not her sentiments
those; quotation from Christina, sister of Lady
Macmaster's favorite poet . . . Or, perhaps,
since she had had a title she would have
found poets more . . . more chic! The poet
who was killed at Gallipoli . . . Gerald Osborne,
was it? Couldn't remember the name!

But for six years then she had been a
member of that . . . triangle.

You couldn't call it *ménage à trois*, even if
you didn't know French. They hadn't lived
together! . . . They had d—d near died
together when the general's car hit their
dog-cart! D—d near! (You *must* not use those
War-time idioms. *Do* break yourself of it!
Remember the maroons!)

An oafish thing to do! To take a school-girl,
just . . . oh, just past the age of consent, out
all night in a dog-cart and then get yourself
run into by the car of the V. C., P. G., champ-
ion-in-red-trouser-stripe of your Legitimate!

You'd think any man who *was* a man would have avoided that!

Most men knew enough to know that the Woman Pays . . . the school-girl too!

But they get it both ways . . . Look here: when Edith Ethel Duchemin, then, just — or perhaps not quite, Lady Macmaster! At any rate, her husband was dead and she had just married that miserable little . . . (Mustn't use that word!) She, Valentine Wannop, had been the only witness of the marriage — as of the previous, discreet, but so praiseworthy adultery! . . . When, then, Edith Ethel had . . . It must have been on the very day of the knighthood, because Edith Ethel made it an excuse not to ask her to the resultant Party . . . Edith Ethel had accused her of having had a baby by . . . oh, Mr. So and So . . . And heaven was her, Valentine Wannop's, witness that, although Mr. So and So was her mother's constant adviser, she, Valentine Wannop, was still in such a state of acquaintance with him that she still called him by his surname . . . When Lady Macmaster, spitting like the South American beast of burden called a Llama, had accused her of having had a baby by her mother's adviser — to her natural astonishment, but, of course, it had been the result of the dog-cart and the motor and the General, and the

General's sister, Lady Pauline Something — or perhaps it was Claudine? Yes, Lady Claudine! — who had been in the car and the Society Wife, who was always striding along the railings of the Row ... When she had been so accused out of the blue, her first thought — and, confound it, her enduring thought! — had not been concern for her own reputation but for *his* ...

That was the *quality* of his entanglements, their very essence. He got into appalling messes, unending and unravellable — no, she meant un-unravellable! — messes and other people suffered for him whilst he mooned on — into more messes! The General charging the dog-cart was symbolical of him. He was perfectly on his right side and all, but it was like him to be in a dog-cart when flagitious automobiles carrying Generals were running a-muck! Then ... the Woman Paid! ... She really did, in this case. It had been her mother's horse they had been driving and, although they had got damages out of the General, the costs were twice that ... And her, Valentine's, reputation had suffered from being in a dog-cart at dawn, alone with a man ... It made no odds that he had — or was it hadn't? — 'insulted' her in any way all through that — oh, that delicious, delirious night ... She had to be said to have a baby by him, and then she had to be dreadfully worried about *his* poor old reputation . . . Of course it *would* have been pretty rotten of him — she so young and innocent, daughter of so preposterously eminent, if so impoverished a man, his father's best friend and all. 'He hadn't oughter'er done it!' He hadn't really oughter . . . She heard them all saying it, still!

Well, he hadn't! . . . But she?

That magic night. It was just before dawn, the mists nearly up to their necks as they drove; the sky going pale in a sort of twilight. And one immense star! She remembered only one immense star, though, historically, there had been also a dilapidated sort of moon. But the star was *her* best boy — what her wagon was hitched on to . . . And they had been quoting — quarrelling over, she remembered:

Flebis et arsuro me, Delia, lecto
Tristibus et . . .

She exclaimed suddenly:

'Twilight and evening star
And one clear call for me
And may there be no moaning at the
    bar
When I . . . '

She said:

'Oh, but you *oughtn't* to, my dear! That's *Tennyson*!' Tennyson, with a difference!

She said:

'All the same, that would have been an inexperienced schoolgirl's prank . . . But if I let him kiss me now I should be . . . ' She would be a what was it . . . a fornicatress? . . . *trix*! Fornicatrix is preferable! Very preferable. Then why not adultrix? You couldn't: you had to be a 'cold-blooded adultress!' or morality was not avenged.

Oh, but surely not cold-blooded! . . . Deliberate, then! . . . That wasn't, either, the word for the process. Of osculation! . . . Comic things, words, as applied to states of feelings!

But if she went now to Lincoln's Inn and the Problem held out its arms . . . That would be 'deliberate.' It would be asking for it in the fullest sense of the term.

She said to herself quickly:

'This way madness lies!' And then:

'What an imbecile thing to say!'

She had had an Affair with a man, she made her mind say to her, two years ago. That was all right. There could not be a, say, a schoolmistress rising twenty-four or twenty-five, in the world who hadn't had *some* affair, even if it were no more than a gentleman in a tea-shop who every afternoon for a week had gazed at her disrespectfully over a slice of plum-cake . . . And then disappeared . . . But you had to have had at least a might-have-been or you couldn't go on being a schoolmistress or a girl in a ministry or a dactylographer of respectability. You packed *that* away in the bottom of your mind and on Sunday mornings before the perfectly insufficient Sunday dinner, you took it out and built castles in Spain in which you were a castanetted heroine turning on wonderful hips, but casting behind you inflaming glances . . . Something like that!

Well, she had had an affair with this honest, simple creature! So good! So unspeakably GOOD . . . Like the late Albert, prince consort! The very, helpless, immobile sort of creature that she ought not to have tempted. It had been like shooting tame pigeons! Because he had had a Society wife always in the illustrated papers whilst he sat at home and evolved Statistics or came to tea with her dear, tremendous, distracted mother, whom he helped to get her articles accurate. So a woman tempted him and he did . . . No; he didn't quite eat!

But why? . . . Because he was GOOD?

Very likely.

Or was it . . . That was the intolerable thought that she shut up within her along

47

with the material for castles in the air! Was it because he had been really indifferent?

They had revolved round each other at tea-parties — or rather he had revolved round her, because at Edith Ethel's affairs she always sat, a fixed starlet, behind the tea-urn and dispensed cups. But he would moon round the room, looking at the backs of books; occasionally laying down the law to some guest; and always drifting in the end to her side where he would say a trifle or two . . . And the beautiful — the quite excruciatingly beautiful wife — striding along the Row with the second son of the Earl of Someone at her side . . . Asking for it . . .

So it had been from the 1/7/12, say, to the 4/8/14!

After that, things had become more rubbled — mixed up with alarums. Excursions on his part to unapproved places. And trouble. He was quite damnably in trouble. With his Superiors; with, so unnecessarily, Hun projectiles, wire, mud; over Money; politics; mooning on without a good word from anyone . . . Unravellable muddles that never got unravelled but that somehow got you caught up in them . . .

Because he needed her moral support! When, during the late Hostilities, he hadn't been out there, he had drifted to the tea-table much earlier of an afternoon and stayed beside it much longer, till after everyone else had gone and they could go and sit on the tall fender side by side, and argue . . . about the rights and wrongs of the War!

Because she was the only soul in the world with whom he could talk . . . They had the same sort of good, bread-and-butter brains; without much of the romantic . . . No doubt a touch . . . in him. Otherwise he would not have always been in these muddles. He gave all he possessed to anyone who asked for it. That was all right. But that those who sponged on him should also involve him in intolerable messes . . . That was not proper. One ought to defend oneself against that!

Because . . . if you do not defend yourself against that, look how you let in your nearest and dearest — those who have to sympathise with you in your confounded troubles whilst you moon on, giving away more and more and getting into more troubles! In this case it was she who was his Nearest and Dearest . . . Or had been! At that her nerves suddenly got the better of her and her mind went mad . . . Supposing that that fellow, from whom she had not heard for two years, *hadn't* now communicated with her . . . Like an ass she had taken it for granted that he had *asked* Lady . . . Blast her! . . . to 'bring them together again'! She had imagined that even Edith Ethel would not have had the cheek to ring her up if he hadn't asked her to!

But she had nothing to go on . . . Feeble, oversexed ass that she was, she had let her mind jump at once to the conclusion, the moment the mere mention of him seemed implied — jump to the conclusion that he was asking her again to come and be his mistress . . . Or nurse him through his present muddle till he should be fit to . . .

Mind, she did not say that she would have succumbed. But if she had not jumped at the idea that it was he, really, speaking through Edith Ethel, she would never have permitted her mind to dwell on . . . on his blasted, complacent perfections!

Because she had taken it for granted that if he had had her rung up he would not have been monkeying with other girls during the two years he hadn't written to her . . . Ah, but hadn't he?

Look here! *Was* it reasonable? Here was a fellow who had all but . . . all BUT . . . 'taken advantage of her' one night just before going out to France, say, two years ago . . . And not another word from him after that! . . . It was all very well to say that he was portentous, looming, luminous, loony: John Peel with his coat so grey, the English Country Gentleman *pur sang*, and then some; saintly, Godlike, Jesus Christ-like . . . He was all that. But you don't seduce, as near as can be, a young woman and then go off to Hell, leaving her, God knows, in Hell, and not so much as send her, in two years, a picture-postcard with MIZPAH on it. You don't. You don't!

Or if you do you have to have your character revised. You have to have it taken for granted that you were only monkeying with her and that you've been monkeying ever since with Waacs in Rouen or some other Base . . .

Of course, if you ring your young woman up when you come back . . . or have her rung up by a titled lady . . . That might restore you in the eyes of the world, or at least in the eyes of the young woman if she was a bit of a softie . . .

But *had* he? *Had* he? It was absurd to think that Edith Ethel hadn't had the face to do it unasked! To save three thousand, two hundred pounds, not to mention interest — which was what Vincent owed *him*! — Edith Ethel with the sweetest possible smile would beg the pillows off a whole hospital ward full of dying . . . She was quite right. She had to save her man. You go to any depths of ignominy to save your man.

But that did not help her, Valentine Wannop!

She sprang off the bench; she clenched her nails into her palms; she stamped her thin-soled shoes into the coke-brise floor that was singularly unresilient. She exclaimed:

'Damn it all, he didn't ask her to ring me up. He didn't ask her to. He didn't ask her to!' still stamping about.

She marched straight at the telephone that was by now uttering long, tinny, night-jar's calls and, with one snap, pulled the receiver right off the twisted, green-blue cord . . . Broke it! With incidental satisfaction.

Then she said:

'Steady the Buffs!' not out of repentance for having damaged School Property, but because she was accustomed to call her thoughts The Buffs because of their practical, unromantic character as a rule . . . A fine regiment, the Buffs!

Of course, if she had not broken the telephone she could have rung up Edith Ethel and have asked her whether he had or hadn't asked to . . . to be brought together again . . . It was like her, Valentine Wannop, to smash the only means of resolving a torturing doubt . . .

It wasn't, really, in the least like her. *She* was practical enough; none of the 'under the ban of fatality' business about her. She had smashed the telephone because it had been

52

like smashing a connection with Edith Ethel; or because she hated tinny night-jars; or because she had smashed it. For nothing in the world; for nothing, nothing, nothing in the world would she ever ring up Edith Ethel and ask her:

'Did *he* put you up to ringing me up?'

That would be to let Edith Ethel come between their intimacy.

A subconscious volition was directing her feet towards the great doors at the end of the Hall, varnished, pitch-pine doors of Gothic architecture; economically decorated as if with straps and tin-lids of Brunswick-blacked cast iron.

She said:

'Of course if it's his wife who has removed his furniture that would be a reason for his wanting to get into communication. They would have split . . . But he does not hold with a man divorcing a woman, and she won't divorce.'

As she went through the sticky postern — all that woodwork seemed sticky on account of its varnish! — beside the great doors she said:

'Who cares!'

The great thing was . . . but she could not formulate what the great thing was. You had to settle the preliminaries.

3

She said eventually to Miss Wanostrocht who had sat down at her table behind two pink carnations:

'I didn't consciously want to bother you but a spirit in my feet has led me who knows how . . . That's Shelley, isn't it?'

And indeed a quite unconscious but shrewd mind had pointed out to her whilst still in the School Hall and even before she had broken the telephone, that Miss Wanostrocht very probably would be able to tell her what she wanted to know and that if she didn't hurry she might miss her, since the Head would probably go now the girls were gone. So she had hurried through gauntish corridors whose Decorated Gothic windows positively had bits of pink glass here and there interspersed in their lattices. Nevertheless a nearly deserted, darkish, locker-lined dressing-room being a short cut, she had paused in it before the figure of a clumsyish girl, freckled, in black and, on a stool, desultorily lacing a dull black boot, an ankle on her knee. She felt an impulse to say: 'Goodbye, Pettigul!' she didn't know why.

The clumsy, fifteenish, bumpy-faced girl was a symbol of that place — healthyish, but not over healthy; honestish but with no craving for intellectual honesty; big-boned in unexpected places . . . and uncomelily blubbering so that her face appeared dirtyish . . . It was in fact all 'ishes' about that Institution. They were all healthyish, honestish, clumsyish, twelve-to-eighteenish, and big-boned in unexpected places because of the late insufficient feeding . . . Emotionalish, too; apt to blubber rather than to go into hysterics.

Instead of saying good-bye to the girl she said:

'Here!' and roughly, since she was exhibiting too much leg, pulled down the girl's shortish skirt and set to work to lace the unyielding boot on the unyielding shin-bone . . . After a period of youthful bloom, which would certainly come and as certainly go, this girl would, normally, find herself one of the Mothers of Europe, marriage being due to the period of youthful bloom . . . Normally that is to say according to a normality that that day might restore. Of course it mightn't!

A tepid drop of moisture fell on Valentine's right knuckle.

'My cousin Bob was killed the day before yesterday,' the girl's voice said above her head. Valentine bent her head still lower over the boot with the patience that, in educational establishments, you must, if you want to be businesslike and shrewd, acquire and display in face of unusual mental vagaries . . . This girl had never had a cousin Bob, or anything else. Pettigul and her two sisters, Pettiguls Two and Three, were all in that Institution at extremely reduced rates precisely because they had not got, apart from their widowed mother, a discoverable relative. The father, a half-pay major, had been killed early in the war. All the mistresses had had to hand in reports on the moral qualities of the Pettiguls, so all the mistresses had this information.

'He gave me his puppy to keep for him before he went out,' the girl said. 'It doesn't seem just!'

Valentine, straightening herself, said:

'I should wash my face if I were you, before I went out. Or you might get yourself taken for a German!' She pulled the girl's clumsyish blouse straight on her shoulders.

'Try,' she added, 'to imagine that you've got someone just come back! It's just as easy and it will make you look more attractive!'

Scurrying along the corridors she said to herself:

'Heaven help me, does it make *me* look more attractive?'

She caught the Head, as she had anticipated, just on the point of going to her home in Fulham, an unattractive suburb but near a bishop's palace nevertheless. It seemed somehow appropriate. The lady was episcopally minded, but experienced in the vicissitudes of suburban children: very astonishing some of them unless you took them very much in the lump.

Miss Head had stood behind her table for the first three questions and answers in an attitude of someone who is a little at bay, but she had sat down just before Valentine had quoted her Shelley at her, and she had now the air of one who is ready to make a night of it. Valentine continued to stand.

'This,' Miss Wanostrocht said very gently, 'is a day on which one might . . . take steps . . . that might influence one's whole life.'

'That's,' Valentine answered, 'exactly why I've come to you. I want to know what that woman said to you so as to know where I stand before I take a step.'

The Head said:

'I had to let the girls go. I don't mind saying that you are very valuable to me. The Governors — I had an express from Lord Boulnois — ordered them to be given a

57

holiday to-morrow. It's very inconsistent. But that makes it all the . . . '

She stopped. Valentine said to herself:

'By Jove, I don't know anything about men; but how little I know about women. What's she getting at?'

She added:

'She's nervous. She must be wanting to say something she thinks I won't like!'

She said chivalrously:

'I don't believe anybody could have kept those girls in to-day. It's a thing one has no experience of. There's never been a day like this before.'

Out there in Piccadilly there would be mobs shoulder to shoulder; she had never seen the Nelson column stand out of a solid mass. They might roast oxen whole in the Strand. Whitechapel would be seething, enamelled iron advertisements looking down on millions of bowler hats. All sordid and immense London stretched out under her gaze. She felt herself *of* London as the grouse feels itself of the heather, and there she was in an emptied suburb looking at two pink carnations. Dyed probably: offering of Lord Boulnois to Miss Wanostrocht! You never saw a natural-grown carnation that shade!

She said:

'I'd be glad to know what that woman

— Lady Macmaster — told you.'

Miss Wanostrocht looked down at her hands. She had the little-fingers hooked together, the hands back to back; it was a demoded gesture . . . Girton of 1897, Valentine thought; indulged in by the thoughtfully blonde . . . Fair girl graduates the sympathetic comic papers of those days had called them. It pointed to a long sitting. Well, she, Valentine, was not going to brusque the issue! . . . French-derived expression that. But how would you put it otherwise?

Miss Wanostrocht said:

'I sat at the feet of your father!'

'You see!' Valentine said to herself. 'But she must then have gone to Oxford, not Newnham!' She could not remember whether there had been woman's colleges at Oxford as early as 1895 or 1897. There must have been.

'The greatest Teacher . . . The greatest influence in the world,' Miss Wanostrocht said.

It was queer, Valentine thought: This woman had known all about her — at any rate all about her distinguished descent all the time she, Valentine, had been Physical Instructress at that Great Public School (Girls'). Yet except for an invariable courtesy such as she imagined Generals might show to non-commissioned officers, Miss Wanostrocht had hitherto taken no more notice of her than she might have taken of a superior parlourmaid. On the other hand she had let Valentine arrange her physical training exactly as she liked, without any interference.

'We used to hear,' Miss Wanostrocht said, 'how he spoke Latin with you and your brother from the day of your births . . . He used to be regarded as eccentric, but how *right*! . . . Miss Hall says that you are the most remarkable Latinist she has ever so much as imagined.'

'It's not true,' Valentine said, 'I can't *think* in Latin. You cannot be a real Latinist unless you do that. He did of course.'

'It was the last thing you would think of him as doing,' the Head answered with a pale gleam of youth. 'He was such a thorough man of the world. So awake!'

'We ought to be a queer lot, my brother and I,' Valentine said. 'With such a father . . . And mother of course!'

Miss Wanostrocht said:

'Oh . . . your *mother* . . . '

And immediately Valentine conjured up the little, adoring female clique of Miss Wanostrocht's youth, all spying on her father and mother in their walks under the Oxford Sunday trees, the father so jaunty and awake, the mother so trailing, large, generous, unobservant. And all the little clique saying: If only he had *us* to look after him . . . She said with a little malice:

'You don't read my mother's novels, I suppose . . . It was she who did all my father's writing for him. He couldn't write, he was too impatient!'

Miss Wanostrocht exclaimed:

'Oh, you *shouldn't* say that!' with almost the pain of someone defending her own personal reputation.

'I don't see why I shouldn't,' Valentine said. 'He was the first person to say it about himself.'

'He shouldn't have said it either,' Miss Wanostrocht answered with a sort of soft unction. 'He should have taken care more of his own reputation for the sake of his Work!'

Valentine considered this thin, ecstatic spinster with ironic curiosity.

'Of course, if you've sat . . . if you're still sitting at father's feet as much as all that,' she conceded, 'it gives you a certain right to be careful about his reputation . . . All the same I wish you would tell me what that person said on the phone!'

The bust of Miss Wanostrocht moved with a sudden eagerness further towards the edge of her table.

'It's precisely because of that,' she said, 'that I want to speak to you first . . . That I want you to consider . . . '

Valentine said:

'Because of my father's reputation . . . Look here, did that person — Lady Macmaster! — speak to you as if you were me? Our names are near enough to make it possible.'

'You're,' Miss Wanostrocht said, 'as one might say, the fine fruit of the product of his views on the education of women. And if you . . . It's been such a satisfaction to me to observe in you such a . . . a sound, instructed head on such a . . . oh, you know, sane body . . . And then . . . An earning capacity. A commercial value. Your father, of course, never minced words . . . ' She added:

'I'm bound to say that my interview with Lady Macmaster . . . who surely isn't a lady of whom you could say that you disapprove. I've read her husband's work. It surely — you'd say, wouldn't you? — conserves some of the ancient fire.'

'He,' Valentine said, 'hasn't a word of Latin to his tail. He makes his quotations out, if he uses them, by means of school-cribs . . . I know his methods of work, you know.'

It occurred to Valentine to think that if Edith Ethel really *had* at first taken Miss

Wanostrocht for herself there might pretty obviously be some cause for Miss Wanostrocht's concern for her father's reputation as an intimate trainer of young women. She figured Edith Ethel suddenly bursting into a description of the circumstances of that man who was without furniture and did not appear to recognise the porter. The relations she might have described as having existed between her and him might well worry the Head of a Great Public School for Middle Class Girls. She had no doubt been described as having had a baby. A disagreeable and outraged current invaded her feelings . . .

It was suddenly obscured by a recrudescence of the thought that had come to her only incidentally in the hall. It rushed over her with extraordinary vividness now, like a wave of warm liquid . . . If it *had* really been that fellow's wife who had removed his furniture what *was* there to keep them apart? He couldn't have pawned or sold or burnt his furniture whilst he had been with the British Expeditionary Force in the Low Countries! He couldn't have without extraordinary difficulty! Then . . . What *should* keep them apart? . . . Middle Class Morality? A pretty gory carnival that had been for the last four years! Was this then Lent, pressing hard on the heels of Saturnalia? Not so hard as that, surely! So that if one hurried . . . What on earth did she want, unknown to herself?

She heard herself saying, almost with a sob, so that she was evidently in a state of emotion:

'Look here, I disapprove of this whole thing: of what my father has brought me to! Those people . . . the brilliant Victorians talked all the time through their hats. They evolved a theory from anywhere and then went brilliantly mad over it. Perfectly recklessly . . . Have you noticed Pettigul One? . . . Hasn't it occurred to you that you *can't* carry on violent physical jerks and mental work side by side? I ought not to be in this school and I ought not to be what I am!'

At Miss Wanostrocht's perturbed expression she said to herself:

'What on earth am I saying all this for? You'd think I was trying to cut loose from this school! Am I?'

Nevertheless her voice was going on:

'There's too much oxygenation of the lungs, here. It's unnatural. It affects the brain, deleteriously. Pettigul One is an example of it. She's earnest with me and earnest with her books. Now she's gone dotty. Most of them it only stupefies.'

It was incredible to her that the mere imagination that that fellow's wife had left him should make her spout out like this — for all the world like her father spouting out one of his ingenious theories! . . . It had really occurred to her once or twice to think that you could not run a dual physical and mental existence without some risk. The military physical developments of the last four years had been responsible for a real exaggeration of physical values. She was aware that in that Institution, for the last four years, she had been regarded as supplementing if not as actually replacing both the doctor and the priest . . . But from that to evolving a complete theory that the Pettigul's lie was the product of an overoxygenated brain was going pretty far . . .

Still, she was prevented from taking part in national rejoicings; pretty certainly Edith Ethel had been talking scandal about her to Miss Wanostrocht. She had the right to take it out in some sort of exaggerated declamation!

'It appears,' Miss Wanostrocht said, 'for we can't now go into the question of the whole curriculum of the school, though I am inclined to agree with you. What by the by is the matter with Pettigul One? I thought her rather a solid sort of girl. But it appears that the wife of a friend . . . perhaps it's only a former friend of yours, is in a nursing home.'

Valentine exclaimed:

65

'Oh, he . . . But that's too ghastly!'

'It appears,' Miss Wanostrocht said, 'to be rather a mess.' She added: 'That appears to be the only expression to use.'

★ ★ ★

For Valentine, that piece of news threw a blinding light upon herself. She was overwhelmingly appalled because that woman was in a nursing home. Because in that case it would not be sporting to go and see the husband!

Miss Wanostrocht went on:

'Lady Macmaster was anxious for your advice . . . It appears that the only other person that could look after the interests of . . . of your friend: his brother . . . '

Valentine missed something out of that sentence. Miss Wanostrocht talked too fluently. If people wanted you to appreciate items of sledge-hammering news they should not use long sentences. They should say:

'He's mad and penniless. His brother's dying, his wife's just been operated on.' Like that! Then you could take it in; even if your mind was rioting about like a cat in a barrel.

'The brother's . . . female companion,' Miss Wanostrocht was wandering on, 'though it appears that she would have been willing is

66

therefore not available . . . The theory is that he — he himself, your friend, has been considerably unhinged by his experiences in the war. Then . . . Who in your opinion should take the responsibility of looking after his interests?'

Valentine heard herself say:

'Me!'

She added:

'Him! Looking after him. I don't know that he has any . . . interests!'

He didn't appear to have any furniture, so how could he have the other things. She wished Miss Wanostrocht would leave off using the word 'appear.' It was irritating . . . and infectious. Could the lady not make a direct statement? But then, no one ever made clear statements and this no doubt appeared to that anæmic spinster a singularly tenebrous affair.

As for clear statements . . . If there had ever been any in precisely this tenebrous mess she, Valentine, would know how she stood with that man's wife. For it was part of the preposterous way in which she herself and all her friends behaved that they never made clear statements — except for Edith Ethel who had the nature of a female costermonger and could not tell the truth, though she could be clear enough. But even Edith Ethel had never hitherto said anything about the way the wife in this case treated the husband. She had given Valentine very clearly to understand that she 'sided' with the wife — but she had never gone as far as to say that the wife was a good wife. If she — Valentine — could only know that.

Miss Wanostrocht was asking:

'When you say 'Me,' do you mean that you would propose to look after that man yourself? I trust not.'

. . . Because, obviously, if she were a good wife, she, Valentine couldn't butt in . . . not generously. As her father's and still more her mother's daughter . . . On the face of it you would say that a wife who was always striding along the palings of the Row, or the paths of other resorts of the fashionable could not be a good — a domestic — wife of a Statistician. On the other hand he was a pretty smart man, Governing class, county family, and the rest of it — so he might like his wife to figure in Society; he might even exact it. He was quite capable of that. Why, for all she knew, the wife might be a retiring, shy person whom he thrust out into the hard world. It was not likely, but it was as possible as anything else.

Miss Wanostrocht was asking:

'Aren't there Institutions . . . Military Sanatoria . . . for cases precisely like that of this Captain Tietjens. It appears to be the war that has broken him down, not merely evil living.'

'It's precisely,' Valentine said, 'because of that that one should want . . . shouldn't one . . . Because it's because of the War . . . '

The sentence would not finish itself.

Miss Wanostrocht said:

'I thought . . . It has been represented to me . . . that you were a Pacifist. Of an extreme type!'

It had given Valentine a turn — like the breaking out of sweat in a case of fever — to hear the name, coldly, 'Captain Tietjens,' for it was like a release. She had been irrationally determined that hers should not be the first tongue to utter that name.

And apparently from her tone Miss Wanostrocht was prepared to detest that Captain Tietjens. Perhaps she detested him already.

She was beginning to say:

'If one is an extreme Pacifist because one cannot bear to think of the sufferings of men isn't that a precise reason why one should wish that a poor devil, all broken up . . .

But Miss Wanostrocht had begun one of her own long sentences. Their voices went on together, like trains dragging along ballast — disagreeably. Miss Wanostrocht's organ,

69

however, won out with the words:

'. . . behaved very badly indeed.'

Valentine said hotly:

'You ought not to believe anything of the sort — on the strength of anything said by a woman like Lady Macmaster.'

Miss Wanostrocht appeared to have been brought to a complete stop: she leaned forward in her chair; her mouth was a little open. And Valentine said: 'Thank Goodness!' to herself.

She had to have a moment to herself to digest what had the air of being new evidence of the baseness of Edith Ethel; she felt herself to be infuriated in regions of her own being that she hardly knew. That seemed to her to be a littleness in herself. She had not thought that she had been as little as that. It ought not to matter what people said of you. She was perfectly accustomed to think of Edith Ethel as telling whole crowds of people very bad things about her, Valentine Wannop. But there was about this a recklessness that was hardly believable. To tell an unknown person, encountered by chance on the telephone, derogatory facts about a third party who might be expected to come to the telephone herself in a minute or two — and, not only that — who must in all probability hear what had been said very soon after, from the first,

70

listener . . . That was surely a recklessness of evil-speaking that almost outpassed sanity . . . Or else it betrayed a contempt for her, Valentine Wannop, and what she could do in the way of reprisals that was extremely hard to bear!

She said suddenly to Miss Wanostrocht:

'Look here! Are you speaking to me as a friend to my father's daughter or as a Headmistress to a Physical Instructor?'

A certain amount of blood came into the lady's pinkish features. She had certainly been ruffled when Valentine had permitted her voice to sound so long alongside her own; for, although Valentine knew next to nothing about the Head's likes or dislikes she had once or twice before seen her evince marked distaste on being interrupted in one of her formal sentences.

Miss Wanostrocht said with a certain coldness:

'I'm speaking at present . . . I'm allowing myself the liberty — as a much older woman — in the capacity of a friend of your father. I have been, in short, trying to recall to you all that you owe to yourself as being an example of his training!'

Involuntarily Valentine's lips formed themselves for a low whistle of incredulity. She said to herself:

'By Jove! I am in the middle of a nasty affair . . . This is a sort of professional cross-examination.'

'I am in a way glad,' the lady was now continuing, 'that you take that line . . . I mean of defending Mrs. Tietjens with such heat against Lady Macmaster. Lady Macmaster appears to dislike Mrs. Tietjens, but I am bound to say that she appears to be in the right of it. I mean of her dislike. Lady Macmaster is a serious personality and, even on her public record Mrs. Tietjens appears to be very much the reverse. No doubt you wish to be loyal to your . . . friends, but . . . '

'We appear,' Valentine said, 'to be getting into an extraordinary muddle.'

She added:

'I haven't, as you seem to think, been defending Mrs. Tietjens. I would have. I would at any time. I have always thought of her as beautiful and kind. But I heard you say the words: *has been behaving very badly*,' and I thought you meant that Captain Tietjens had. I denied it. If you meant that his wife has, I deny it, too. She's an admirable wife . . . and mother . . . that sort of thing, for all I know . . . '

She said to herself:

'Now why do I say that? What's Hecuba to me?' and then:

72

'It's to defend *his* honour, of course
. . . I'm trying to present Captain Tietjens as
English Country Gentleman complete with
admirably arranged establishment, stables,
kennels, spouse, offspring . . . That's a queer
thing to want to do!'

Miss Wanostrocht who had breathed deeply
said now:

'I'm extremely glad to hear that. Lady
Macmaster certainly said that Mrs. Tietjens
was — let us say — at least a neglectful wife
. . . Vain, you know; idle; overdressed . . . All
that . . . And you appeared to defend Mrs.
Tietjens.'

'She's a smart woman in smart Society,'
Valentine said, 'but it's with her husband's
concurrence. She has a right to be . . . '

'We shouldn't,' Miss Wanostrocht said, 'be
in the extraordinary muddle to which you
referred if you did not so continually
interrupt me. I was trying to say that, for you,
an inexperienced girl, brought up in a
sheltered home, no pitfall could be more
dangerous than a man with a wife who
neglected her duties!'

Valentine said:

'You will have to excuse my interrupting
you. It *is*, you know, rather more my funeral
than yours.'

Miss Wanostrocht said quickly:

73

'You can't say that. You don't know how ardently . . . '

Valentine said:

'Yes, yes . . . Your *schwaerm* for my father's memory and all. But my father couldn't bring it about that I should lead a sheltered life . . . I'm about as experienced as any girl of the lower classes . . . No doubt it was his doing, but don't make any mistakes.'

She added:

'Still, it's I that's the corpse. You're conducting the inquest. So it's more fun for you.'

Miss Wanostrocht had grown slightly pale:

'I, if . . . ' she stammered slightly, 'by 'experience' you mean . . . '

'I don't,' Valentine exclaimed, 'and you have no right to infer that I do on the strength of a conversation you've had, but shouldn't have had, with one of the worst tongues in London . . . I mean that my father left us so that I had to earn my and my mother's living as a servant for some months after his death. That was what his training came to. But I can look after myself . . . In consequence . . . '

Miss Wanostrocht had thrown herself back in her chair.

'But . . . ' she exclaimed; she had grown completely pale — like discoloured wax.

'There was a subscription . . . We . . . ' she began: 'We knew that he hadn't . . . '

'You subscribed,' Valentine said, 'to purchase his library and presented it to his wife . . . who had nothing to eat but what my wages as a tweeny maid got for her.' But before the pallor of the other lady she tried to add a touch of generosity: 'Of course the subscribers wanted, very naturally, to preserve as much as they could of his personality. A man's books are very much himself. That was all right.' She added: 'All the same I had that training: in a suburban basement. So you cannot teach me a great deal about the shady in life. I was in the family of a Middlesex County Councillor. In Ealing.'

Miss Wanostrocht said faintly:

'This is very dreadful!'

'It isn't really!' Valentine said. 'I wasn't badly treated as tweeny maids go. It would have been better if the Mistress hadn't been a constant invalid and the cook constantly drunk . . . After that I did a little office work. For the suffragettes. That was after old Mr. Tietjens came back from abroad and gave mother some work on a paper he owned. We scrambled along then, somehow. Old Mr. Tietjens was father's greatest friend, so father's side, as you might say, turned up

75

trumps — if you like to think that to console you . . . '

Miss Wanostrocht was bending her face down over her table, presumably to hide a little of it from Valentine or to avoid the girl's eyes.

Valentine went on:

'One knows all about the conflict between a man's private duties and his public achievements. But with a very little less of the flamboyant in his life my father might have left us very much better off. It isn't what I *want* — to be a cross between a sergeant in the army and an upper housemaid. Any more than I wanted to be an under one.'

Miss Wanostrotch uttered an 'Oh!' of pain. She exclaimed rapidly:

'It was your moral rather than your mere athletic influence that made me so glad to have you here . . . It was because I felt that you did not set such a high value on the physical . . . '

'Well, you aren't going to have me here much longer,' Valentine said. 'Not an instant more than I can in decency help. I'm going to . . . '

She said to herself:

'What on earth am I going to do? . . . What do I want?'

She wanted to lie in a hammock beside a

76

blue, tideless sea and think about Tibullus
. . . There was no nonsense about her. She
did not want to engage in intellectual pursuits
herself. She had not the training. But she
intended to enjoy the more luxurious forms
of the intellectual products of others . . .
That appeared to be the moral of the day!

And, looking rather minutely at Miss
Wanostrocht's inclined face, she wondered if,
in the history of the world, there had ever
been such another day. Had Miss Wanostrocht, for instance, ever known what it was to
have a man come back. Ah, but amid the
tumult of a million other men coming back!
A collective impulse to slacken off! Immense!
Softening!

Miss Wanostrocht had apparently loved her
father. No doubt in company with fifty
damsels. Did they ever get a collective kick
out of that affair? It was even possible that
she had spoken as she had . . . *pour cause.*
Warning her, Valentine, against the deleterious effect of being connected with a man
whose wife was unsatisfactory . . . Because
the fifty damsels had all, in duty bound,
thought that her mother was an unsatisfactory wife for the brilliant, grey-black-haired
Eminence with the figure of a stripling that
her father had been . . . They had probably
thought that, without the untidy figure of

Mrs. Wannop as a weight upon him, he might have become ... Well, with one of *them*! ... anything! Any sort of figure in the councils of the nation. Why not Prime Minister? For along with his pedagogic theories he had had political occupations. He had certainly had the friendship of Disraeli. He supplied — it was historic! — materials for eternally famous, meretricious speeches. He would have been head-trainer of the Empire's pro-consuls if the other fellow, at Balliol, had not got in first ... As it was he had had to specialise in the Education of Women. Building up Primrose Dames ...

So Miss Wanostrocht warned her against the deleterious effect of neglected wives upon young, attached virgins! It probably *was* deleterious. Where would she, Valentine Wannop, have been by now if she had thought that Sylvia Tietjens was really a bad one?

Miss Wanostrocht said, as if with sudden anxiety:

'You are going to do what? You propose to do what?'

Valentine said:

'Obviously after your conversation with Edith Ethel you won't be so glad to have me here. My moral influence has not been brightened in aspect!' A wave of passionate resentment swept over her.

'Look here,' she said, 'if you think that I am prepared to . . . '

She stopped however, 'No,' she said, 'I am not going to introduce the housemaid note. But you will probably see that this is irritating.' She added: 'I would have the case of Pettigul One looked into, if I were you. It might become epidemic in a big school like this. And we've no means of knowing where we stand nowadays!'

Part Two

1

Months and months before Christopher Tietjens had stood extremely wishing that his head were level with a particular splash of purposeless whitewash. Something behind his mind forced him to the conviction that, if his head — and of course the rest of his trunk and lower limbs — were suspended by a process of levitation to that distance above the duckboard on which, now, his feet were, he would be in an inviolable sphere. These waves of conviction recurred continually: he was constantly glancing aside and upwards at that splash; it was in the shape of the comb of a healthy rooster; it gleamed, with five serrations, in the just-beginning light that shone along the thin, unroofed channel in the gravel slope. Wet half-light, just flickering; more visible there than in the surrounding desolation because the deep, narrow channel framed a section of just-illuminated rift in the watery eastwards!

Twice he had stood up on a rifleman's step enforced by a bully-beef case to look over — in the last few minutes. Each time, on stepping down again, he had been struck by that phenomenon: the light seen from the trench seemed if not brighter, then more definite. So, from the bottom of a pit-shaft in broad day you can see the stars. The wind was light, but from the north-west. They had there the weariness of a beaten army, the weariness of having to begin always new days again . . .

He glanced aside and upwards: that cockscomb of phosphorescence . . . He felt waves of some X force propelling his temples towards it. He wondered if perhaps the night before he had not observed that that was a patch of reinforced concrete, therefore more resistant. He might of course have observed that and then forgotten it. He hadn't! It was therefore irrational.

If you are lying down under fire — flat under pretty smart fire — and you have only a paper bag in front of your head for cover you feel immeasurably safer than you do without it. You have a mind at rest. This must be the same thing.

It remained dark and quiet. It was forty-five minutes. It became forty-four . . . Forty-three . . . Forty-two minutes and thirty seconds before a crucial moment and the slate grey cases of miniature metal pineapples had not come from the bothering place . . . Who knew if there was anyone in charge there?

Twice that night he had sent runners back. No results yet. That bothering fellow might quite well have forgotten to leave a substitute. That was not likely. A careful man. But a man with a mania might forget. Still it was not likely! . . .

Thoughts menaced him as clouds threaten the heads of mountains, but for the moment they kept away. It was quiet; the wet cool air was agreeable. They had autumn mornings that felt like that in Yorkshire. The wheels of his physique moved smoothly; he was more free in the chest than he had been for months.

A single immense cannon, at a tremendous distance said something. Something sulky. Aroused in its sleep and protesting. But it was not a signal to begin anything. Too heavy. Firing at something at a tremendous distance. At Paris, maybe, or the North Pole, or the moon! They were capable of that, those fellows!

It would be a tremendous piece of frightfulness to hit the moon. Great gain in prestige. And useless. There was no knowing what they would not be up to, as long as it was stupid and useless. And, naturally, boring . . . And it was a mistake to be boring. One went on fighting to get rid of those bores — as you would to get rid of a bore in a club.

It was more descriptive to call what had spoken a cannon than a gun — though it was not done in the best local circles. It was all right to call 75's or the implements of the horse artillery 'guns'; they were mobile and toy-like. But those immense things were cannons; the sullen muzzles always elevated. Sullen, like cathedral dignitaries or butlers. The thickness of barrel compared to the bore appeared enormous as they pointed at the moon, or Paris, or Nova Scotia.

Well, that cannon had not announced anything except itself! It was not the beginning of any barrage; our own fellows were not pooping off to shut it up. It had just announced itself, saying protestingly, 'CAN ... NON,' and its shell soaring away to an enormous height caught the reflection of the unrisen sun on its base. A shining disc, like a halo in flight . . . Pretty! A pretty motive for a decoration, tiny pretty planes up on a blue sky amongst shiny, flying haloes! Dragon-flies amongst saints . . . No, 'with angels and archangels!' . . . Well, one had seen it!

Cannon . . . Yes, that was the right thing to call them. Like the up-ended, rusted things that stuck up out of parades when one had been a child.

No, not the signal for a barrage! A good thing! One might as well say 'Thank

Goodness,' for the later they began the less long it lasted . . . Less long it lasted was ugly alliteration. Sooner it was over was better . . . No doubt half-past eight or at half-past eight to the stroke those boring fellows would let off their usual offering, probably plump, right on top of that spot . . . As far as one could tell three salvoes of a dozen shells each at half-minute intervals between the salvoes. Perhaps salvoes was not the right word. Damn all artillery, anyhow!

Why did those fellows do it! Every morning at half-past eight; every afternoon at half-past two. Presumably just to show that they were still alive, and still boring. They were methodical. That was their secret. The secret of their boredom. Trying to kill them was like trying to shut up Liberals who would talk party politics in a non-political club . . . Had to be done, though! Otherwise the world was no place for . . . Oh, post-prandial naps! . . . Simple philosophy of the contest! . . . Forty minutes! And he glanced aside and upwards at the phosphorescent cockscomb! Within his mind something said that if he were only suspended up there . . .

He stepped once more on to the rifle-step and on to the bully-beef-case. He elevated his head cautiously: grey desolation sloped down and away F.R.R.R.r.r.r.! A gentle purring sound!

He was automatically back, on the duckboard, his breakfast hurting his chest. He said:

'By Jove! I got the fright of my life!' A laugh was called for; he managed it, his whole stomach shaking. And cold!

A head in a metal pudding-basin — a Suffolk type of blond head, pushed itself from a withdrawn curtain of sacking in the gravel wall beside him, at his back. A voice said with concern:

'There ain't no beastly snipers, is there, sir. I did 'ope there would'n be henny beastly snipers 'ere. It gives such a beastly lot of extra trouble warning the men.'

Tietjens said it was a beastly skylark that almost walked into his mouth. The acting sergeant-major said with enthusiasm that them 'ere skylarks could fair scare the guts out of you. He remembered a raid in the dark, crawling on 'is 'ands 'n knees wen 'e put 'is 'and on a skylark on its nest. Never left 'is nest till 'is 'and was on 'im! Then it went up and fair scared the wind out of 'im. Cor! Never would 'e forget that!

With an air of carefully pulling parcels out of a carrier's cart he produced from the cavern behind the sacking two blinking assemblages of tubular khaki-clad limbs. They wavered to erectness, pink cheeses of faces yawning beside tall rifles and bayonets. The sergeant said:

'Keep yer 'eds down as you go along. You never knows!'

Tietjens told the lance-corporal of that party of two that his confounded gas-mask nozzle was broken. Hadn't he seen that for himself? The dismembered object bobbed on the man's chest. He was to go and borrow another from another man and see the other drew a new one at once.

Tietjens' eyes were drawn aside and upwards. His knees were still weak. If he were levitated to the level of that thing he would not have to use his legs for support.

The elderly sergeant went on with enthusiasm about skylarks. Wonderful the trust they showed in hus 'uman beens! Never left ther nesteses till you trod on them tho hall 'ell was rockin' around them.

An appropriate skylark from above and before the parapet made its shrill and heartless noise heard. No doubt the skylark that Tietjens had frightened — that had frightened him.

'Therd bin,' the sergeant went on still enthusiastically, pointing a hand in the direction of the noise, skylarks singing on the mornin' of every straf'e'd ever bin in! Woner'ful trust in yumanity! Woner'ful hinstinck set in the fethered brest by the Halmighty! for 'oo was goin' to 'it a skylark on a battlefield?

The solitary Man dropped beside his long, bayonetted rifle that was muddied from stock to bayonet attachment. Tietjens said mildly that he thought the sergeant had got his natural history wrong. He must divide the males from the females. The females sat on the nest through obstinate attachment to their eggs; the males obstinately soared above the nests in order to pour out abuse at other male skylarks in the vicinity.

He said to himself that he must get the doctor to give him a bromide. A filthy state his nerves had got into unknown to himself. The agitation communicated to him by that bird was still turning his stomach round . . .

'Gilbert White of Shelbourne,' he said to the sergeant 'called the behaviour of the female 'storge': a good word for it.' But, as for trust in humanity, the sergeant might take it that larks never gave us a thought. We were part of the landscape and if what destroyed their nests whilst they sat on them was a bit of H.E. shell or the coulter of a plough it was all one to them.

The sergeant said to the rejoined lance

corporal whose box now hung correctly on his muddied chest:

'Now its HAY post you gotter wait at!' They were to go along the trench and wait where another trench ran into it and there was a great A in whitewash on a bit of corrugated iron that was half-buried. 'You can tell a great HAY from a bull's foot as well as another, can't you Corporal?' patiently.

'Wen they Mills bombs come 'e was to send 'is Man into Hay Cumpny dugout fer a fatigue to bring 'em along 'ere, but Hay Cumpny could keep *is* little lot fer 'isself.'

'An if they Mills bombs did'n' come the corporal'd better manufacture them on 'is own. An not make no mistakes!'

The lance-corporal said 'Yes sargint, no sargint!' and the two went desultorily wavering along the duckboards, grey silhouettes against the wet bar of light, equilibrating themselves with hands on the walls of the trench.

'Ju 'eer what the orfcer said, Corporal,' the one said to the other. 'Wottever'll 'e say next! Skylarks not trust 'uman beens in battles! Cor!' The other grunted and, mournfully, the voices died out.

The cockscomb-shaped splash became of overwhelming interest momentarily to Tietjens; at the same time his mind began upon abstruse

91

calculation of chances. Of his chances! A bad sign when the mind takes to doing that. Chances of direct hits by shells, by rifle bullets, by grenades, by fragments of shells or grenades. By any fragment of metal impinging on soft flesh. He was aware that he was going to be hit in the soft spot behind the collar-bone. He was conscious of that spot — the right-hand one; he felt none of the rest of his body. It is bad when the mind takes charge like that. A bromide was needed. The doctor must give him one. His mind felt pleasure at the thought of the M.O. A pleasant little fellow of the no-account order that knows his job. And carried liquor cheerfully. Confoundedly cheerfully!

He saw the doctor — plainly! It was one of the plainest things he could see of this whole show . . . The doctor, a slight figure, vault on to the parapet, like a vaulting horse for height; stand up in the early morning sun . . . Blind to the world, but humming *Father O'Flynn*. And stroll in the sunlight, a swagger cane of all things in the world, under his arms, right straight over to the German trench . . . Then throw his cap down into that trench. And walk back! Delicately avoiding the strands in the cut apron of wire that he had to walk through!

The doctor said he had seen a Hun

— probably an officer's batman — cleaning a top-boot with an apron over his knees. The Hun had shied a boot-brush at him and he had shied his cap at the Hun. The blinking Hun, he called him! No doubt the fellow had blinked!

No doubt you could do the unthinkable with impunity!

No manner of doubt: if you were blind drunk and all! . . . And however you strained, in an army you fell into routine. Of a quiet morning you do not expect drunken doctors strolling along your parapet. Besides, the German front lines were very thinly held. Amazingly! There might not have been a Hun with a gun within half a mile of that boot-black!

If he, Tietjens, stood in space, his head level with that cockscomb, he would be in an inviolable vacuum — as far as projectiles were concerned!

He was asking desultorily of the sergeant whether he often shocked the men by what he said and the sergeant was answering with blushes: Well, you do *say* things, sir! Not believing in skylarks now! If there was one thing the men believed hit was in the hinstincks of them little creatures!

'So that,' Tietjens said, 'they look at me as a sort of an atheist.'

He forced himself to look over the parapet again, climbing heavily to his place of observation. It was sheer impatience and purely culpable technically. But he was in command of the regiment, of an establishment of a thousand and eighteen men, or that used to be the establishment of a battalion; of a strength of three hundred and thirty-three. Say seventy-five per company. And two companies in command of second lieutenants, one just out . . . The last four days . . . There ought to be, say, eighty pairs of eyes surveying what he was going to survey. If there were fifteen it was as much as there were! . . . Figures were clean and comforting things. The chance against being struck by a shell-fragment that day, if the Germans came in any force, was fourteen-to-one against. There were battalions worse off than they. The sixth had only one one six left!

The tortured ground sloped down into mists. Say a quarter of a mile away. The German front lines were just shadows, like the corrugations of photographs of the moon: the paradoses of our own trenches two nights ago! The Germans did not seem to have troubled to chuck up much in the way of parapets. They didn't. They were coming on.

Anyhow they held their front lines always very sparsely . . . Was that the phrase? Was it even English?

Above the shadows the mist behaved tortuously, mounting up into umbrella shapes. Like snow-covered umbrella pines.

Disagreeable to force the eye to examine that mist. His stomach turned over . . . That was the sacks. A flat, slightly disordered pile of wet sacks, half-right at two hundred yards. No doubt a shell had hit a G.S. wagon coming up with sacks for trenching. Or the bearers had bolted, chucking the sacks down. His eyes had fallen on that scattered pile four times already that morning. Each time his stomach had turned over. The resemblance to prostrate men was appalling. The enemy creeping up . . . Christ! Within two hundred yards. So his stomach said. Each time, in spite of the preparation.

Otherwise the ground had been so smashed that it was flat; went down into holes but did not rise up into mounds. That made it look gentle. It sloped down, to the untidiness. They appeared mostly to lie on their faces; why? Presumably they were mostly Germans pushed back in the last counter-attack. Anyhow you saw mostly the seats of their trousers. When you did not, how profound was their repose! You must phrase it a little like that — rhetorically. There was no other way to get the effect of that profoundness. Call it profundity!

It was different from sleep; flatter. No doubt when the appalled soul left the weary body, the panting lungs . . . Well, you can't go on with a sentence like that . . . But you collapsed inwards. Like the dying pig they sold on trays in the street. Painter fellows doing battlefields never got that *intimate* effect. Intimate to them there. Unknown to the corridors in Whitehall . . . Probably because they — the painters — drew from living models or had ideas as to the human form . . . But these were not limbs, muscles, torsi. Collections of tubular shapes in field-grey or mud-colour they were. Chucked about by Almighty God? As if He had dropped them from on high to make them flatten into the earth . . . Good gravel soil, that slope and relatively dry. No dew to speak of. The night had been covered . . .

Dawn on the battlefield . . . Damn it all, why sneer? It *was* dawn on the battlefield . . . The trouble was that *this* battle was not over. By no means over. There would be a hundred and eleven years, nine months, and twenty-seven days of it still . . . No, you could not get the effect of that endless monotony of effort by numbers. Nor yet by saying 'Endless monotony of effort.' . . . It was like bending down to look into darkness of corridors under dark curtains. Under clouds . . . Mist . . .

At that, with dreadful reluctance his eyes went back to the spectral mists over the photographic shadows. He forced himself to put his glasses on the mists. They mopped and mowed, fantastically; grey, with black shadows; dropping like the dishevelled veils of murdered bodies. They were engaged in fantastic and horrifying laying out of corpses of vast dimensions; in silence, but in accord, they performed unthinkable tasks. They were the Germans. This was fear. This was the intimate fear of black, quiet nights, in dugouts where you heard the obscene suggestions of the miners' picks below you: tranquil, engrossed. Infinitely threatening . . . But not FEAR.

It was in effect the desire for privacy. What he dreaded at those normal times when fear visited him at lunch; whilst seeing that the men got their baths or when writing, in a trench, in support, a letter to his bank-manager, was finding himself unhurt, surrounded by figures like the brothers of the Misericordia, going unconcerned about their tasks, noticing him hardly at all . . . Whole hillsides, whole stretches of territory, alive with myriads of whitish-grey, long cagoules, with slits for eyeholes. Occasionally one would look at him through the eye-slits in the hoods . . . The prisoner!

He would be the prisoner, liable to physical contracts — to being handled and being questioned. An invasion of his privacy!

As a matter of fact that wasn't so far out; not so dotty as it sounded. If the Huns got him — as they precious near had the night before last! — they would be — they had then been — in gas-masks of various patterns. They must be short of these things, but they looked, certainly, like goblin pigs with sore eyes, the hood with the askew, blind-looking eyeholes and the mouthpiece or the other nose attachment going down into a box, astonishingly like snouts! . . . Mopping and mowing — no doubt shouting through the masks!

They had appeared with startling suddenness and as if with a supernatural silence, beneath a din so overwhelming that you could not any longer bother to notice it. They were there, as it were, under a glass dome of silence that sheltered beneath that dark tumult, in the white illumination of Verey lights that went on. They were there, those of them that had already emerged from holes — astonishingly alert hooded figures with the long rifles that always looked rather amateurish — though, Hell, they weren't. The hoods and the white light gave them the aspects of Canadian trappers in snow; made them no doubt look still more husky fellows as against our poor rats of Derby men. The heads of goblin pigs were emerging from shell-holes, from rifts in the torn earth, from old trenches ... This ground had been fought over again and again. Then the counter-attack had come through his, Tietjens' own crowd. One disorderly mob, as you might think, going through a disordered crowd that was damn glad to let them through, realising slowly, in the midst of a general not knowing what was going to happen, that the fellows were reliefs. They shot past you clumsily in a darkness spangled with shafts of light coming from God knows where and appeared going forward, whilst you at least had the satisfaction that, by order, you were going back. In an atmosphere of questioning. What was happening? What was going to happen? ... What the bloody hell ... What ...

Tidy-sized shells began to drop among them saying: 'Wee ... ee ... ry ... Whack!' Some fellow showed Tietjens the way through an immense apron of wire that was beginning to fly about. He, Tietjens, was carrying a hell of a lot of paper folders and books. They ought to have evacuated an hour ago; or the Huns ought not to have got out of their holes for an hour . . . But the Colonel had been too . . . too exalted. Call it too exalted. He was not going to evacuate for a pack of . . . damn orders! . . . The fellow McKechnie, had at last had to beg Tietjens to give the order . . . Not that the order mattered. The men could not have held ten minutes longer. The ghostly Huns would have been in the trenches. But the Company Commanders knew that there was a Divisional Order to retire, and no doubt they had passed it on to their subalterns before getting killed. Still, that Bn. H.Q. should have given the order made it better even if there was no one to take it to the companies. It turned a practical expulsion into an officially strategic retreat . . . And damn good divisional staff work at that. They had been fitted into beautiful, clean, new trenches, all ready for them — like chessmen fitting into their boxes. Damn good for a beaten army that was being forced off the face of the earth. Into the English Channel . . . What made them stick it? What the devil made the men stick it? They were unbelievable.

There was a stroking on his leg. A gentle,

100

timid stroking! Well, he *ought* to get down: it was setting a bad example. The admirable trenches were perfectly efficiently fitted up with spy-holes. For himself he always disliked them. You thought of a rifle bullet coming smack through them and guided by the telescope into your right eye. Or perhaps you would not have a telescope. Anyhow you wouldn't know . . .

There were still the three wheels, a-tilt, attached to slanting axles, in a haze of disintegrated wire, that, be-dewed, made profuse patterns like frost on a window. There was their own apron — a perfect village! — of wire over which he looked. Fairly intact. The Germans had put up some of their own in front of the lost trenches, a quarter of a mile off, over the reposing untidinesses. In between there was a perfect maze: their own of the night before last. How the deuce had it not been *all* mashed to pieces by the last Hun barrage? Yet there were three frosty erections — like fairy sheds, half-way between the two lines. And, suspended in them, as there would have to be, three bundles of rags and what appeared to be a very large, squashed crow. How the devil had that fellow managed to get smashed into that shape? It was improbable. There was also — suspended, too, a tall melodramatic object, the head cast back to

101

the sky. One arm raised in the attitude of, say, a Walter Scott Highland officer waving his men on. Waving a sword that wasn't there . . . That was what wire did for you. Supported you in grotesque attitudes, even in death! The beastly stuff! The men said that was Lieutenant Constantine. It might well be. The night before last he, Tietjens, had looked round at all the officers that were in H.Q. dug-out, come for a last moment conference. He had speculated on which of them would be killed. Ghostly! Well, they had all been killed, and more on to that. But his premonition hadn't run to thinking that Constantine would get caught up in the wire. But perhaps it was not Constantine. Probably they would never know. The Huns would be where he stood by lunch-time, if the attack of which Brigade H.Q. had warned them came off. But it mightn't . . .

As a final salute to the on the whole not thrilling landscape, he wetted his forefinger by inserting it in his mouth and held it in the air. It was comfortingly chilly on the exterior, towards his back. Light airs were going right in the other fellows' faces. It might be only the dawn wind. But if it stiffened a very little or even held, those blessed Wurtembergers would never that day get out of their trenches. They couldn't come without gas.

They were probably pretty well weakened, too . . . You were not traditionally supposed to think much of Wurtembergers. Mild, dull creatures they were supposed to be. With funny hats. Good Lord! Traditions were going by the board!

He dropped down into the trench. The rather reddish soil with flakes of flint and little, pinkish nodules of pebbles was a friendly thing to face closely.

That sergeant was saying:

'You hadn't ought to do it, sir. Give me the creeps.' He added rather lachrymosely that they couldn't do without superior officers *al*together. Odd creatures these Derby N.C.O.'s! They tried to get the tone of the old, time-serving N.C.O. They couldn't; all the same you couldn't say they weren't creditable achievements.

Yes, it was friendly, the trench face. And singularly unbellicose. When you looked at it you hardly believed that it was part of this affair . . . Friendly! You felt at peace looking at its flints and pebbles. Like being in the butts up above Groby on the moor, waiting for the grouse to come over. The soil was not of course like those butts which were built of turfs . . .

He asked, not so much for information, as to get the note of this fellow:

Why? What difference did it make whether there were senior officers or not? Anyone above eighteen would do, wouldn't they? They would keep on going on. It was a young man's war!

'It hasn't got that comfortable feeling, sir!' the sergeant expressed it. The young officers were very well for keeping you going through wire and barrages. But when you looked at them you didn't feel they knew so well what you were doing it for, if he might put it that way.

Tietjens said:

'Why? What are you doing it for?'

It wanted thirty-two minutes to the crucial moment. He said:

'Where are those bloody bombs?'

A trench cut in gravel wasn't, for all its friendly reddish-orange coloration, the ideal trench. Particularly against rifle-fire. There were rifts, presumably alongside flakes of flint that a rifle-bullet would get along. Still, the chances against a hit by a rifle-bullet were eighty thousand-to-one in a deep gravel trench like that. And he had had poor Jimmy Johns killed beside him by a bullet like that. So that gave him, say 140,000 chances-to-one against. He wished his mind would not go on and on figuring. It did it whilst you weren't looking. As a well-trained dog will do when you tell it to stay in one part of a room and it prefers another. It prefers to do figuring. Creeps from the rug by the door to the hearth-rug, its eyes on your unconscious face . . . That was what your mind was like. Like a dog!

The sergeant said:

'They do say the first consignment of bombs was it not smashed. Hin a gully; well behind the line. Another was coming down.'

'Then you'd better whistle,' Tietjens said, 'Whistle for all you're worth.'

The sergeant said:

'Fer a wind, sir? Keep the 'Uns' beck, sir?'

Looking up at the whitewash cockscomb Tietjens lectured the sergeant on Gas. He always *had* said, and he said now, that the Germans had ruined themselves with their gas.

He went on lecturing that sergeant on gas . . . He considered his mind: it was alarming him. All through the war he had had one dread — that a wound, the physical shock of a wound, would cause his mind to fail. He was going to be hit behind the collar-bone. He could feel the spot; not itching, but the blood pulsing just a little warmer. Just as you can become conscious of the end of your nose if you think about it!

The sergeant said that 'e wished 'e could

feel the Germans 'ad ruined theirselves: they seemed to be drivin' us into the Channel. Tietjens gave his reasons. They were driving us. But not fast enough. Not fast enough. It was a race between our disappearance and their endurance. They had been hung up yesterday by the wind, they were as like as not going to be held up to-day . . . They were not going fast enough. They could not keep it up.

The sergeant said 'e wished, sir, you'd tell the men that. That was what the men ought to be told; not the stuff that was hin Divisional Comic Cuts and the 'ome pipers . . .

A key-bugle of singular sweetness — at least Tietjens supposed it to be a key-bugle, for he knew the identities of practically no wind-instruments; it was certainly not a cavalry bugle, for there were no cavalry and even no Army Service Corps at all near — a bugle, then, of astounding sweetness made some remarks to the cool, wet dawn. It induced an astonishingly melting mood. He remarked:

'Do you mean to say, then, that your men, Sergeant, are really damned heroes? I suppose they are!'

He said 'your men,' instead of 'our' or even 'the' men, because he had been till the day before yesterday merely the second-in-command — and was likely to be to-morrow again merely the perfectly inactive second-in-command of what was called a rag-time collection that was astonishingly a clique and mutely combined to regard him as an outsider. So he really regarded himself as rather a spectator; as if a railway passenger had taken charge of a locomotive whilst the engine-driver had gone to have a drink.

The sergeant flushed with pleasure. 'Hit was,' he said, 'good to 'ave prise from Regular officers.' Tietjens said that he was not a Regular. The sergeant stammered:

'*Hain't* you, sir, a Ranker. The men all thinks you are a promoted Ranker.'

No, Tietjens said, he was not a promoted Ranker. He added, after consideration, that he was a militiaman. The men would have, by the will of chance, to put up with his leadership for at least that day. They might as well feel as good about it as they could — as settled in their stomachs! It certainly made a difference that the men should feel assured about their officers; what exact difference there was no knowing. This crowd was not going to get any satisfaction out of being led by a 'gentleman.' They did not know what a gentleman was: a quite un-feudal crowd.

Mostly Derby men. Small drapers, rate-collectors' clerks, gas-inspectors. There were even three music-hall performers, two scene shifters and several milkmen.

It was another tradition that was gone. Still, they desired the companionship of elder, heavier men who had certain knowledges. A militiaman probably filled the bill! Well, he was that, officially!

He glanced aside and upwards at the whitewash cockscomb. He regarded it carefully and with amusement. He knew what it was that had made his mind take the particular turn it had insisted on taking . . . The picks going in the dark under the H.Q. dug-out in the Cassenoisette section. The men called it Crackerjack.

He had been all his life familiar with the idea of picks going in the dark, underground. There is no North Country man who is not. All through that country, if you awake at night you hear the sound, and always it appears supernatural. You know it is the miners, at the pit-face, hundred and hundreds of feet down.

But just because it was familiar, it was familiarly rather dreadful. Haunting. And the silence had come at a bad moment. After a perfect hell of noise; after so much of noise that he had been forced to ascend the slippery clay stairs of the dug-out . . . And heaven knew if there was one thing that on account of his heavy-breathing chest he loathed, it was slippery clay . . . he had been forced to pant up those slippery stairs . . . His chest had been much worse, then . . . two months ago!

Curiosity had forced him up. And no doubt FEAR. The large battle fear; not the constant little, haunting misgivings. God knew! Curiosity or fear. In terrific noise; noise like the rushing up of innumerable noises determined not to be late, whilst the earth rocks or bumps or quakes or protests, you cannot be very coherent about your thoughts. So it might have been cool curiosity or it might have been sheer panic at the thought of being buried alive in that dug-out, its mouth sealed up. Anyhow, he had gone up from the dug-out where in his capacity of second-in-command, detested as an interloper by his C.O., he had sat ignominiously in that idleness of the second-in-command that it is in the power of the C.O. to inflict. He was to sit there till the C.O. dropped dead: then, however much the C.O. might detest him, to step into his shoes. Nothing the C.O. could do could stop that. In the meantime, as long as the C.O. existed, the second-in-command must be idle; he would be given nothing to do. For fear he got kudos!

Tietjens flattered himself that he cared nothing about kudos. He was still Tietjens of Groby; no man could give him anything, no man could take anything from him. He flattered himself that he in no way feared death, pain, dishonour, the afterdeath, feared very little disease — except for choking sensations! . . . But his Colonel got in on him.

He had no disagreeable feelings, thinking of the Colonel. A good boy, as boys go; perfectly warranted in hating his second-in-command . . . There are positions like that! But the fellow got in on him. He shut him up in that reeling cellar. And, of course, you might lose control of your mind in a reeling cellar where you cannot hear your thoughts. If you cannot hear your thoughts how the hell are you going to tell what your thoughts are doing?

You couldn't hear. There was an orderly with fever or shell-shock or something — a rather favourite orderly of the orderly room — asleep on a pile of rugs. Earlier in the night Orderly Room had asked permission to dump the boy in there because he was making such a beastly row in his sleep that they could not hear themselves speak and they had a lot of paper work to do. They could not tell what had happened to the boy, whom they liked.

The acting sergeant-major thought he must have got at some methylated spirits.

Immediately, that *strafe* had begun. The boy had lain, his face to the light of the lamp, on his pile of rugs — army blankets, that is to say . . . A very blond boy's face, contorted in the strong light, shrieking — positively shrieking obscenities at the flame. But with his eyes shut. And two minutes after that *strafe* had begun you could see his lips move, that was all.

Well, he, Tietjens, had gone up. Curiosity or fear? In the trench you could see nothing and noise rushed like black angels gone mad; solid noise that swept you off your feet . . . Swept your brain off its feet. Something else took control of it. You became second-in-command of your own soul. Waiting for its C.O. to be squashed flat by the direct hit of a four point two before you got control again.

There was nothing to see; mad lights whirled over the black heavens. He moved along the mud of the trench. It amazed him to find that it was raining. In torrents. You imagined that the heavenly powers in decency suspended their activities at such moments. But there was positively lightning. They didn't! A Verey light or something extinguished *that* — not very efficient lightning, really. Just at that moment he fell on his nose at an angle of forty-five degrees against some squashed earth where, as he remembered, the parapet had been revetted. The trench had been squashed in, level with the outside ground. A pair of boots emerged from the pile of mud. How the deuce did the fellow get into that position?

Broadside on to the hostilities in progress! . . . But, naturally, he had been running along the trench when that stuff buried him. Clean buried, anyhow. The obliging Verey light showed to Tietjens, just level with his left hand, a number of small smoking fragments. The white smoke ran level with the ground in a stiff breeze. Other little patches of smoke added themselves quickly. The Verey light went out. Things were coming over. Something hit his foot; the heel of his boot. Not unpleasantly, a smarting feeling as if his sole had been slapped.

It suggested itself to him, under all the noise, that there being no parapet there . . . He got back into the trench towards the dug-out, skating in the sticky mud. The duckboards were completely sunk in it. In the whole affair it was the slippery mud he hated most. Again a Verey light obliged, but the trench being deep there was nothing to see except the backside of a man. Tietjens said:

'If he's wounded . . . Even if he's dead one

ought to pull him down . . . And get the Victoria Cross!'

The figure slid down into the trench. Speedily, with drill-movements, engrossed, it crammed two clips of cartridges into a rifle correctly held at the loading angle. In a rift of the noise, like a crack in the wall of a house, it remarked:

'Can't reload lying up there, sir. Mud gets into your magazine.' He became again merely the sitting portion of a man, presenting to view the only part of him that was not caked with mud. The Verey light faded. Another reinforced the blinking effect. From just overhead.

Round the next traverse after the mouth of their dug-out a rapt face of a tiny subaltern, gazing upwards at a Verey illumination, with an elbow on an inequality of the trench and the forearm pointing upwards suggested — the rapt face suggested The Soul's Awakening! . . . In another rift in the sound the voice of the tiny subaltern stated that he had to economise the Verey cartridges. The battalion was very short. At the same time it was difficult to time them so as to keep the lights going . . . This seemed fantastic! The Huns were just coming over.

With the finger of his upward pointing hand the tiny subaltern pulled the trigger of his upward pointing pistol. A second later more brilliant illumination descended from above. The subaltern pointed the clumsy pistol to the ground in the considerable physical effort — for such a tiny person! — to reload the large implement. A very gallant child — name of Aranjuez. Maltese, or Portuguese, or Levantine — in origin.

The pointing of the pistol downwards revealed that he had practically coiled around his little feet, a collection of tubular, dead, khaki limbs. It didn't need any rift in the sound to make you understand that his loader had been killed on him ... By signs and removing his pistol from his grasp Tietjens made the subaltern — he was only two days out from England — understand that he had better go and get a drink and some bearers for the man who might not be dead.

He was, however. When they removed him a little to make room for Tietjens' immensely larger boots his arms just flopped in the mud, the tin hat that covered the face, to the sky. Like a lay figure, but a little less stiff. Not yet cold.

Tietjens became like a solitary statue of the Bard of Avon, the shelf for his elbow being rather low. Noise increased. The orchestra was bringing in *all* the brass, *all* the strings, *all* the wood-wind, all the percussion instruments. The performers threw about biscuit tins filled with horse-shoes; they emptied sacks of coal on cracked gongs, they threw down forty-storey iron houses. It was comic to the extent that an operatic orchestra's crescendo is comic. Crescendo! ... Crescendo! C R R R R R E S C ... The Hero *must* be coming! He didn't!

Still like Shakespeare contemplating the creation of, say, Cordelia, Tietjens leaned against his shelf. From time to time he pulled the trigger of the horse-pistol; from time to time he rested the butt on his ledge and rammed a charge home. When one jammed he took another. He found himself keeping up a fairly steady illumination.

The Hero arrived. Naturally, he was a Hun. He came over, all legs and arms going, like a catamount; struck the face of the parados, fell into the trench on the dead body, with his hands to his eyes, sprang up again and danced. With heavy deliberation Tietjens drew his great trench-knife rather than his revolver. Why? The butcher instinct? Or trying to think himself with the Exmoor stag-hounds. The man's shoulders had come heavily on him as he had rebounded from the parados-face. He felt outraged. Watching that performing Hun he held the knife pointed and tried to think of the German for *Hands*

Up. He imagined it to be *Hoch die Haende!* He looked for a nice spot in the Hun's side.

His excursion into a foreign tongue proved supererogatory. The German threw his arm abroad, his — considerably mashed! — face to the sky.

Always dramatic, Cousin Fritz! Too dramatic, really.

He fell, crumbling, into his untidy boot. Nasty boots, all crumpled too, up the calves! But he didn't say *Hoch der Kaiser,* or *Deutschland über alles,* or anything valedictory.

Tietjens fired another light upwards and filled in another charge, then, down on his hams in the mud he squatted over the German's head, the fingers of both hands under the head. He could feel the great groans thrill his fingers. He let go and felt tentatively for his brandy flask.

But there was a muddy group round the traverse end. The noise reduced itself to half. It was bearers for the corpse. And the absurdly wee Aranjuez and a new loader . . . In those days they had not been so short of men! Shouts were coming along the trench. No doubt other Huns were in.

Noise reduced itself to a third. A bumpy diminuendo. Bumpy! Sacks of coal continued to fall down the stairs with a regular cadence;

more irregularly, Bloody Mary, who was just behind the trench, or seemed like it, shook the whole house as you might say and there were other naval howitzers or something, somewhere.

Tietjens said to the bearers:

'Take the Hun first. He's alive. Our man's dead.' He was quite remarkably dead. He hadn't, Tietjens had observed, when he bent over the German, really got what you might call a head, though there was something in its place. What had done that?

Aranjuez, taking his place beside the trench-face, said:

'Damn cool you were, sir. Damn cool. I never saw a knife drawn so slow!' They had watched the Hun do the *danse du ventre*! The poor beggar had had rifles and the young feller's revolver turned on him all the time. They would probably have shot him some more but for the fear of hitting Tietjens. Half a dozen Germans had jumped into that sector of trenches in various places. As mad as March hares! . . . That fellow had been shot through both eyes, a fact that seemed to fill the little Aranjuez with singular horror. He said he would go mad if he thought he would be blinded, because there was a girl in the teashop at Bailleul, and a fellow called Spofforth of the Wiltshires would get her if his, Aranjuez's, beauty was spoiled. He positively whimpered at the thought and then gave the information that this was considered to be a false alarm, he meant a feigned attack to draw off troops from somewhere else where the real attempt was being made. There must be pretty good hell going on somewhere else, then.

It looked like that. For almost immediately all the guns had fallen silent except for one or two that bumped and grumped . . . It had all been just for fun, then!

Well, they were damn near Bailleul now. They would be driven past it in a day or two. On the way to the Channel. Aranjuez would have to hurry to see his girl. The little devil! He had overdrawn his confounded little account over his girl, and Tietjens had had to guarantee his overdraft — which he could not afford to do. Now the little wretch would probably overdraw still more — and Tietjens would have to guarantee still more of an overdraft.

But that night, when Tietjens had gone down into the black silence of his own particular branch of a cellar — they really had been in wine-cellars at that date, cellars stretching for hundreds of yards under chalk with strata of clay which made the mud so particularly sticky and offensive — he had found the sound of the pickaxes beneath his flea-bag almost unbearable. They were probably our own men. Obviously they were our own men. But it had not made much difference, for, of course, if they were there they would be an attraction, and the Germans might just as well be below them, counter-mining.

His nerves had been put in a bad way by that rotten *strafe* — that had been just for fun. He knew his nerves were in a bad way because he had a ghostly visit from O Nine Morgan, a fellow whose head had been smashed, as it were, on his, Tietjens', own hands, just after Tietjens had refused him home leave to go and get killed by a prize-fighter who had taken up with his, O Nine Morgan's, wife. It was complicated, but Tietjens wished that fellows who wished to fall on him when they were stopping things would choose to stop things with something else than their heads. That wretched Hun dropping on his shoulder, when, by the laws of war, he ought to have been running back to his own lines, had given him a jar that still shook his whole body. And, of course, a shock. The fellow had looked something positively Apocalyptic, his whitey-grey arms and legs spread abroad ... And it had been an imbecile

119

affair, with no basis of real fighting . . .

That thin surge of whitey-grey objects of whom not more than a dozen had reached the line — Tietjens knew that, because, with a melodramatically drawn revolver and the fellows who would have been really better employed carrying away the unfortunate Hun who had had in consequence to wait half an hour before being attended to — with those fellows loaded up with Mills bombs like people carrying pears, he had dodged, revolver first, round half a dozen traverses, and in quite enough of remains of gas to make his lungs unpleasant . . . Like a child playing a game of 'I spy!' Just like that.

. . . But only to come on several lots of Tommies standing round unfortunate objects who were either trembling with fear and wet and sweat, or panting with their nice little run.

This surge then of whitey-grey objects, sacrificed for fun, was intended . . . was intended ulti . . . ultim . . . then . . .

A voice, just under his camp-bed, said:

'*Bringt dem Hauptmann eine Kerze* . . . .'
As who should say: 'Bring a candle for the Captain . . . ' Just like that! A dream!

It hadn't been as considerable of a shock as you might have thought to a man just dozing off. Not really as bad as the falling dream, but quite as awakening ... His mind had resumed that sentence.

The handful of Germans who had reached the trench had been sacrificed for the stupid sort of fun called Strategy, probably. Stupid! ... It was, of course, just like German spooks to go mining by candle-light. Obsoletely Nibelungen-like. Dwarfs probably! ... They had sent over that thin waft of men under a blessed lot of barrage and stuff ... A lot! A *whole* lot! It had been really quite an artillery *strafe*. Ten thousand shells as like as not. Then, somewhere up the line they had probably made a demonstration in force. *Great* bodies of men, an immense surge. And twenty to thirty thousand shells. Very likely some miles of esplanade, as it were, with the sea battering against it. And only a demonstration in force ...

It could not be real fighting. They had not been ready for their spring advance.

It had been meant to impress somebody imbecile ... Somebody imbecile in Wallachia, or Sofia, or Asia Minor. Or Whitehall, very likely. Or the White House! ... Perhaps they had killed a lot of Yankees — to make themselves Trans-Atlantically popular. There were no doubt, by then, whole American Army Corps in the line somewhere. By then! Poor devils, coming so late into such an

accentuated hell. Damnably accentuated . . .
The sound of even that little bit of fun had
been portentously more awful than even quite
a big show say in '15. It was better to have
been in then and got used to it . . . If it
hadn't broken you, just by duration . . .

Might be to impress anybody . . . But, who
was going to be impressed? Of course, our
legislators with the stewed-pear brains running about the ignoble corridors with coke-
brize floors and mahogany doors . . . might be
impressed . . . You must not rhyme! . . . Or,
of course, our own legislators might have been
trying a nice little demonstration in force,
equally idiotic somewhere else, to impress
someone just as unlikely to be impressed . . .
This, then, would be the answer! But no one
ever would be impressed again. We all had
each other's measures. So it was just wearisome . . .

It was remarkably quiet in that thick
darkness. Down below, the picks continued
their sinister confidences in each other's ears
. . . It was really like that. Like children in
the corner of a schoolroom whispering nasty
comments about their masters, one to the
other . . . Girls, for choice . . . Chop, chop,
chop, a pick whispered. Chop? another asked
in an undertone. The first said Chopchopchop.
Then *Chup* . . . . And a silence of irregular

duration . . . Like what happens when you listen to typewriting and the young woman has to stop to put in another page . . .

Nice young women with typewriters in Whitehall had very likely taken from dictation, on hot-pressed, square sheets with embossed royal arms, the plan for that very *strafe* . . . . Because, obviously it might have been dictated from Whitehall almost as directly as from Unter den Linden. We might have been making a demonstration in force on the Dwolologda in order to get the Huns to make a counter-demonstration in Flanders. Hoping poor old Puffles would get it in the neck. For they were trying still to smash poor old General Puffles and stop the single command . . . They might very well be hoping that our losses through the counter-demonstration would be so heavy that the country would cry out for the evacuation of the Western Front . . . If they could get half a million of us killed perhaps the country might . . . They, no doubt, thought it worth trying. But it was wearisome: those fellows in Whitehall never learned. Any more than Brother Boche . . .

Nice to be in poor old Puffles' army. Nice but wearisome . . . Nice girls with typewriters in well-ventilated offices. Did they still put paper cuffs on to keep their sleeves from ink?

He would ask Valen . . . Valen . . . It was warm and still . . . On such a night . . .

'Bringt dem Hauptmann eine Kerze!' A voice from under his camp bed! He imagined that the Hauptmann spark must be myopic; short-sightedly examining a tamping fuse . . . If they used tamping fuses or if that was what they called them in the army!

He could not see the face or the spectacles of the Hauptmann any more than he could see the faces of his men. Not through his flea-bag and shins! They were packed in the tunnel; whitish-grey, tubular agglomerations . . . Large! Like the maggots that are eaten by Australian natives . . . Fear possessed him!

He sat up in his flea-bag, dripping with icy sweat.

'By jove, I'm for it!' he said. He imagined that his brain was going; he was mad and seeing himself go mad. He cast about in his mind for some subject about which to think so that he could prove to himself that he had not gone mad.

2

The key-bugle remarked with singular distinctness to the dawn:

                    dy
I know a la   fair   kind
                        and
    Was never face
                    so   mind
                pleased my
                            y

A sudden waft of pleasure at the seventeenth-century air that the tones gave to the landscape went all over Tietjens . . . Herrick and Purcell! . . . Or it was perhaps a modern imitation. Good enough. He asked:

'What the devil's that row, Sergeant?'

The sergeant disappeared behind the muddied sacking curtain. There was a guard-room in there. The key-bugle said:

Fair   kind . . .
        and
Fair   Fair   Fair
                                kind . . .
    and . . .   and . . .   and . . .

125

It might be two hundred yards off along the trenches. Astonishing pleasure came to him from that seventeenth-century air and the remembrance of those exact, quiet words . . . Or perhaps he had not got them right. Nevertheless, they were exact and quiet. As efficient working beneath the soul as the picks of miners in the dark.

The sergeant returned with the obvious information that it was O Nine Griffiths practising on the cornet. Captain McKechnie 'ad promised to 'ear 'im after breakfast 'n recommend 'im to the Divisional Follies to play at the concert to-night, if 'e likes 'im.

Tietjens said:

'Well, I hope Captain McKechnie likes him!'

He hoped McKechnie, with his mad eyes and his pestilential accent, would like that fellow. That fellow spread seventeenth-century atmosphere across the landscape over which the sun's rays were beginning to flood a yellow wash. Then, might the seventeenth century save the fellow's life, for his good taste! For his life would probably be saved. He, Tietjens, would give him a pass back to Division to get ready for the concert. So he would be out of the *strafe* . . . . Probably none of them would be alive after the *strafe* that Brigade reported to be coming in . . .

Twenty-seven minutes, by now! Three hundred and twenty-eight fighting men against . . . say, a Division. Any preposterous number . . . Well, the seventeenth century might as well save one man!

What had become of the seventeenth century? And Herbert and Donne and Crashaw and Vaughan, the Silurist? . . . Sweet day so cool, so calm, so bright, the bridal of the earth and sky! . . . By Jove, it was that! Old Campion, flashing like a popinjay in the scarlet and gilt of the major-general, had quoted that in the base camp, years ago. Or was it months? Or wasn't it: 'But at my back I always hear Time's winged chariots hurrying near,' that he had quoted?

Anyhow, not bad for an old general!

He wondered what had become of that elegant collection of light yellow, scarlet, and gilt . . . Somehow he always thought of Campion as in light yellow, rather than khaki, so much did he radiate light . . . Campion and his, Tietjens', wife, radiating light together — she in a golden gown!

Campion was about due in these latitudes. It was astonishing that he had not turned up before. But poor old Puffles with his abominably weakened Army had done too jolly well to be replaced. Even at the request of the Minister who hated him. Good for him!

It occurred to him that if he . . . call it 'stopped one' that day, Campion would probably marry his, Tietjens', widow . . . Sylvia in crêpe. With perhaps a little white about it!

The cornet — obviously it was not a key-bugle — remarked:

  : *her pass   by . . .*
      ing

I did but view . . .

and then stopped to reflect. After a moment it added meditatively:

        .her . . .
         .   .
And   .   .
  now   .   .
    I   .   .
      love   *.till*
          I die!

That would scarcely refer to Sylvia . . . Still, perhaps in crêpe, with a touch of white, passing by, very tall . . . Say, in a seventeenth-century street . . .

The only satisfactory age in England! ... Yet what chance had it to-day. Or, still more, to-morrow. In the sense that the age of, say, Shakespeare had a chance. Or Pericles! Or Augustus!

Heaven knew, we did not want a preposterous drum-beating such as the Elizabethans produced — and received. Like lions at a fair ... But what chance had quiet fields, Anglican sainthood, accuracy of thought, heavy-leaved, timbered hedge-rows, slowly creeping plough-lands moving up the slopes? ... Still, the land remains ...

The land remains ... It remains! ... At that same moment the dawn was wetly revealing; over there in George Herbert's parish ... What was it called? ... What the devil was its name? Oh, Hell! ... Between Salisbury and Wilton ... The tiny church ... But he refused to consider the plough-lands, the heavy groves, the slow high-road above the church that the dawn was at that moment wetly revealing — until he could remember that name ... He refused to consider that, probably even to-day, that land ran to ... produced the stock of ... Anglican sainthood. The quiet thing!

But until he could remember the name he would consider nothing ...

He said:

'Are those damned Mills bombs coming?'
The sergeant said:
'In ten minutes they'll be 'ere, sir. HAY Cumpny had just telephoned that they were coming in now.'

It was almost a disappointment; in an hour or so, without bombs, they might all have been done with. As quiet as the seventeenth century: in heaven . . . The beastly bombs would have to explode before that, now! They might, in consequence, survive . . . Then what was he, Tietjens, going to do! Take orders! It was thinkable . . .

He said:

'Those bloody imbeciles of Huns are coming over in an hour's time, Brigade says. Get the beastly bombs served out, but keep enough in store to serve as an emergency ration if we should want to advance . . . Say a third. For C and D Companies . . . Tell the Adjutant I'm going along all the trenches and I want the Assistant-Adjutant, Mr. Aranjuez, and Orderly-Corporal Colley to come with me . . . As soon as the bombs come for certain! . . . I don't want the men to think they've got to stop a Hun rush without bombs . . . They're due to begin their barrage in fourteen minutes, but they won't really come over without a hell of a lot of preparation . . . I don't know how Brigade knows all this!'

The name *Bemerton* suddenly came on to his tongue. Yes, Bemerton, Bemerton, Bemerton was George Herbert's parsonage. Bemerton, outside Salisbury . . . The cradle of the race as far as our race was worth thinking about. He imagined himself standing up on a little hill, a lean contemplative parson, looking at the land sloping down to Salisbury spire. A large, clumsily bound seventeenth-century testament, Greek, beneath his elbow . . . Imagine standing up on a hill! It was the unthinkable thing there!

The sergeant was lamenting, a little wearily, that the Huns were coming.

'Hi did think them bleeding 'uns, 'xcuse me, sir, wasn' per'aps coming this morning . . . Giv us a rest an' a chance to clear up a bit . . . ' He had the tone of a resigned schoolboy saying that the Head *might* have given the school a holiday on the Queen's birthday. But what the devil did that man think about his approaching dissolution?

That was the unanswerable question. He, Tietjens, had been asked several times what death was like . . . Once, in a cattle-truck under a bridge, near a Red-Cross Clearing Station, by a miserable fellow called Perowne. In the presence of the troublesome lunatic called McKechnie. You would have thought that even a Movement Order Officer would have managed to send up the line that triangle differently arranged. Perowne was known to have been his wife's lover; he, Tietjens, against his will, had been given the job, as second-in-command of the battalion, that McKechnie wanted madly. And indeed he had a right to it. They *ought* not to have been sent up together.

But there they had been — Perowne broken down, principally at the thought that he was not going to see his, Tietjens', wife ever again in a golden gown . . . Unless, perhaps, with a golden harp on a cloud, for he looked at things like that . . . And, positively, as soon as that baggage-car — it had been a baggage-car, not a cattle-truck! — had discharged the deserter with escort and the three wounded Cochin-Chinese platelayers whom the French authorities had palmed off on them . . . And where the devil had they all been going? Obviously up into the line, and already pretty near it: near Division Headquarters. But where? . . . God knew? Or when? God knew too! . . . A fine-ish day with a scanty remains of not quite melted snow in the cutting and the robins singing in the coppice above. Say February . . . Say St. Valentine's Day, which,

of course, would agitate Perowne some more
. . . Well, positively as soon as the baggage-car had discharged the wounded who had groaned, and the sheepish escort who did not know whether they ought to be civil to the deserter in the presence of the orfcers, and the deserter who kept on defiantly — or if you like broken-heartedly, for there was no telling the difference — asking the escort questions as to the nature of their girls, or volunteering information as to the intimate behaviour of *his* . . . . The deserter a gipsyfied, black-eyed fellow with an immense jeering mouth; the escort a corporal and two Tommies, blond and blushing East Kents, remarkably polished about the buttons and brass numerals, with beautifully neatly-put-on puttees: obviously Regulars, coming from behind the lines; the Cochin-Chinese, with indistinguishable broad yellow faces, brown poetic eyes, furred topboots and blue furred hoods over their bandaged heads and swathed faces. Seated, leaning back against the side of the box-truck and groaning now and then and shivering all the time . . .

Well, the moment they had been cleared out at the Deputy Sub. R.T.O.'s tin shed by the railway bridge, the fellow Perowne with his well-padded presence and his dark babu-Hindooish aspect had bubbled out with questions as to the hereafter according to Tietjens and as to the nature of Death; the immediate process of dissolution: dying . . . And in between Perowne's questions McKechnie, with his unspeakable intonation and his dark eyes as mad as a cat's, had asked Tietjens how he dared get himself appointed second-in-command of his, McKechnie's, own battalion . . . 'You're no soldier,' he would burst out. 'Do you think you are a b—y infantryman? You're a mealsack, and what the devil's to become of *my* battalion . . . Mine . . . My battalion! *Our* battalion of pals!'

That had been in, presumably, February, and, presumably, it was now April. The way the dawn came up looked like April . . . What did it matter? . . . That damned truck had stayed under that bridge for two hours and a half . . . in the process of the eternal waiting that is War. You hung about and you hung about, and you kicked your heels and you kicked your heels: waiting for Mills bombs to come, or for jam, or for generals, or for the tanks, or transport, or the clearance of the road ahead. You waited in offices under the eyes of somnolent orderlies, under fire on the banks of canals, you waited in hotels, dug-outs, tin sheds, ruined houses. There will be no man who survives of His Majesty's

Armed Forces that shall not remember those eternal hours when Time itself stayed still as the true image of bloody War! . . .

Well, in that case Providence seemed to have decreed a waiting just long enough to allow Tietjens to persuade the unhappy mortal called Perowne that death was not a very dreadful affair . . . He had enough intellectual authority to persuade the fellow with his glued-down black hair that Death supplied His own anæsthetics. That was the argument. On the approach of Death all the faculties are so numbed that you feel neither pain nor apprehension . . . He could still hear the heavy, authoritative words that, on that occasion, he had used.

The Providence of Perowne! For, when he was dug out after, next night having been buried in going up into the trenches, they said, he had a smile like a young baby's on his face. He didn't have long to wait and died with a smile on his face . . . nothing having so much become him during the life as . . . well, a becoming smile! During life he had seemed a worried, fussing sort of chap.

Bully for Perowne . . . But what about him, Tietjens? Was that the sort of thing that Providence ought to do to one? . . . That's Tempting God!

The sergeant beside him said:

'Then a man could stand hup on an 'ill
. . . You really mean to say, sir, that you think
a man will be able to stand up on a bleedin'
'ill . . . '

Presumably Tietjens had been putting
heart into that acting temporary sergeant-
major. He could not remember what he had
been saying to the N.C.O. because his mind
had been so deeply occupied with the image
of Perowne . . . He said:

'You're a Lincolnshire man, aren't you? You
come from a Fen country. What do you want
to stand up on a hill for?'

The man said:

'Ah, but you *do*, sir!'

He added:

'You want to stand up! Take a look
around . . . ' He struggled for expression:
'Like as if you wanted to breathe deep after
bein' in a stoopin' posture for a long time!'

Tietjens said:

'Well, you can do that here. With
discretion. I did it just now . . . '

The man said:

'You, sir . . . You're a law hunto yourself!'

It was the most considerable shock that
Tietjens received in the course of his military
career. And the most considerable reward.

There were all these inscrutable beings: the
Other Ranks, a brownish mass, spreading

underground, like clay strata in the gravel, beneath all this waving country that the sun would soon be warming; they were in holes, in tunnels, behind sack cloth curtains, carrying on . . . carrying on some sort of life, conversing, breathing, desiring. But completely mysterious, in the mass. Now and then you got a glimpse of a passionate desire: 'A man could stand up on a bleedin' 'ill'; now and then you got — though you knew that they watched you eternally and knew the minutest gestures of your sleep — you got some sort of indication as to how they regarded you: 'You are a law unto yourself!'

That must be hero-worship: an acting temporary regimental sergeant-major, without any real knowledge of his job, extemporising, not so long ago a carrier in an eastern county of remarkable flatness does not tell his Acting Commanding Officer that he is a law unto himself without meaning it to be a flattering testimony: a certificate, as far as it went, of trustworthiness . . .

They were now crawling out into the light of day; from behind the sacking, six files that he had last night transferred from C to D Coy., D having been reduced to forty-three rank and file. They shuffled out, an extraordinary Falstaff's battalion of muddy odd-come shorts, fell into some sort of

137

alignment in the trench, shuffled an inch further this way, an inch further that; pushed up their chinstraps and pulled them down; humped up their packs by hunching their shoulders and jerking; adjusted their water bottles and fell into some sort of immobility, their rifles, more or less aligned, poked out before them. In that small company they were men of all sorts of sizes, of all sorts of disparities and grotesquenesses of physique. Two of them were music-hall comedians and the whole lot looked as if they made up a knock-about turn . . . The Rag-Time Army at its vocation, living and breathing.

The sergeant called them to attention and they wavered back and forward. The sergeant said:

'The Commandin' Officer's lookin' at you. FIX . . . B'ts!'

And, positively, a dwarf concealed under a pudding basin shuffled a foot-length and a half forward in the mud, protruded his rifle-muzzle between his bent knees, jerked his head swiftly to strain his sight along the minute line . . . It was like a blurred fairy-tale! Why did that dwarf behave in a smart and soldierly manner? Through despair? It wasn't likely!

The men wavered like the edge of a field of tall grass with the wind running along it; they felt round themselves for their bayonet-handles, like women attempting difficult feats with their skirts . . . The dwarf cut his hand smartly away to his side, as the saying is, the men pulled their rifles up into line. Tietjens exclaimed:

'Stand at ease, stand easy,' negligently enough, then he burst out in uncontrollable irritation: 'For *God's* sake, put your beastly hats straight!' The men shuffled uneasily, this being no order known to them, and Tietjens explained: 'No, this isn't drill. It's only that your hats all at sixes and sevens give me the pip!' And the whispers of the men went down the little line:

'You 'eer the orfcer . . . Gives 'im the pip, we do! . . . Goin' for a wawk in the pawk wiv our gels, we are . . . ' They glanced nevertheless aside and upwards at each other's tin-hat rims and said: 'Shove 'im a shade forward, 'Orace . . . You tighten your martingale, 'Erb!' They were gaily rueful and impenitently profane; they had let thirty-six hours of let-off. A fellow louder-than-hummed:

'As I wawk erlong ther Bor dee Berlong
Wiv an indipendent air . . .
W'ere's me swegger-kine, you fellers!'

Tietjens addressed him:

'Did you ever hear Coborn sing that, Runt?' and Runt replied:

'Yes, sir. I was the hind legs of the elephant when he sung it in the Old Drury panto!' A little, dark, beady-eyed Cockney, his enormous mouth moved lip on lip as if he were chewing a pebble in pride at the reminiscence. The men's voices went on: ''Ind legs 'f the elephink! . . . good ol' Helefink . . . I'll go 'n see 'n elephink first thing I do in Blighty!'

Tietjens said:

'I'll give every man of you a ticket for Drury Lane next Boxing Day. We'll all be in London for the next Boxing Day. Or Berlin!'

They exclaimed polyphonically and low:

'Oo-er! Djee 'eer 'im? Di'djee 'eer the orfcer? The noo C.O.?'

A hidden man said:

'Mike it the old Shoreditch Empire, sir, 'n we'll thenk you!'

Another:

'I never keered fer the Lane meself! Give me the old Balliam for Boxing Day.' The sergeant made the sounds for them to move off.

They shuffled off up the trench. An unseen man said:

'Better'n a bleedin' dipso!' Lips said 'Shhh!'

140

The sergeant shouted — with an astonishing, brutal panic:

'You shut your bleedin' mouth, you man, or I'll shove you in the b—y clink!' He looked nevertheless at Tietjens with calm satisfaction a second later.

'A good lot of chaps, sir,' he said. 'The best!' He was anxious to wipe out the remembrance of the last spoken word. 'Give 'em the right sort of officers 'n they'll beat the world!'

'Do you think it makes any difference to them what officers they have?' Tietjens asked. 'Wouldn't it be all the same if they had just anyone?'

The sergeant said:

'No, sir. They bin frightened these last few days. Now they're better.'

This was just exactly what Tietjens did not want to hear. He hardly knew why. Or he did . . . He said:

'I should have thought these men knew their job so well — for this sort of thing — that they hardly needed orders. It cannot make much difference whether they receive orders or not.'

The sergeant said:

'It *does* make a difference, sir,' in a tone as near that of cold obstinacy as he dare attain to; the feeling of the approaching *strafe* was growing on them. It hung over them.

McKechnie stuck his head out from behind the sacking. The sacking had the lettering P X L in red and the word *Minn* in black. McKechnie's eyes were blazing maniacally, jumping maniacally in his head. They always were jumping maniacally in his head. He was a tiring fellow. He was wearing not a tin hat, but an officer's helmet. The gilt dragon on it glittered. The sun was practically up, somewhere. As soon as its disc cleared the horizon, the Huns, according to Brigade, were to begin sending over their wearisome stuff. In thirteen and a half minutes.

McKechnie gripped Tietjens by the arm, a familiarity that Tietjens detested. He hissed — he really hissed because he was trying to speak under his breath:

'Come past the next traverse. I want to speak to you.'

In correctly prepared trenches, made according to order as these had been to receive them in retreat, by a regular battalion acting under the orders of the Royal Engineers, you go along a straight ditch of trench for some yards, then you find a square block of earth protruding inwards from the parapet round which you must walk; then you come to another straight piece, then to another traverse, and so on to the end of the line, the lengths and dimensions varying to suit the nature of the terrain or the character of the soil. These outjuttings were designed to prevent the lateral spreading of fragments of shell bursting in the trench which would otherwise serve as a funnel, like the barrel of a gun to direct those parts of missiles into men's bodies. It was also exciting — as Tietjens expected to be doing before the setting of the not quite risen sun — to crouch rapidly along past one of them, the heart moving very disagreeably, the revolver protruded well in advance, with half a dozen careless fellows with grenades of sorts just behind you. And you not knowing whether, crouching against the side that was just round the corner you would or would not find a whitish, pallid, dangerous object that you would have no time to scrutinise closely.

Past the nearest of these McKechnie led Tietjens. He was portentous and agitated.

At the end of the next stretch of trench, leaning, as it were, against a buttress in an attitude of intense fatigue was a mud-coloured, very thin, tall fellow; squatting dozing on his heels in the mud just beside that one's foot was another, a proper Glamorganshire man of whom not many more than ten were left in the battalion. The standing man was leaning like that to look

143

through a loophole that had been placed very close to the buttress of raw earth. He grunted something to his companion and continued looking intently. The other man grunted too.

McKechnie withdrew precipitately into the recessed pathway. The column of earth in their faces gave a sense of oppression. He said:

'Did you put that fellow up to saying that damnable thing? . . . ' He repeated: 'That perfectly damnable thing! Damnable!' Besides hating Tietjens he was shocked, pained, femininely lachrymose. He gazed into Tietjens' eyes like a forsaken mistress fit to do a murder, with a sort of wistful incredulity of despair.

To that Tietjens was accustomed. For the last two months McKechnie whispering in the ear of the C.O. wherever Battalion Headquarters might happen to be — McKechnie, with his arms spread abroad on the table and his chin nearly on the cloth that they had always managed to retain in spite of three precipitate moves, McKechnie, with his mad eyes every now and then moving in the direction of Tietjens, had been almost the most familiar object of Tietjens' night landscapes. They wanted him gone so that McKechnie might once again become Second in Command of that body of pals . . .

That indeed was what they were . . . with the addition of a great deal too much of what they called 'Ooch.

Tietjens obviously could not go. There was no way of managing it: he had been put there by old Campion and there he must remain. So that by the agreeable irony of Providence there was Tietjens who had wanted above all McKechnie's present relatively bucolic job hated to hell by half a dozen quite decent if trying young squits — the pals — because Tietjens was in his, McKechnie's, desired position. It seemed to make it all the worse that they were all, with the exception of the Commanding Officer himself, of the little, dark, Cockney type and had the Cockney's voice, gesture, and intonation, so that Tietjens felt himself like a blond Gulliver with hair very silver in patches, rising up amongst a lot of Lilliputian brown creatures . . . Portentous and unreasonably noticeable.

A large cannon, nearer than the one that had lately spoken, but as it were with a larger but softer voice, remarked: 'Phohhhhhhhhh,' the sound wandering round the landscape for a long while. After a time about four coupled railway-trains hurtled jovially amongst the clouds and went a long way away — four in one. They were probably trying to impress the North Sea.

It might of course be the signal for the German barrage to begin. Tietjens' heart stopped; his skin on the nape of the neck began to prickle; his hands were cold. That was fear: the Battle Fear, experienced in *strafes*. He might not again be able to hear himself think. Not ever. What did he want of life? . . . Well, just not to lose his reason. One would pray. Not that . . . Otherwise, perhaps a nice parsonage might do. It was just thinkable. A place in which for ever to work at the theory of waves . . . But of course it was not thinkable . . .

He was saying to McKechnie:

'You ought not to be here without a tin hat. You will have to put a tin hat on if you mean to stop here. I can give you four minutes if that is not the *strafe* beginning. Who's been saying what?'

McKechnie said.

'I'm not stopping here. I'm going back, after I've given you a piece of my mind, to the beastly job you have got me defiled with.'

Tietjens said:

'Well, you'll put on a tin hat to go there, please. And don't ride your horse, if you've got it here, till after you're a hundred yards, at least, down a communication trench.'

McKechnie asked how Tietjens dared give him orders and Tietjens said: Fine he would look with Divisional Transport dead in his lines at five in the morning in a parade hat. McKechnie with objurgations said that the Transport Officer had the right to consult the C.O. of a battalion he supplied. Tietjens said:

'I'm commanding here. You've not consulted me.'

It appeared to him queer that they should be behaving like that when you could hear . . . oh, say, the wings of the angel of death . . . You can 'almost hear the very rustling of his wings' was the quotation. Good enough rhetoric. But of course that was how armed men would behave . . . At all times!

He had been trying the old trick of the military, clipped voice on the half-dotty subject. It had before then reduced McKechnie to some sort of military behaviour.

It reduced him in this case to a maudlin state. He exclaimed with a sort of lachrymose agony:

'This is what it has come to with the old battalion . . . the b—y; b—w, b—y old battalion of z—rs!' Each imprecation was a sob. 'How we worked at it . . . And now . . . you've got it!'

Tietjens said:

'Well, you were Vice-Chancellor's Latin Prize-man once. It's what we get reduced to.' He added: '*Vos mellificatis apes!*'

147

McKechnie said with gloomy contempt:
'You . . . You're no Latinist!'

By now Tietjens had counted two hundred and eighty since the big cannon had said 'Phooooh.' Perhaps then it was not the signal for the barrage to begin . . . Had it been it would have begun before now; it would have come thumping along on the heels of the 'Phoooh.' His hands and the nape of his neck were preparing to become normal.

Perhaps the *strafe* would not come at all that day.

There was the wind. If anything it was strengthening. Yesterday he had suspected that the Germans hadn't got any tanks handy. Perhaps the ugly, senseless armadillos — and incapable at that! under-engined! — had all got stuck in the marshes in front of G section. Perhaps the heavy artillery fire of ours that had gone on most of yesterday had been meant to pound the beastly things to pieces. Moving, they looked like slow rats, their noses to the ground, snouting crumbs of garbage. When they were still they looked merely pensive!

Perhaps the *strafe* would not come. He hoped it would not. He did not want a *strafe* with himself in command of the battalion. He did not know what to do, what he ought to do by the book. He knew what he would do. He would stroll about along those deep trenches. Stroll. With his hands in his pockets. Like General Gordon in pictures. He would say contemplative things as the time dragged on . . . A rather abominable sort of Time, really . . . But that would introduce into the Battalion a spirit of calm that it had lately lacked . . . The night before last the C.O. with a bottle in each hand had hurled them both at Huns who did not materialise for an hour and a half. Even the Pals had omitted to laugh. After that he, Tietjens, had taken command. With lots of the Orderly Room papers under both arms. They had had to be in a hurry, at night; with men suggesting pale grey Canadian trappers coming out of holes!

He did not want to command in a *strafe*, or at any other time! He hoped the unfortunate C.O. would get over his trouble by the evening . . . But he supposed that he, Tietjens, would get through it all right if he had to. Like the man who had never tried playing the violin!

McKechnie had suddenly become lachry-mosely feminine, like a woman pleading, large-eyed, for her lover, his eyes explored Tietjens' face for signs of treachery, for signs that what he said was not what he meant in his heart. He said:

'What are you going to do about Bill? Poor

old Bill that has sweated for his Battalion as you never . . . ' He began again:

'Think of poor old Bill! You can't be *thinking* of doing the dirty on him . . . *No* man could be such a swine!'

It was curious how those circumstances brought out the feminine that was in man. What was that ass of a German Professor's theory . . . formula? M^y *plus* W^x equals Man? . . . Well, if God hadn't invented woman men would have had to do so. In that sort of place. You grew sentimental. He, Tietjens, was growing sentimental. He said:

'What does Terence say about him this morning?'

The nice thing to have said would have been:

'Of course, old man, I'll do all I can to keep it dark!' Terence was the M.O. — the man who had chucked his cap at the Hun orderly.

McKechnie said:

'That's the damnable thing! Terence is ratty with him. He won't take a pill!'

Tietjens said:

'What's that? What's that?'

McKechnie wavered; his desire for comfort became overpowering.

He said:

'Look here! *Do* the decent thing! You know

150

how poor Bill has worked for us! Get Terence not to report him to Brigade!'

This was wearisome, but it had to be faced.

A very minute subaltern — Aranjuez — in a perfectly impossible tin hat peered round the side of the bank. Tietjens sent him away for a moment . . . These tin hats were probably all right, but they were the curse of the army. They bred distrust! How could you trust a man whose incapable hat tumbled forward on his nose? Or another, with his hat on the back of his head, giving him the air of a ruined gambler? Or a fellow who had put on a soap-dish, to amuse the children — not a serious proceeding . . . The Germans' things were better — coming down over the nape of the neck and rising over the brows. When you saw a Hun sideways he looked something: a serious proposition. Full of ferocity. A Hun up against a Tommie looked like a Holbein *lansknecht* fighting a music-hall turn. It made you feel that you were indeed a rag-time army. Rubbed it in!

McKechnie was reporting that the C.O. had refused to take a pill ordered him by the M.O. Unfortunately the M.O. was ratty that morning — too much hooch overnight! So he said he should report the C.O. to Brigade. Not as being unfit for further service, for he wasn't. But for refusing to take the pill. It was damnable. Because if Bill wouldn't take a pill he wouldn't . . . The M.O. said that if he took a pill, and stayed in bed that day — without hooch of course! — he would be perfectly fit on the morrow. He had been like that often enough before. The C.O. had always been given the dose before as a drench. He swore he would not take it as a ball. Sheer contrariety!

Tietjens was accustomed to think of the C.O. as a lad — a good lad, but young. They were, all the same, much of an age, and, for the matter of that, because of his deeply-lined forehead the Colonel looked the older often enough. But when he was fit he was fine. He had a hooked nose, a forcible, grey moustache, like two badger-haired paint-brushes joined beneath the nose, pink skin as polished as the surface of a billiard ball, a noticeably narrow but high forehead, an extremely piercing glance from rather colour-less eyes; his hair was black and most polished in slight waves. He was a soldier.

He was, that is to say, the ranker. Of soldiering in the English sense — the real soldiering of peace-time, parades, social events, spit and polish, hard-worked sum-mers, leisurely winters, India, the Bahamas, Cairo seasons, and the rest he only knew the outside, having looked at it from the barrack windows, the parade ground and, luckily for him, from his Colonel's house. He had been a most admirable batman to that Colonel, had — in Simla — married the Colonel's memsahib's lady's maid, had been promoted to the orderly-room, to the corporals' and sergeants' messes, had become a Musketry-colour sergeant and, two months before the war had been given a commission. He would have gained this before but for a slight — a very slight — tendency to overdrinking, which had given on occasion a similarly slight tone of insolence to his answers to field-officers. Elderly field-officers on parade are apt to make slight mistakes in their drill, giving the command to move to the right when technically, though troops are moving to the right, the command should be: 'Move to the left!'; and the officer's left being the troops' right, on a field-day, after lunch, field-officers of a little rustiness are apt to grow confused. It then becomes the duty of warrant-officers present if possible to rectify, or if not, to accept the responsibility for the resultant commotion. On two occasions during his brilliant career, being slightly elated, this war-time C.O. had neglected this military duty, the result being subsequent Orderly Room *strafes* which remained as black patches when he looked back on his past life and which constantly embittered his remembrances. Professional soldiers are like that.

In spite of an exceptionally fine service record he remained bitter, and upon occasion he became unreasonable. Being what the men — and for the matter of that the officers of the battalion, too — called a b—y h—ll of a pusher, he had brought his battalion up to a great state of efficiency; he had earned a double string of ribbons and by pushing his battalion into extremely tight places, by volunteering it for difficult services which, even during trench warfare did present themselves, and by extricating what remained of it with singular skill during the first battle of the Somme on an occasion — perhaps the most lamentable of the whole war — when an entire division commanded by a political rather than a military general had been wiped out, he had earned for his battalion a French decoration called a *Fourragère* which is seldom given to other than French regiments. These exploits and the spirit which dictated them were perhaps less appreciated by the men under his command than was imagined by the C.O. and his bosom friend Captain McKechnie who had loyally aided him, but they *did* justify the two in attaching to the battalion the sort of almost maudlin sentimentality that certain parents will bestow upon their children.

In spite, however, of the appreciation that his services had received, the C.O. remained embittered. He considered that, by this time, he ought at least to have been given a brigade, if not a division, and he considered that, if that was not the case, it was largely due to the two black marks against him as well as to the fact of his low social origin. And, when he had taken a little liquor these obsessions exaggerated themselves very quickly to a degree that very nearly endangered his career. It was not that he soaked — but there were occasions during that period of warfare when the consumption of a certain amount of alcohol was a necessity if the human being were to keep on carrying on and through rough places. Then, happy was the man who carried his liquor well.

Unfortunately the C.O. was not one of these. Worn out by continual attention to papers — at which he was no great hand — and by fighting that would continue for days on end, he would fortify himself with whisky and immediately his bitternesses would overwhelm his mentality, the aspect of the world would change and he would rail at his superiors in the army and sometimes would completely refuse to obey orders, as had been the occasion a few nights before, when he had refused to let his battalion take part in the concerted retreat of the Army Corps. Tietjens had had to see to this.

Now, exasperated by the aftereffects of several day's great anxieties and alcoholisms, he was refusing to take a pill. This was a token of his contempt for his superiors, the outcome of his obsession of bitterness.

3

An army — especially in peace time — is a very complex and nicely adjusted affair, and though active operations against an enemy force are apt to blunt nicenesses and upset compensations — as they might for a chronometer — and although this of ours, according to its own computation was only a rag-time aggregation, certain customs of times when this force was also Regular had an enormous power of survival.

It may seem a comic affair that a Colonel commanding a regiment in the midst of the most breathless period of hostilities, should refuse to take a pill. But the refusal, precisely like a grain of sand in the works of a chronometer, may cause the most singular perturbations. It was so in this case.

A sick officer of the very highest rank is the subordinate of his doctor the moment he puts himself into the M.O.'s hands: he must obey orders as if he were a Tommy. A Colonel whole and in his senses may obviously order his M.O. to go here and there and to perform this or that duty; the moment he becomes sick the fact that his body is the property of

His Majesty the King, comes forcibly into operation, and the M.O. is the representative of the sovereign in so far as bodies are concerned. This is very reasonable and proper, because sick bodies are not only of no use to the King, but are enormously detrimental to the army that has to cart them about.

In the case that Tietjens had perforce to worry over, the matter was very much complicated in the first place by the fact of the great personal dislike that the C.O. had manifested — though always with a sort of field-officer's monumental courtesy — towards himself, and then because Tietjens had a very great respect for the abilities of the Commanding Officer as Commanding Officer. His rag-time battalion of a rag-time army was as nearly on the level of an impeccable regular battalion as such a unit with its constantly changing personnel could possibly be. Nothing had much more impressed Tietjens in the course of even the whole war, than the demeanour of the soldier whom the other night he had seen firing engrossedly into invisibility. The man had fired with care, had come down to re-load with exact drill movements — which are the quickest possible. He had muttered some words which showed that his mind was entirely on his job like a mathematician engrossed in an abstruse calculation. He had climbed back on to the parapet; continued to fire engrossedly into invisibility; had returned and re-loaded and had again climbed back. He might have been firing off a tie at the butts!

It was a very great achievement to have got men to fire at moments of such stress with such complete tranquillity. For discipline works in two ways: in the first place it enables the soldier in action to get through his movements in the shortest possible time; and then the engrossment in the exact performance begets a great indifference to danger. When, with various-sized pieces of metal flying all round you, you go composedly through efficient bodily movements, you are not only wrapped up in your task, but you have the knowledge that that exact performance is every minute decreasing your personal danger. In addition you have the feeling that Providence ought to — and very frequently does — specially protect you. It would not be right that a man exactly and scrupulously performing his duty to his sovereign, his native land and those it holds dear, should not be protected by a special Providence. And he is!

It is not only that that engrossed marksman might — and very probably did — pick off an advancing enemy with every second shot, and thus diminish his personal danger to that extent, it is that the regular and as if mechanical falling of comrades spreads disproportionate dismay in advancing or halted troops. It is no doubt terrible to you to have large numbers of your comrades instantaneously annihilated by the explosion of some huge engine, but huge engines are blind and thus accidental; a slow, regular picking off of the men beside you is evidence that human terribleness that is not blind or accidental is cold-bloodedly and unshakably turning its attention to a spot very near you. It may very shortly turn its attention to yourself.

Of course, it is disagreeable when artillery is bracketting across your line: a shell falls a hundred yards in front of you, another a hundred yards behind you; the next will be half-way between, and you are half-way between. The waiting wrings your soul; but it does not induce panic or the desire to run — at any rate to nearly the same extent. Where, in any event, could you run to?

But from coldly and mechanically advancing and firing troops you *can* run. And the C.O. was accustomed to boast that on the several occasions when imitating the second battalion of the regiment he had been able to line his men up on tapes before letting them go in an attack and had insisted that they should advance at a very slow double indeed, and in exact alignment, his losses had been not only less than those of every other battalion in the Division, but they had been almost farcically negligible. Faced with troops advancing remorselessly and with complete equanimity the good Wurtembergers had fired so wildly and so high that you could hear their bullets overhead like a flock of wild-geese at night. The effect of panic is to make men fire high. They pull too sharply on their triggers.

These boasts of their Old Man naturally reached the men; they would be uttered before warrant officers and the orderly room staff; and the men — than whom in this matter none are keener mathematicians — were quick to see that the losses of their battalion until lately, at any rate, had been remarkably smaller than those of other units engaged in the same places. So that hitherto, though the men had regarded their Colonel with mixed feelings, he had certainly come out on top. That he was a b—y h—ll of a pusher did not elate them; they would have preferred to be reserved for less dangerous enterprises than those by which the battalion gained its remarkable prestige. On the other hand; though they were constantly being pushed into nasty scrapes, they lost less than units in quieter positions, and that pleased them. But they still asked themselves: 'If the Old Man let us be quiet shouldn't we lose proportionately still less? No one at all?'

That had been the position until very lately: until a week or so, or even a day or so before.

But for more than a fortnight this Army had been what amounted to on-the-run. It retreated with some personal stubbornness and upon prepared positions, but these prepared positions were taken with such great speed and method by the enormous forces attacking it, that hostilities had assumed the aspect almost of a war of movement. For this these troops were singularly ill-adapted, their training having been almost purely that suited for the process of attrition known as trench-warfare. In fact, though good with bombs and even with the bayonet, and though coura-geous and composed when not in motion, these troops were singularly inept when it was a matter of keeping in communication with the units on either side of them, or even within their own unit, and they had practi-cally no experience in the use of the rifle when in motion. To both these branches the Enemy had devoted untiring attention all through the period of relative inaction of the winter that had now closed and in both particulars their troops, though by now apparently inferior in morale, were remarkably superior. So it appeared to be merely a matter of waiting for a period of easterly winds for this Army to be pushed into the North Sea. The easterly winds were needed for the use of the gas without which, in the idea of the German leaders, it was impossible to attack.

The position, nevertheless, had been desperate and remained desperate, and standing there in the complete tranquillity and inaction of an April morning with a slight westerly breeze, Tietjens realised that he was experiencing what were the emotions of an army practically in flight. So at least he saw it. The use of gas had always been extremely disliked by the enemy's men, and its employment in cylinders had long since been abandoned. But the German Higher Staff persisted in preparing their attacks by dense screens of gas put over by huge plasterings of shells. These screens the enemy forces refused to enter if the wind blew in their direction.

There had come in, then, the factor which caused him himself to feel particular discomfort.

The fact that the battalion was remarkably ably commanded and unusually well-disciplined had not, of course, been overlooked by either brigade or division. And the brigade, too, happened to be admirable. Thus — these things did happen even in the confused periods that preceded the final breaking up of trench warfare — the brigade was selected to occupy positions where the enemy divisions might be expected to be hottest in attack, the battalion was selected to occupy the hottest points in that hottest sector of the line. The chickens of the C.O.'s efficiency had come home to roost.

It had been, as Tietjens felt all over his body, nearly more than flesh and blood could stand. Do what the C.O. had been able to do to husband his men, and, do what discipline could do to aid in the process, the battalion was reduced to not more than a third of what would have been a reasonable strength for the position it had had to occupy — and to abandon. And it was small comfort to the men that the Wiltshires on their right and the Cheshires on their left were in far worse case. So the aspect of the Old Man as a b—y h—ll of a pusher became foremost in their considerations.

To a sensitive officer — and all good officers in this respect are sensitive — the psychology of the men makes itself felt in innumerable ways. He can afford to be blind to the feelings of his officers, for officers have

164

to stand so much at the hands of their seniors before the rules of the service give them a chance to retaliate, that it takes a really bad Colonel to put his own mess in a bad way. As officer you *have* to jump to your C.O.'s orders, to applaud his sentiments, to smile at his lighter witticisms and to guffaw at those that are more gross. That is the Service. With the Other Ranks it is different. A discreet warrant-officer will discreetly applaud his officer's eccentricities and good humours, as will a sergeant desirous of promotion; but the rank and file are under no such compulsion. As long as a man comes to attention when spoken to that is all that can be expected of him. He is under no obligation to understand his officer's witticisms so he can still less be expected to laugh at or to repeat them with gusto. He need not even come very smartly to attention . . .

And for some days the rank and file of the battalion had gone dead, and the C.O. was aware that it had gone dead. Of the various types of field-officer upon whom he could have modelled himself as regards the men, he had chosen that of the genial, rubicund, slightly whiskyfied C.O. who finishes every sentence with the words: 'Eh, what?' In him it was a perfectly cold-blooded game for the benefit of the senior non-commissioned officers and the Other Ranks, but it had gradually become automatic.

For some days now, this mannerism had refused to work. It was as if Napoleon the Great had suddenly found that the device of pinching the ear of a grenadier on parade, had suddenly become ineffective. After the 'Eh, what!' like a pistol shot the man to whom it was addressed had not all but shuffled nor had any other men within earshot tittered and whispered to their pals. They had all remained just loutish. And it is a considerable test of courage to remain loutish under the Old Man's eyes!

All this the C.O. knew by the book, having been through it. And Tietjens knew that the C.O. knew it; and he half suspected that the C.O. knew that he, Tietjens, knew it . . . And that the Pals and the Other Ranks also knew: that, in fact, everyone knew that everyone knew. It was like a nightmare game of bridge with all hands exposed and all the players ready to snatch pistols from their hip-pockets.

And Tietjens, for his sins, now held the trump card and was in play!

It was a loathsome position. He loathed having to decide the fate of the C.O. as he loathed the prospect of having to restore the *morale* of the men — if they survived.

And he was faced now by the conviction

that he could do it. If he hadn't felt himself get his hand in with that dozen of disreputable tramps he would not have felt that he could do it. Then he must have used his moral authority with the doctor to get the Old Man patched up, drugged up, bucked up, sufficiently to carry the battalion at least to the end of the retreat of the next few days. It was obvious that that must be done if there was no one else to take command — no one else that was pretty well certain to handle the men all right. But if there *was* anyone else to take over didn't the C.O.'s condition make it too risky to let him remain in authority? Did it, or didn't it? Did it, or didn't it?

Looking at McKechnie coolly as if to see where next he should plant his fist he had thus speculated. And he was aware that, at the most dreadful moment of his whole life his besetting sin, as the saying is, was getting back on him. With the dreadful dread of the approaching *strafe* all over him, with a weight on his forehead, his eyebrows, his heavily labouring chest, he had to take . . . Responsibility. And to realise that he was a fit person to take responsibility.

He said to McKechnie:

'The M.O. is the person who has to dispose of the Colonel.'

McKechnie exclaimed:

'By God, if that drunken little squit dares . . . '

Tietjens said:

'Terry will act along the lines of my suggestions. He doesn't have to take orders from me. But he has said that he will act along the lines of my suggestions. I shall accept the moral responsibility.'

He felt the desire to pant, as if he had just drunk at a draft a too great quantity of liquid. He did not pant. He looked at his wrist-watch. Of the time he had decided to give McKechnie, thirty seconds remained.

McKechnie made wonderful use of the time. The Germans sent over several shells. Not such very long-distance shells either. For ten seconds McKechnie went mad. He was always going mad. He was a bore. If that were only the German customary popping off . . . But it was heavier. Unusual obscenities dropped from the lips of McKechnie. There was no knowing where the German projectiles were going. Or aimed at. A steam laundry in Bailleul as like as not. He said:

'Yes! Yes! Aranjuez!'

The tiny subaltern had peeped again, with his comic hat, round the corner of the pinkish gravel buttress . . . A good, nervous boy. Imagining that the fact that he had reported had not been noticed! The gravel certainly

looked more pink now the sun was come up
. . . It was rising on Bemerton! Or perhaps
not so far to the west yet. The parsonage of
George Herbert, author of *Sweet day so cool,
so calm, so bright, the bridal of the earth and
sky!*

It was odd where McKechnie who was still
shouting got his words for unnatural vice. He
had been Latin Prize Man. But he was
probably quite pure. The words very likely
meant nothing to him . . .   As to the
Tommies! . . . Then, why did they use them?

The German artillery thumped on! Heavier
than the usual salvoes with which methodically they saluted the dawn. But there were
no shells falling in that neighbourhood. So it
might not be the barrage opening the Great
Strafe! Very likely they were being visited by
some little German Prince and wanted to
show him what shooting was. Or by Field
Marshal Count von Brunkersdorf! Who had
ordered them to shoot down the chimney of
the Bailleul steam laundry. Or it might be
sheer irresponsibility such as distinguished all
gunners. Few Germans were imaginative
enough to be irresponsible, but no doubt
their gunners were more imaginative than
other Germans.

He remembered being up in the artillery
O.P. — what the devil was its name? — before

169

Albert. On the Albert-Bécourt-Bécordel Road! What the *devil* was its name? A gunner had been looking through his glasses. He had said to Tietjens: 'Look at that fat! . . . ' And through the glasses lent him, Tietjens had seen, on a hillside in the direction of Martinpuich, a fat Hun, in shirt and trousers, carrying in his right hand a food tin from which he was feeding himself with his left. A fat, lousy object, suggesting an angler on a quiet day. The gunner had said to Tietjens:

'Keep your glass on him!'

And they had chased that miserable German about that naked hillside, with shells, for ten minutes. Whichever way he bolted, they put a shell in front of him. Then they let him go. His action, when he had realised that they were really attending to him, had been exactly that of a rabbit dodging out of the wheat the reapers have just reached. At last he just lay down. He wasn't killed. They had seen him get up and walk off later. Still carrying his bait can!

His antics had afforded those gunners infinite amusement. It afforded them almost more when all the German artillery on that front, imagining that God knew what was the matter, had awakened and plastered heaven and earth and everything between for a quarter of an hour with every imaginable kind of missile. And had then, abruptly, shut up. Yes . . . Irresponsible people, gunners!

The incident had really occurred because Tietjens had happened to ask that gunner how much he imagined it had cost in shells to smash to pieces an indescribably smashed field of about twenty acres that lay between Bazentin-le-petit and Mametz Wood. The field was unimaginably smashed, pulverised, powdered . . . The gunner had replied that with shells from all the forces employed it might have cost three million sterling. Tietjens asked how many men the gunner imagined might have been killed there. The gunner said he didn't begin to know. None at all, as like as not! No one was very likely to have been strolling about there for pleasure, and it hadn't contained any trenches. It was just a field. Nevertheless, when Tietjens had remarked that in that case two Italian labourers with a steam plough could have pulverised that field about as completely for, say, thirty shillings, the gunner had taken it quite badly. He had made his men poop off after that inoffensive Hun with the bait can, just to show what artillery can *do*.

. . . At that point Tietjens had remarked to McKechnie:

'For my part, I shall advise the M.O. to recommend that the Colonel should be sent

171

back on sick leave for a couple of months. It is within his power to do that.'

McKechnie had exhausted all his obscene expletives. He was thus sane. His jaw dropped:

'Send the C.O. back!' he exclaimed lamentably. 'At the very moment when . . . '

Tietjens exclaimed:

'Don't be an ass. Or don't imagine that I'm an ass. No one is going to reap any glory in this Army. Here and now!'

McKechnie said:

'But what price the money? Command pay! Nearly four quid a day. You could do with two-fifty quid at the end of his two months!'

Not so very long ago it would have seemed impossible that any man *could* speak to him about either his private financial affairs or his intimate motives.

He said:

'I have obvious responsibilities . . . '

'Some say,' McKechnie went on, 'that you're a b—y millionaire. One of the richest men in England. Giving coal mines to duchesses. So they say. Some say you're such a pauper that you hire your wife out to generals . . . Any generals. That's how you get your jobs.'

To that Tietjens had had to listen before . . .

Max Redoubt . . . It had come suddenly on to his tongue — just as, before, the name of Bemerton had come, belatedly. The name of the artillery observation post between Albert and Bécourt-Bécordel had been Max Redoubt! During the intolerable waitings of that half-forgotten July and August the name had been as familiar on his lips as . . . say, as Bemerton itself . . . When I forget thee, oh, my Bemerton . . . or, oh, my Max Redoubt . . . may my right hand forget its cunning! . . . The unforgettables! . . . Yet he had forgotten them!

If only for a time he had forgotten them. Then, his right hand might forget its cunning. If only for a time . . . But even that might be disastrous, might come at a disastrous moment . . . The Germans had suppressed themselves. Perhaps they had knocked down the laundry chimney. Or hit some G.S. wagons loaded with coal . . . At any rate, that was not the usual morning *strafe*. That was to come. Sweet day so cool — began again.

McKechnie hadn't suppressed himself. He was going to get suppressed. He had just been declaring that Tietjens had not displayed any chivalry in not reporting the C.O. if he, Tietjens, considered him to be drunk — or even chronically alcoholic. No chivalry . . .

This was like a nightmare! . . . No it wasn't. It was like fever when things appear

173

stiffly unreal . . . And exaggeratedly real!
Stereoscopic, you might say!

McKechnie with an accent of sardonic hate
begged to remind Tietjens that if he
considered the C.O. to be a drunkard he
ought to have him put under arrest. King's
Regs. exacted that. But Tietjens was too
cunning. He meant to have that two-fifty
quid. He might be a poor man and need it.
Or a millionaire, and mean. They said that
was how millionaires became millionaires: by
snapping up trifles of money that, God
knows, would be godsends to people like
himself, McKechnie.

It occurred to Tietjens that two hundred
and fifty pounds after this was over, might be
a godsend to himself in a manner of speaking.
And then he thought:

'Why the devil shouldn't I earn it?'

What was he going to do? After this was
over.

And it was going over. Every minute the
Germans were not advancing they were
losing. Losing the power to advance . . .
Now, this minute! It was exciting.

'No!' McKechnie said. 'You're too cunning. If you got poor Bill cashiered for
drunkenness you'd have no chance of
commanding. They'd put in another pukka
colonel. As a stop-gap, whilst Bill's on sick

leave, you're pretty certain to get it. That's why you're doing the damnable thing you're doing.'

Tietjens had a desire to go and wash himself. He felt physically dirty.

Yet what McKechnie said was true enough! It was true! . . . The mechanical impulse to divest himself of money was so strong that he began to say:

'In that case . . . ' He was going to finish: 'I'll *get* the damned fellow cashiered.' But he didn't.

He was in a beastly hole. But decency demanded that he shouldn't act in panic. He had a mechanical, normal panic that made him divest himself of money. Gentlemen don't earn money. Gentlemen, as a matter of fact, don't do anything. They exist. Perfuming the air like Madonna lilies. Money comes into them as air through petals and foliage. Thus the world is made better and brighter. And, of course, thus political life can be kept clean! . . . So you can't make money.

But look here: This unit was the critical spot of the whole affair. The weak spots of Brigade, Division, Army, British Expeditionary Force, Allied Forces . . . If the Hun went through there . . . *Fuit Ilium et magna gloria* . . . . Not much glory!

He was bound to do his best for that unit.

175

That poor b—y unit. And for the b—y knockabout comedians to whom he had lately promised tickets for Drury Lane at Christmas . . . The poor devils had said they preferred the Shoreditch Empire or the old Balham. That was typical of England. The Lane was the *locus classicus* of the race, but those rag-time . . . heroes, call them heroes! — preferred Shoreditch and Balham!

An immense sense of those grimy, shuffling, grouching, dirty-nosed pantomime-supers came over him and an intense desire to give them a bit of luck, and he said:

'Captain McKechnie, you can fall out. And you will return to duty. Your own duty. In proper head-dress.'

McKechnie, who had been talking, stopped with his head on one side like a listening magpie. He said:

'What's this? What's this?' stupidly. Then he remarked:

'Oh, well, I suppose if you're in command . . . '

Tietjens said:

'It's usual to say 'sir,' when addressing a senior officer on parade. Even if you don't belong to his unit.'

McKechnie said:

'Don't belong! . . . *I* don't . . . To the poor b—y old pals! . . . '

Tietjens said:

'You're attached to Division Headquarters, and you'll get back to it! Now! At once! . . . And you won't come back here. Not while I'm in command . . . Fall out . . . '

That was really a duty — a feudal duty! — performed for the sake of the rag-time fellows. They wanted to be rid — and at once! — of dipsomaniacs in command of that unit and having the disposal of their lives . . . Well, the moment McKechnie had uttered the words: 'To the poor b—y old pals,' an illuminating flash had presented Tietjens with the conviction that, alone, the C.O. was too damn good an officer to appear a dipsomaniac, even if he were observably drunk quite often. But, seen together with this fellow McKechnie, the two of them must present a formidable appearance of being alcoholic lunatics!

The rest of the poor b—y old pals didn't really any more exist. They were a tradition — of ghosts! Four of them were dead: four in hospital, two awaiting court martial for giving worthless cheques. The last of them, practically, if you excepted McKechnie, was the collection of putrescence and rags at that moment hanging in the wire apron . . . The whole complexion of Headquarters would change with the going of McKechnie.

177

He considered with satisfaction that he would command a very decent lot. The Adjutant was so inconspicuous you did not even notice him. Beady-eyed, like a bird! Always preoccupied. And little Aranjuez, the signalling officer! And a fat fellow called Dunne, who had represented Intelligence since the Night Before Last! 'A' Company Commander was fifty, thin as a pipe-stem, and bald; 'B' was a good, fair boy, of good family; 'C' and 'D' were subalterns, just out. But clean . . . Satisfactory!

What a handful of frail grass with which to stop an aperture in the dam of — of the Empire! Damn the Empire! It was England! It was Bemerton Parsonage that mattered! What did we want with an Empire! It was only a jerry-building Jew like Disraeli that could have provided us with that jerry-built name! The Tories said they had to have someone to do their dirty work . . . Well, they'd had it!

He said to McKechnie:

'There's a fellow called Bemer — I mean Griffiths, O Nine — Griffiths, I understand you're interested in for the Divisional Follies. I'll send him along to you as soon as he's had his breakfast. He's first-rate with the cornet.'

McKechnie said:

'Yes, sir,' saluted rather limply and took a step.

That was McKechnie all over. He never brought his mad fists to a crisis. That made him still more of a bore. His face would be distorted like that of a wildcat in front of its kittens' hole in a stone wall. But he became the submissive subordinate. Suddenly! Without rhyme or reason!

Tiring people! Without manners! . . . They would presumably run the world now. It would be a tiresome world.

McKechnie, however, was saluting. He held a sealed envelope, rather small and crumpled, as if from long carrying. He was talking in a controlled voice after permission asked. He desired Tietjens to observe that the seal on the envelope was unbroken. The envelope contained 'The Sonnet.'

McKechnie must, then, have gone mad! His eyes, if his voice was quiet, though with an Oxford-Cockney accent — his prune-coloured eyes were certainly mad . . . Hot prunes!

Men shuffled along the trenches, carrying by rope-handles very heavy, lead-coloured wooden cases; two men to each case. Tietjens said:

'You're 'D' Company . . . Get a move on!'

McKechnie, however, wasn't mad. He was

only pointing out that he could pit his Intellect and his Latinity against those of Tietjens; that he could do it when the great day came!

The envelope, in fact, contained a sonnet. A sonnet Tietjens, for distraction, had written to rhymes dictated by McKechnie . . . for distraction in a moment of stress.

Several moments of stress they had been in together. It ought to have formed a bond between them. It hadn't . . . Imagine having a bond with a Highland-Oxford-Cockney!

Or perhaps it had! There was certainly the sonnet. Tietjens had written it in two and a half minutes, he remembered, to stave off the thought of his wife who was then being a nuisance . . . Two and a half minutes of forgetting Sylvia! A bit of luck! . . . But McKechnie had insisted on regarding it as a challenge. A challenge to his Latinity. He had then and there undertaken to turn that sonnet into Latin hexameters in two minutes. Or perhaps four . . .

But things had got in the way. A fellow called O Nine Morgan had got himself killed over their feet. In the hut. Then they had been busy with the Draft!

Apparently McKechnie had sealed up that sonnet in an envelope. In *that* envelope. Then and there. Apparently McKechnie had been inspired with a blind, Celtic, snorting rage to prove that he was better as a Latinist than Tietjens as a sonneteer. Apparently he was still so inspired. He was mad to engage in competition with Tietjens.

It was perhaps that that made him not quite mad. He kept sane in order to be fit for this competition. He was now repeating, holding out the envelope, seal upwards:

'I suppose you believe I have not read your sonnet, sir. I suppose you believe I have not read your sonnet, sir . . . To prepare myself to translate it more quickly.'

Tietjens said:

'Yes! No! . . . I don't care.'

He couldn't tell the fellow that the idea of a competition was loathsome to him. Any sort of competition was loathsome to Tietjens. Even competitive games. He liked playing tennis. Real tennis. But he very rarely played because he couldn't get fellows to play with, that beating would not be disagreeable . . . And it would be loathsome to be drawn into any sort of competition with this Prize Man . . . They were moving very slowly along the trench, McKechnie retreating sideways and holding out the seal.

'It's your seal, sir!' he was repeating. 'Your own seal. You see, it isn't broken . . . You don't perhaps imagine that I read the sonnet

181

quickly and made a copy from memory?'

... The fellow wasn't even a decent Latinist. Or verse-maker, though he was always boasting about it to the impossible, adenoidy, Cockney subalterns who made up the battalion's mess. He would translate their chits into Latin verse ... But it was always into tags. Generally from the Æneid. Like:

'*Conticuere omnes*, or *Vino somnoque sepultum!*'

That was, presumably, what Oxford of just before the War was doing.

He said:

'I'm not a beastly detective ... Yes, of course, I quite believe it.'

He thought of emerging into the society of little Aranjuez who was some sort of gentle earnest Levantine. Think of thinking of a Levantine with pleasure! He said:

'Yes. It's all right, McKechnie.'

He felt himself solid. He was really in a competition with this fellow. It was deterioration. He, Tietjens, was crumpling up morally. He had accepted responsibility; he had thought of two hundred and fifty pounds with pleasure; now he was competing with a Cockney-Celtic-Prize Man. He was reduced to that level ... Well, as like as not he would be dead before the afternoon. And no one would know.

Think of thinking about whether any one would know or no! . . . But it was Valentine Wannop that wasn't to know. That he had deteriorated under the strain! . . . That enormously surprised him. He said to his subconscious self:

'What! Is *that* still there?'

That girl was at least an admirable Latinist. He remarked, with a sort of sardonic glee that, years before, in a dog-cart, emerging from mist, somewhere in Sussex — Udimore! — she had made him look silly. Over Catullus! Him, Tietjens! . . . Shortly afterwards old Campion had run into them with his motor that he couldn't drive but *would* drive.

McKechnie, apparently assuaged, said:

'I don't know if you know, sir, that General Campion is to take over this Army the day after to-morrow . . . But, of course, you would know.'

Tietjens said:

'No. I didn't . . . You fellows in touch with Headquarters get to hear of things long before us.' He added:

'It means that we shall be getting reinforcements . . . It means the Single Command.'

4

It meant that the end of the war was in sight.

In the next sector, in front of the Headquarters' dug-out sacking they found only Second-Lieutenant Aranjuez and Lance-Corporal Duckett of the Orderly Room. Both good boys, the lance-corporal, with very long graceful legs. He picked up his feet well, but continually moved his ankles with his soles when he talked earnestly. Somebody's bastard.

McKechnie plunged at once into the story of the sonnet. The lance-corporal had, of course, a large number of papers for Tietjens to sign. An untidy, buff and white sheaf, so McKechnie had time to talk. He wished to establish himself as on a level with the temporary C.O. At least intellectually.

He didn't. Aranjuez kept on exclaiming: 'The Major wrote a sonnet in two and a half minutes! The Major! Who would have thought it!' Ingenuous boy!

Tietjens looked at the papers with some attention. He had been so kept out of contact with the affairs of the battalion, that he wanted to know. As he had suspected, the

184

paper business of the unit was in a shocking state. Brigade, Division, even Army and, positively, Whitehall were *strafing* for information about everything imaginable from jam, toothbrushes and braces, to religions, vaccination, and barrack damages ... This was interesting matter. A relief to contemplate ... You would almost think all-wise Authority snowed under and broke the backs of Commanding Officers with papers in order to relieve their minds of affording alternative interests ... alternative to the exigencies of active hostilities! It was certainly a relief whilst waiting for a *strafe* to come to the right stage — to have to read a violent enquiry about P.R.I. funds, whilst the battalion had been resting near a place called Béhencourt ...

It appeared that Tietjens might well be thankful that he had not been allowed to handle the P.R.I. funds.

The second-in-command is the titular administrator of the Regimental Institute: he is the President, supposed to attend to the men's billiard tables, almanacks, backgammon boards, football boots. But the C.O. had preferred to keep these books in his own hands. Tietjens regarded that as a slight. Perhaps it had not been!

It went quickly through his head that the

C.O. perhaps had financial difficulties — though that was no real affair of his . . . The House Guards was pressingly interested in the pre-enlistment affairs of a private called 64 Smith. They asked violently and for the third time for particulars of his religion, previous address and real name. That was no doubt the espionage branch at work . . . But Whitehall was also more violently interested in answers to queries about the disposal of regimental funds of a training camp in January, 1915 . . . As long ago as that! The mills of God grind slowly . . . That query was covered by a private note from the Brigadier saying that he wished for goodness' sake the C.O. would answer these queries or there would have to be a Court of Enquiry.

These particular two papers ought not to have been brought to Tietjens. He held them between the thumb and forefinger of his left hand and the query upon 64 Smith — which seemed rather urgent — between his first and second, and so handed them to Lance-Corporal Duckett. That nice, clean, fair boy was, at the moment, talking in intimate undertones to Second-Lieutenant Aranjuez about the resemblances between the Petrarchan and the Shakespearean sonnet form . . .

This was what His Majesty's Expeditionary Force had come to. You had four of its warriors, four minutes before the zero of a complete advance of the whole German line, all interested in sonnets . . . Drake and his game of bowls — in fact repeated itself! Differently, of course! But times change.

He handed the two selected papers to Duckett.

'Give this one to the Commanding Officer,' he said, 'and tell the Sergeant-Major to find what Company 64 Smith is in and have him brought to me, wherever I am . . . I'm going right along the trenches now. Come after me when you've been to the C.O. and the Sergeant-Major. Aranjuez will make notes of what I want done about revetting, you can put down anything about the personnel of the companies . . . Get a move on!'

He told McKechnie amiably to be out of those lines forthwith. He didn't want him killed on his hands.

The sun was now shining into the trench.

He looked again through Brigade's morning communication concerning dispositions the unit was to make in the event of the expected German attack . . . Due to begin — the preparatory artillery at least — in three minutes' time.

Don't we say prayers before battle? . . . He could not imagine himself doing it . . . He just hoped that nothing would happen that

187

would make him lose control of his mind . . . Otherwise he found that he was meditating on how to get the paper affair of the unit into a better state . . . 'Who sweeps a room as for Thy cause . . . ' It was the equivalent of prayer probably.

He noted that Brigade's injunctions about the coming fight were not only endorsed with earnestness by Division but also by very serious exhortations from Army. The chit from Brigade was in handwriting, that from Division in fairly clear typescript, that from Army in very pale type characters . . . It amounted to this: that they were that day to stick it till they burst . . . That meant that there was nothing behind their backs — from there to the North Sea! . . . The French were hurrying along probably . . . He imagined a lot of little blue fellows in red breeches trotting along pink, sunlit plains.

(You cannot control your imagination's pictures. Of course the French no longer wore red trousers.) He saw the line breaking just where the blue section came to; the rest, swept back into the sea. He saw the whole of the terrain behind them. On the horizon was a glistening haze. That was where they were going to be swept to. Or of course they would not be swept. They would be lying on their faces, exposing the seats of their breeches.

188

Too negligible for the large dust-pan and broom . . . What was death like — the immediate process of dissolution? He stuffed the papers into his tunic pocket.

He remembered with grim amusement that one chit promised him reinforcements. Sixteen men! Sixteen! Worcesters! From a Worcester training camp . . . Why the deuce weren't they sent to the Worcester battalion just next door? Good fellows, no doubt. But they hadn't got the drill quiffs of our lot; they were not pals with our men; they did not know the officers by name. There would be no welcome to cheer them . . . It was a queer idea, the deliberate destruction of regimental esprit de corps that the Home Authorities now insisted on. It was said to be imitated at the suggestion of a civilian of advanced social views from the French who in turn had imitated it from the Germans. It is of course lawful to learn of the Enemy; but is it sensible?

Perhaps it is. The Feudal Spirit was broken. Perhaps it would therefore be harmful to Trench-Warfare. It used to be comfortable and cosy. You fought beside men from your own hamlet under the leadership of the parson's son. Perhaps that was not good for you?

At any rate, as at present arranged, dying

was a lonely affair.

He, Tietjens, and little Aranjuez there, if something hit them would die — a Yorkshire territorial magnate's son and the son of, positively, an Oporto Protestant minister, if you can imagine such a thing! — the dissimilar souls winging their way to heaven side by side. You'd think God would find it more appropriate if Yorkshiremen went with other North Country fellows, and Dagoes with other Papists. For Aranjuez, though the son of a Non-conformist of sorts, had reverted to the faith of his fathers.

He said:

'Come along, Aranjuez . . . I want to see that wet bit of trench before the Hun shells hit it.'

Well . . . They were getting reinforcements. The Home Authorities had awakened to their prayers. They sent them sixteen Worcesters. They would be three hundred and forty-four — no, forty-three, because he had sent back O Nine Griffiths, the fellow with the cornet — three hundred and forty-three lonely souls against . . . say two Divisions! Against about eighteen thousand, very likely. And they were to stick it till they burst. Reinforced!

Reinforced. Good God! . . . Sixteen Worcesters!

What was at the bottom of it all?

Campion was going to command that Army. That meant that real reinforcements had been promised from the millions of men that filled the base camps. And it meant the Single Command! Campion would not have consented to take the command of that Army if he had not had those very definite promises.

But it would take time. Months! Anything like adequate reinforcements would take months.

And at that moment, in the most crucial point of the line of the Army, of the Expeditionary Force, the Allied Forces, the Empire, the Universe, the Solar System, they had three hundred and sixty-six men commanded by the last surviving Tory. To face wave on wave of the Enemy.

In one minute the German barrage was due.

Aranjuez said to him:

'You can write a sonnet in two and a half minutes, sir . . . And your siphon works like anything in that damp trench . . . It took my mother's great-uncle, the canon of Oporto, fifteen weeks to finish his celebrated sonnet. I know because my mother told me . . . But you oughtn't to be here, sir.'

Aranjuez then was the nephew of the author of the *Sonnet to Night*. He could be.

You had to have that sort of oddity to make up this world. So naturally he was interested in sonnets.

And, having got hold of a battalion with a stretch of damp trench, Tietjens had had the opportunity of trying a thing he had often thought of — of drying out vertically cut, damp soil by means of a siphon of soil-pipes put in, not horizontally, but vertically. Fortunately Hackett, the commander of B Company, that had the wet trench, had been an engineer in civil life. Aranjuez had been along, out of sheer hero-worship, to B trenches to see how his hero's siphons had worked. He reported that they worked like a dream.

Little Aranjuez said:

'These trenches are like Pompeii, sir.'

Tietjens had never seen Pompeii, but he understood that Aranjuez was referring to the empty square-cut excavations in the earth. Particularly to their emptiness. And to the deadly stillness in the sunlight . . . Admirable trenches. Made to hold an establishment of several thousand men. To bustle with Cockney life. Now dead empty. They passed three sentries in the pinkish gravel passage and two men, one with a pick, the other with a shovel. They were exactly squaring the juncture of the wall and the path, as they might have done in Pompeii. Or in Hyde Park! A perfect devil for tidiness, 'A' Company Commander. But the men seemed to like it. They were sniggering, though they stopped that, of course, when Tietjens passed . . .

A nice, dark, tiny boy, Aranjuez; his adoration was charming. From the very first — and naturally, frightened out of his little life, he had clung to Tietjens as a child clings to an omnipotent father. Tietjens, all-wise, could direct the awful courses of war and decree safety for the frightened! Tietjens needed that sort of worship. The boy said it would be awful to have anything happen to your eyes. Your girl naturally would not look at you. Not more than three miles away, Nancy Truefitt was now. Unless they had evacuated her. Nancy was his flame. In a tea-shop at Bailleul.

A man was sitting outside the mouth of 'A' dug-out, just after they passed the mouth of the communication trench . . . Comforting that channel in the soil looked, running uphill. You could saunter away up there, out of all this . . . But you couldn't! There was no turning here either to the right or to the left!

The man writing in a copy-book had his tin hat right over his eyes. Engrossed, he sat on a gravel-step, his copy-book on his knees. His name was Slocombe and he was a dramatist. Like Shakespeare. He made fifty pounds a time writing music-hall sketches, for the outer halls. The outer halls were the cheap music-halls that go in a ring round the suburbs of London. Slocombe never missed a second, writing in his copy-books. If you fell the men out for a rest when marching, Slocombe would sit by the roadside — and out would come his copy-book and his pencil. His wife would type out what he sent home. And write him grumbling letters if the supply of copy failed. How was she to keep up the Sunday best of George and Flossie if he did not keep on writing one-act sketches? Tietjens had this information through censoring one of the man's letters containing manuscript . . . Slocombe was slovenly as a soldier, but he kept the other men in a good humour, his mind being a perfect repertoire of Cockney jests at the expense of Big and Little Willy and Brother Fritz. Slocombe wrote on, wetting his pencil with his tongue.

The sergeant in the mouth of 'A' Company headquarters dugout started to turn out some sort of a guard, but Tietjens stopped him. 'A' Company ran itself on the lines of regulars in the depot. The O.C. had a conduct sheet-book as neat as a ledger! The old, bald, grim fellow. Tietjens asked the sergeant questions. Had they their Mills bombs all right? They weren't short of rifles — first-class order? . . . But how could they be! Were there any sick? . . . Two! . . . Well, it was a healthy life! . . . Keep the men under cover until the Hun barrage began. It was due now.

It was due now. The second hand of Tietjens' watch, like an animated pointer of hair, kicked a little on the stroke of the minute . . . 'Crumb!' said the punctual, distant sound.

Tietjens said to Aranjuez:

'It's presumably coming now!' Aranjuez pulled at the chin strap of his tin hat.

Tietjen's mouth filled itself with a dreadful salty flavour, the back of his tongue being dry. His chest and heart laboured heavily. Aranjuez said:

'If I stop one, sir, you'll tell Nancy Truefitt that . . . '

Tietjens said:

'Little nippers like you don't stop things . . . Besides, feel the wind!'

They were at the highest point of the trenches that ran along a hillside. So they were exposed. The wind had undoubtedly freshened, coming down the hill. In front and behind, along the trench, they could see views. Land, some green; greyish trees.

Aranjuez said:

'You think the wind will stop them, sir,' appealingly.

Tietjens exclaimed with gruffness:

'Of course it will stop them. They won't work without gas. Yet their men hate to have to face the gas-screens. It's our great advantage. It saps their *morale*. Nothing else would. They can't put up smoke-screens either.'

Aranjuez said:

'I know you think their gas has ruined them, sir . . . It was wicked of them to use it. You can't do a wicked thing without suffering for it, can you, sir?'

It remained indecently quiet. Like Sunday in a village with the people in church. But it was not pleasurable.

Tietjens wondered how long physical irregularities would inconvenience his mind. You cannot think well with a parched back to your tongue. This was practically his first day in the open during a *strafe*. His first whole day for quite a time. Since Noircourt! . . . How long ago? . . . Two years? . . . Maybe! . . . Then he had nothing to go on to tell him how long he would be inconvenienced!

It remained indecently quiet! Running footsteps, at first on duck-boards, then on the dry path of trench! They made Tietjens start violently, inside himself. The house must be on fire!

He said to Aranjuez:

'Some one is in a hurry!'

The lad's teeth chattered. They must have made him feel bad, too, the footsteps. The knocking on the gate in *Macbeth*!

They began. It had come. Pam . . . Pamperi . . . Pam! Pam! . . . Pa . . . Pamperi . . . Pam! Pam! . . . Pampamperipampampam . . . Pam . . . They were the ones that sound like drums. They continued incessantly. Immensely big drums, the ones that go at it with real zest . . . You know how it is, looking at an opera orchestra when the fellow with the big drum-sticks really begins. Your own heart beats like hell. Tietjens' heart did. The drummer appears to go mad.

Tietjens was never much good at identifying artillery by the sound. He would have said that these were anti-aircraft guns. And he remembered that, for some minutes, the drone of plane engines had pervaded the indecent silence . . . But that drone was so normal it was part of the silence. Like your own thoughts. A filtered and engrossed sound, drifting down from overhead. More like fine dust than noise.

A familiar noise said: 'We . . . e . . . e . . . ry!' Shells always appeared tired of life. As if after a long, long journey they said: 'Weary!' Very much prolonging the 'e' sound.

Then 'Whack!' when they burst.

This was the beginning of the *strafe* . . . . Though he had been convinced the *strafe* was coming he had hoped for a prolongation of the . . . say Bemerton! . . . conditions. The life Peaceful. And Contemplative. But here it was beginning. 'Oh well . . . '

This shell appeared heavier and to be more than usually tired. Desultory. It seemed to pass within six feet over the heads of Aranjuez and himself. Then, just twenty yards up the hill it said, invisibly, 'Dud!' . . . And it *was* a dud!

It had not, very likely, been aimed at their trench at all. It was probably just an air-craft shrapnel shell that had not exploded. The Germans were firing a great number of duds — these days.

So it might not be a sign of the beginning! It was tantalising. But as long as it ended the right way one could bear it.

Lance-Corporal Duckett, the fair boy, ran to within two foot of Tietjens' feet and pulled up with a Guardee's stamp and a terrific salute. There was life in the old dog yet. Meaning that a zest for spit and polish survived in places in these rag-time days.

The boy said, panting — it might have been agitation, or that he had run so fast . . .

But why had he run so fast if he were not agitated:

'If you please, sir,' . . . Pant . . . 'Will you come to the Colonel?' . . . Pant. 'With as little delay as possible!' He remained panting.

It went through Tietjens' mind that he was going to spend the rest of that day in a comfortable, dark hole. Not in the blinding daylight . . . Let us be thankful!

Leaving Lance-Corporal Duckett . . . it came suddenly into his head that he liked that boy because he suggested Valentine Wannop! . . . to converse in intimate tones with Aranjuez and so to distract him from the fear of imminent death or blindness that would mean the loss of his girl, Tietjens went smartly back along the trenches. He didn't hurry. He was determined that the men should not see him hurry. Even if the Colonel should refuse to be relieved of the command, Tietjens was determined that the men should have the consolation of knowing that Headquarters numbered one cool, sauntering soul amongst its members.

They had had, when they took over the Trasna Valley trenches before the Mametz Wood affair, a rather good Major who wore an eyeglass and was of good family. He had something the matter with him, for he committed suicide later . . . But, as they went

199

in, the Huns, say fifty yards, began to shout various national battle-cries of the Allies or the melodies of regimental quicksteps of British regiments. The idea was that if they heard, say: 'Some talk of Alexander . . . .' resounding from an opposite trench, H.M. Second Grenadier Guards would burst into cheers and Brother Hun would know what he had before him.

Well, this Major Grosvenor shut his men up, naturally, and stood listening with his eyeglass screwed into his face and the air of a connoisseur at a quartette party. At last he took his eyeglass out, threw it in the air and caught it again.

'Shout *Banzai*! men,' he said.

That, on the off-chance, might give the enemy a scunner at the thought that we had Japanese troops in the line in front of them, or it would show them that we were making game of them, a form of offensive that sent these owlish fellows mad with rage . . . So the Huns shut up!

That was the sort of humour in an officer that the men still liked . . . The sort of humour Tietjens himself had not got; but he could appear unconcernedly reflective and all there — and he could tell them, at trying moments that, say, their ideas about skylarks were all wrong . . . That was tranquillising.

Once he had heard a Papist Padre preaching in a barn, under shell-fire. At any rate shells were going overhead and pigs underfoot. The Padre had preached about very difficult points in the doctrine of the Immaculate Conception, and the men had listened raptly. He said that was common sense. They didn't want lachrymose or mortuary orations. They wanted their minds taken off . . . So did the Padre!

Thus you talk to the men, just before the event, about skylarks, or the hind-legs of the elephant at the old Lane! And you don't hurry when the Colonel sends for you.

He walked along, for a moment or two, thinking nothing. The pebbles in the gravel of the trench grew clear and individual. Some one had dropped a letter. Slocombe, the dramatist, was closing his copy-book. Sighing, apparently, he reached for his rifle. 'A' Company Sergeant-Major was turning out some men of sorts. He said: 'Get a move on!' Tietjens said as he passed: 'Keep them under cover as much as you can, Sergeant-Major.'

It occurred to him suddenly that he had committed a military misdemeanour in leaving Lance-Corporal Duckett with Aranjuez. An officer should not walk along a stretch of lonely trench without escort. Some Hun offering might hit him and there would be loss of property to His Majesty. No one to fetch a doctor or stretcher-bearers while you bled to death. That was the Army . . .

Well, he had left Duckett with Aranjuez to comfort him. That minute subaltern was suffering. God knew what little agonies ran about in his little mind, like mice! He was as brave as a lion when *strafes* were on: when they weren't, his little, blackamoor, nobbly face quivered as the thought visited him . . .

He had really left Valentine Wannop with Aranjuez! That, he realised, was what he had really done. The boy Duckett *was* Valentine Wannop. Clean, blond, small, with the ordinary face, the courageous eyes, the obstinately, slightly peaked nose . . . It was just as if, Valentine Wannop being in his possession, they had been walking along a road and seen someone in distress. And he, Tietjens, had said:

'I've got to get along. You stop and see what you can do!'

And, amazingly, he was walking along a country road beside Valentine Wannop, being silent, with the quiet intimacy that comes with possession. She belonged to him . . . Not a mountain road: not Yorkshire. Not a valley road: not Bemerton. A country parsonage was not for him. So he wouldn't take orders!

A dawn-land road, with some old thorn trees. They only grew really in Kent. And the sky coming down on all sides. The flat top of a down!

Amazing! He had not thought of that girl for over a fortnight now, except in moments of great *strafes,* when he had hoped she would not be too worried if she knew where he was. Because he had the sense that, all the time she knew where he was. He had thought of her less and less. At longer intervals . . . As with his nightmare of the mining Germans who desired that a candle should be brought to the Captain. At first, every night, three or four times every night, it had visited him . . . Now it came only once every night . . .

The physical semblance of that boy had brought the girl back to his mind. That was accidental, so it was not part of any psychological rhythm. It did not show him, that is to say, whether, in the natural course of events and without accidents she was ceasing to obsess him.

She was certainly now obsessing him! Beyond bearing or belief. His whole being was overwhelmed by her . . . by her mentality, really. For of course the physical resemblance of the lance-corporal was mere subterfuge. Lance-corporals do not resemble young ladies . . . And, as a matter of fact, he did not remember exactly what Valentine Wannop looked like. Not vividly. He had not that sort of mind. It was words that his mind found that let him know that she was fair, snub-nosed, rather broad-faced, and square on her feet. As if he had made a note of it and referred to it when he wanted to think of her. His mind didn't make any mental picture; it brought up a sort of blur of sunlight.

It was the mentality that obsessed him: the exact mind, the impatience of solecisms and facile generalisations! . . . A queer catalogue of the charms of one's lady love! . . . But he wanted to hear her say: 'Oh, chuck it, Edith Ethel!' when Edith Ethel Duchemin, now of course Lady Macmaster, quoted some of the opinions expressed in Macmaster's critical monograph about the late Mr. Rossetti . . . How *very* late now!

It would rest him to hear that. She was, in effect, the only person in the world that he wanted to hear speak. Certainly the only person in the world that he wanted to talk to. The only clear intelligence! . . . The repose that his mind needed from the crackling of thorns under all the pots of the world . . . From the eternal, imbecile 'Pampamperipam Pam Pamperi Pam Pam!' of the German guns that all the while continued.

Why couldn't they chuck that? What good

did it do them to keep that mad drummer incessantly thundering on his stupid instrument? ... Possibly they might bring down some of our planes, but they generally didn't. You saw the black ball of their shells exploding and slowly expand like pocket-handkerchiefs about the unconcerned planes, like black peas aimed at dragon-fleas, against the blue; the illuminated, pinkish, pretty things! ... But his dislike of those guns was just dislike — a Tory prejudice. They were probably worth while. Just ...

You naturally tried every argument in the unseen contest of wills that went on across the firmament. 'Ho!' says our Staff, 'they are going to attack in force at such an hour ackemma,' because naturally the staff thought in terms of ackemma years after the twenty-four-hour day had been established. 'Well, we'll send out a million machine-gun planes to wipe out any men they've got moving up into support!'

It was of course unusual to move bodies of men by daylight. But this game had only two resources: you used the usual; or the unusual. *Usually* you didn't begin your barrage after dawn and launch your attack at ten-thirty or so. So you might do it — the Huns might be trying it on — as a surprise measure.

On the other hand, our people might be sending over the planes, whose immense droning was then making your very bones vibrate, in order to tell the Huns that we were ready to be surprised, that the time had now about come round when we might be expecting the Hun brain to think out a surprise. So we sent out those deathly, dreadful things to run along just over the tops of the hedgerows, in spite of all the guns! For there was nothing more terrifying in the whole war than that span of lightness, swaying, approaching a few feet above the heads of your column of men: instinct with wrath, dispensing the dreadful rain! So we had sent them. In a moment they would be tearing down . . .

Of course if this were merely a demonstration; if, say, there were no reinforcements moving, no troops detraining at the distant railhead, the correct Hun answer would be to hammer some of our trenches to hell with all the heavy stuff they could put into them. That was like saying sardonically:

'God, if you interfere with our peace and quiet on a fine day we'll interfere with yours!' And . . . Kerumph . . . the wagons of coal would fly over until we recalled our planes and all went to sleep again over the chess-board . . . You would probably be just as well off if you refrained from either demonstration or counter-demonstration. But Great General Staff liked to exchange these witticisms in iron. And a little blood!

A sergeant of sorts approached him from Bn.H.2 way, shepherding a man with a head wound. His tin hat, that is to say, was perched jauntily forward over a bandage. He was Jewish-nosed, appeared not to have shaved, though he had, and appeared as if he ought to have worn pince-nez to complete his style of Oriental manhood. Private Smith. Tietjens said:

'Look here, what was your confounded occupation before the war?'

The man replied with an agreeable, cultured throaty intonation:

'I was a journalist, sir. On a Socialist paper. Extreme Left!'

'And what,' Tietjens asked, 'was your agreeable name? . . . I'm obliged to ask you that question. I don't want to insult you.'

In the old regular army it was an insult to ask a private if he was not going under his real name. Most men enlisted under false names.

The man said:

'Eisenstein, sir!'

Tietjens asked if the man were a Derby recruit or compulsorily enlisted. He said he had enlisted voluntarily. Tietjens said: 'Why?' If the fellow was a capable journalist and on the right side he would be more useful outside the army. The man said he had been foreign correspondent of a Left paper. Being correspondent of a Left paper with a name like Eisenstein deprived one of one's chance of usefulness. Besides he wanted to have a whack at the Prussians. He was of Polish extraction. Tietjens asked the sergeant if the man had a good record. The Sergeant said: 'First-class man. First-class soldier.' He had been recommended for the D.C.M., Tietjens said:

'I shall apply to have you transferred to the Jewish regiment. In the meantime you can go back to the First Line Transport. You shouldn't have been a Left journalist and have a name like Eisenstein. One or the other. Not both.' The man said the name had been inflicted on his ancestry in the Middle Ages. He would prefer to be called Esau, as a son of that tribe. He pleaded not to be sent to the Jewish regiment, which was believed to be in Mesopotamia,, just when the fighting there was at its most interesting.

'You're probably thinking of writing a book,' Tietjens said. 'Well, there are all Abanar and Pharpar to write about. I'm sorry. But you're intelligent enough to see that I can't take . . . ' He stopped, fearing that if the sergeant heard any more the men might make it hot for the fellow as a suspect. He was annoyed at having asked his name before the sergeant. He appeared to be a good man. Jews could fight . . . And hunt! . . . But he wasn't going to take any risks. The man, dark-eyed and erect, flinched a little, gazing into Tietjens' eyes.

'I suppose you can't, sir,' he said. 'It's a disappointment. I'm not writing anything. I want to go on in the Army. I like the life.'

Tietjens said:

'I'm sorry, Smith. I can't help it. Fall out!' He was sorry. He believed the fellow. But responsibility hardens the heart. It must. A very short time ago he would have taken trouble over that fellow. A great deal of trouble, very likely. Now he wasn't going to . . .

A large capital 'A' in whitewash decorated the piece of corrugated iron that was derelictly propped against a channel at right angles to the trench. To Tietjens' astonishment a strong impulse like a wave of passion influenced his being towards the left — up that channel. It wasn't funk: it wasn't any sort of funk. He had been rather irritatedly wrapped up in the case of Private Smith-Eisenstein. It had undeniably irritated him to have to break the chances of a Jew and Red Socialist. It was the sort of thing one did not do if one were omnipotent — as he was. Then . . . this strong impulse? . . . It was a passionate desire to go where you could find exact intellect: rest.

He thought he suddenly understood. For the Lincolnshire sergeant-major the word Peace meant that a man could stand up on a hill. For him it meant someone to talk to.

5

The Colonel said:

'Look here, Tietjens, lend me two hundred and fifty quid. They say you're a damn beastly rich fellow. My accounts are all out. I've got a loathsome complaint. My friends have all gone back on me. I shall have to face a Court of Enquiry if I go home. But my nerve's gone. I've got to go home.'

He added:

'I daresay you knew all that.'

From the sudden fierce hatred that he felt at the thought of giving money to this man, Tietjens knew that his inner mind based all its calculations on the idea of living with Valentine Wannop . . . when men could stand up on hills.

He had found the Colonel in his cellar — it really, actually was a cellar, the remains of a farm — sitting on the edge of his camp-bed, in his shorts, his khaki shirt very open at the neck. His eyes were a little bloodshot, but his cropped, silver-grey hair was accurately waved, his grey moustache beautifully pointed. His silver-backed hair-brushes and a small mirror were indeed on the table in front of him. By the rays of the lamp that, hung overhead, rendered that damp stone place faintly nauseating, he looked keen, clean, and resolute. Tietjens wondered how he would look by daylight. He had remarkably seldom seen the fellow by daylight. Beside the mirror and the brushes lay, limply, an unfilled pipe, a red pencil and the white buff papers from Whitehall that Tietjens had already read.

He had begun by looking at Tietjens with a keen, hard, bloodshot glance. He had said:

'You think you can command this battalion? Have you had any experience? It appears you suggest that I take two months' leave.'

Tietjens had expected a violent outbreak. Threats even. None had come. The Colonel had continued to regard him with intentness, nothing more. He sat motionless, his long arms, bare to the elbow, dependent over each of his knees, which were far apart. He said that if he decided to go he didn't want to leave his battalion to a man that would knock it about. He continued staring hard at Tietjens. The phrase was singular in that place and at that hour, but Tietjens understood it to mean that he did not want his battalion discipline to go to pieces.

Tietjens answered that he did not think he

would let the discipline go to pieces. The Colonel had said:

'How do you know? You're no soldier, are you?'

Tietjens said he had commanded in the line a Company at full strength — nearly as large as the battalion and, out of it, a unit of exactly eight times its present strength. He did not think any complaints had been made of him. The Colonel said, frostily:

'Well! I know nothing about you.' He had added:

'You seem to have moved the battalion all right the night before last. I wasn't in a condition to do it myself. I'm not well. I'm obliged to you. The men appear to like you. They're tired of me.'

Tietjens felt himself on tenterhooks. He had, now, a passionate desire to command that battalion. It was the last thing he would have expected of himself. He said:

'If it becomes a question of a war of motion, sir, I don't know that I should have much experience.'

The Colonel answered:

'It won't become a war of motion before I come back. If I ever do come back.'

Tietjens said:

'Isn't it rather like a war of motion now, sir?' It was perhaps the first time in his life he

213

had ever asked for information from a superior in rank — with an implicit belief that he would get an exact answer. The Colonel said:

'No. This is only falling back on prepared positions. There will be positions prepared for us right back to the sea. If the Staff has done its work properly. If it hasn't, the war's over. We're done, finished, smashed, annihilated, non-existent.'

Tietjens said:

'But if the great *strafe* that, according to Division, is due now . . . '

The Colonel said: 'What?' Tietjens repeated his words and added:

'We might get pushed beyond the next prepared position.'

The Colonel appeared to withdraw his thoughts from a great distance.

'There isn't going to be any great *strafe*,' he said. He was beginning to add: 'Division has got . . . ' A considerable thump shook the hill behind their backs. The Colonel sat listening without much attention. His eyes gloomily rested on the papers before him. He said, without looking up:

'Yes, I don't want my battalion knocked about!' He went on reading again — the communication from Whitehall. He said: 'You've read this?' and then:

'Falling back on prepared positions isn't the same as moving in the open. You don't have to do more than you do in a trench-to-trench attack. I suppose you can get your direction by compass all right. Or get someone to, for you.'

Another considerable Crump of sound shook the earth, but from a little further away. The Colonel turned the sheet of paper from Whitehall over. Pinned to the back of it was the private note of the Brigadier. He perused this also with gloomy and unsurprised eyes.

'Pretty stiff, all this,' he said, 'you've read it? I shall have to go back and see about this.'

He exclaimed:

'It's rough luck. I should have liked to leave my battalion to someone that knew it. I don't suppose you do. Perhaps you do, though.'

An immense collection of fire-irons: all the fire-irons in the world fell just above their heads. The sound seemed to prolong itself in echoes, though of course it could not have; it was repeated.

The Colonel looked upwards negligently. Tietjens proposed to go to see. The Colonel said:

'No, don't. Notting will tell us if anything's wanted . . . Though nothing can be wanted!' Notting was the beady-eyed Adjutant in the adjoining cellar. 'How could they expect us to keep accounts straight in August 1914? How can they expect me to remember what happened? At the Depot. Then!' He appeared listless, but without resentment. 'Rotten luck . . . ' he said. 'In the battalion and . . . with this!' He rapped the back of his hand on the papers. He looked up at Tietjens.

'I suppose I could get rid of you; with a bad report,' he said. 'Or perhaps I couldn't . . . General Campion put you here. You're said to be his bastard.'

'He's my god-father,' Tietjens said. 'If you put in a bad report of me I should not protest. That is, if it were on the grounds of lack of experience. I should go to the Brigadier over anything else.'

'It's the same thing,' the Colonel said. 'I mean a god-son. If I had thought you were General Campion's bastard, I should not have said it . . . No; I don't want to put in a bad report of you. It's my own fault if you don't know the battalion. I've kept you out of it. I didn't want you to see what a rotten state the papers are in. They say you're the devil of a paper soldier. You used to be in a Government office, didn't you?'

Heavy blows were being delivered to the earth with some regularity on each side of the cellar. It was as if a boxer of the size of a mountain were delivering rights and lefts in heavy alternation. And it made hearing rather difficult.

'Rotten luck,' the Colonel said. 'And McKechnie's dotty. Clean dotty.' Tietjens missed some words. He said that he would probably be able to get the paper work of the battalion straight before the Colonel came back.

The noise rolled down hill like a heavy cloud. The Colonel continued talking and Tietjens, not being very accustomed to his voice, lost a good deal of what he said but, as if in a rift, he did hear:

'I'm not going to burn my fingers with a bad report on you that may bring a General on my back — to get back McKechnie who's dotty . . . Not fit to . . . '

The noise rolled in again. Once the Colonel listened to it, turning his head on one side and looking upwards. But he appeared satisfied with what he heard and recommenced his perusal of the Horse Guards letter. He took the pencil, underlined words and then sat idly stabbing the paper with the point.

With every minute Tietjens' respect for him increased. This man at least knew his job — as an engine-driver does, or the captain of a steam tramp. His nerves might have gone to pieces. They probably had; probably he could not go very far without stimulants: he was probably under bromides now.

And, all things considered, his treatment of Tietjens had been admirable and Tietjens had to revise his view of it. He realised that it was McKechnie who had given him the idea that the Colonel hated him, but he would not have said anything. He was too old a hand in the Army to give Tietjens a handle by saying anything definite . . . And he had always treated Tietjens with the sort of monumental deference that, in a Mess, the Colonel should bestow on his chief assistant. Going through a door at meal-times, for instance, if they happened to be side by side, he would motion with his hand for Tietjens to go first, naturally though, taking his proper precedence when Tietjens halted. And here he was, perfectly calm. And quite ready to be instructive.

Tietjens was not calm: he was too much bothered by Valentine Wannop and by the thought that, if the *strafe* was on, he ought to be seeing about his battalion. And of course, by the bombardment. But the Colonel said, when Tietjens with the aid of signs again made proposals to take a look around:

'No. Stop where you are. This isn't the *strafe*. There is not going to be a *strafe*. This is only a little extra Morning Hate. You can tell by the noise. That's only four point twos. There's nothing really heavy. The really heavies don't come so fast. They'll be turning on to the Worcesters now and only giving us one every half-minute . . . That's their game. If you don't know that, what are you doing here?' He added! 'You hear?' pointing his forefinger to the roof. The noise shifted. It went away to the right as a slow coal-wagon might. He went on:

'This is your place. Not doing things up above. They'll come and tell you if they want things. And you've got a first-rate Adjutant in Notting and Dunne's a good man . . . The men are all under cover: that's an advantage in having your strength down to three hundred. There's dug-outs for all and to spare . . . All the same, this is no place for you. Nor for me. This is a young man's war. We're old 'uns. Three and a half years of it have done for me. Three and a half months will do for you.'

He looked gloomily at his reflection in the mirror that stood before him.

'You're a gone coon!' he said to it. Then he took it and, holding it for a moment poised at the end of a bare white arm, flung it violently at the rough stones of the wall behind Tietjens. The fragments tinkled to the ground.

'There's seven years' bad luck,' he said. 'God take 'em, if they can give me seven years worse than this last I'd find it instructive!'

He looked at Tietjens with infuriated eyes.

'Look here you!' he said. 'You're an educated man . . . What's the worst thing about this war? What's the *worst* thing? Tell me that!' His chest began to heave. 'It's that they won't let us alone. Never! Not one of us! If they'd let us alone we could fight. But never . . . No one! It's not only the beastly papers of the battalion, though I'm no good with papers. Never was and never shall be . . . But it's the people at home. One's own people. God help us, you'd think that when a poor devil was in the trenches they'd let him alone . . . Damn it: I've had solicitors' letters about family quarrels when I was in hospital. Imagine that! . . . Imagine it! I don't mean tradesmen's dunnings. But one's own people. I haven't even got a bad wife as McKechnie has and they say you have. My wife's a bit extravagant and the children are expensive. That's worry enough . . . But my father died eighteen months ago. He was in partnership with my uncle. A builder. And they tried to do his estate out of his share of the business and leave my old mother with nothing. And my brother and sister threw the estate into

Chancery in order to get back the little bit my father spent on my wife and children. My wife and children lived with my father whilst I was in India . . . And out here . . . My solicitor says they can get it out of my share: the cost of their keep. He calls it the doctrine of ademption . . . Ademption . . . Doctrine of . . . I was better off as a sergeant,' he added gloomily. 'But sergeants don't get let alone. They've always got women after them. Or their wives take up with Belgians and they get written to about it. Sergeant Cutts of 'D' Company gets an anonymous letter every week about his wife. How's he to do his duty! But he does. So have I till now . . . ' He added with renewed violence:

'Look here. You're an educated man, aren't you? The sort of man that could write a book. You write a book about that. You write to the papers about it. You'd be more use to the Army doing that than being here. I daresay you're a good enough officer. Old Campion is too keen a commander to stick a rotten officer into this job, god-son or no god-son . . . Besides, I don't believe the whole story about you. If a General wanted to give a soft god-son's job to a fellow, it would be a soft job and a fat one. He wouldn't send him here. So take the battalion with my blessing. You won't worry over it more than I have: the poor bloody Glamorgans.'

So he had his battalion! He drew an immense breath. The bumps began to come back along the line. He figured those shells as being like sparrow-hawks beating along a hedge. They were probably pretty accurate. The Germans were pretty accurate. The trenches were probably being knocked about a good deal, the pretty, pinkish gravel falling about in heaps as it would lie in a park, ready to be spread on paths. He remembered how he had been up on the Montagne Noire, still, thank God, behind where they were now. Why did he thank God? Did he really care where the Army was. Probably! But enough to say 'thank God' about? Probably too . . . But as long as they kept on at the job did anything matter? Anything else? It was keeping on that mattered. From the Montagne Noire he had seen our shells bursting on a thinnish line in the distance, in shining weather. Each shell existing in a white puff, beautifully. Forward and backward along the line . . . Under Messines village. He had felt exhilaration to think that our gunners were making such good practice. Now some Hun on a hill was feeling exhilaration over puffs of smoke in our line. But he, Tietjens, was . . . Damn it, he was going to make two hundred and fifty quid towards living with Valentine Wannop

— when you really *could* stand up on a hill
. . . anywhere!

The Adjutant, Notting, looked in and said:
'Brigade wants to know if we're suffering
any, sir?'

The Colonel surveyed Tietjens with irony:

'Well, what are you going to report?' he
asked . . . 'This officer is taking over from
me,' he said to Notting. Notting's beady eyes
and red-varnished cheeks expressed no
emotions.

'Oh, tell Brigade,' the Colonel said, 'that
we're all as happy as sand-boys. We could
stand this till Kingdom Come.' He asked: 'We
aren't suffering any, are we?'

Notting said: 'No, not in particular. 'C'
Company was grumbling that all its beautiful
revetments had been knocked to pieces. The
sentry near their own dug-out complained
that the pebbles in the gravel were nearly as
bad as shrapnel.'

'Well, tell Brigade what I said. With Major
Tietjens' compliments, not mine. He's in
command.'

' . . . You may as well make a cheerful
impression to begin with,' he added to
Tietjens.

It was then that, suddenly, he burst out with:

'Look here! Lend me two hundred and fifty
quid!'

He remained staring fixedly at Tietjens with an odd air of a man who has just asked a teasing, jocular conundrum . . .

Tietjens had recoiled — really half an inch. The man said he was suffering from a loathsome disease: it was being near something dirty. You don't contract loathsome diseases except from the cheapest kind of women or through being untidy-minded . . . The man's pals had gone back on him. That sort of man's pals do go back on him! His accounts were all out . . . He was in short the sort of swindling, unclean scoundrel to whom one lent money . . . Irresistibly!

A crash of the sort that you couldn't ignore, as is the case with certain claps in thunderstorms, sent a good deal of gravel down their cellar steps. It crashed against their shaky door. They heard Notting come out of his cellar and tell someone to shovel the beastly stuff back again where it had come from.

The Colonel looked up at the roof. He said that had knocked their parapet about a bit. Then he resumed his fixed glaze at Tietjens.

Tietjens said to himself:

'I'm losing my nerve . . . It's the damned news that Campion is coming . . . I'm becoming a wretched, irresolute Johnny.'

The Colonel said:

'I'm not a beastly sponger. I never borrowed before!' His chest heaved . . . It really expanded and then got smaller again, the orifice in the khaki at his throat contracting. Perhaps he never had borrowed before . . .

After all, it didn't matter what kind of man this was, it was a question of what sort of a man Tietjens was becoming. He said:

'I can't lend you the money. I'll guarantee an overdraft to your agents. For two hundred and fifty.'

Well, then, he remained the sort of man who automatically lent money. He was glad.

The Colonel's face fell. His martially erect shoulders indeed collapsed. He exclaimed ruefully:

'Oh, I say, I thought you were the sort one could go to.'

Tietjens said:

'It's the same thing. You can draw a cheque on your bank exactly as if I paid the money, in.'

The Colonel said:

'I *can*? It's the same thing? You're *sure*?' His questions were like the pleas of a young woman asking you not to murder her.

. . . He obviously was not a sponger. He was a financial virgin. There could not be a subaltern of eighteen in the whole army who did not know what it meant to have an overdraft guaranteed after a fortnight's leave . . . Tietjens only wished they didn't. He said:

'You've practically got the money in your hand as you sit there. I've only to write the letter. It's impossible your agents should refuse my guarantee. If they do, I'll raise the money and send it you.'

He wondered why he didn't do that last in any case. A year or so ago he would have had no hesitation about overdrawing his account to any extent. Now he had an insupportable objection. Like a hatred!

He said:

'You'd better let me have your address.' He added, for his mind was really wandering a little. There was too much talk! 'I suppose you'll go to No. IX Red Cross at Rouen for a bit.'

The Colonel sprang to his feet:

'My God, what's that?' he cried out. 'Me . . . to No. IX.'

Tietjens exclaimed:

'I don't know the procedure. You said you had . . . '

The other cried out:

'I've got cancer. A big swelling under the armpit.' He passed his hand over his bare flesh through the opening of his shirt, the long arm disappearing to the elbow. 'Good God . . . I suppose when I said my pals had gone back on me you thought I'd asked them for help and been refused. I haven't . . . They're all killed. That's the worst way you can go back on a pal, isn't it! Don't you understand men's language?'

He sat heavily down on his bed again.

He said:

'By jove, if you hadn't promised to let me have the money there would have been nothing for me but to make a hole in the water.'

Tietjens said:

'Well, don't contemplate it now. Get yourself well looked after. What does Derry say?'

The Colonel again started violently:

'Derry! The M.O . . . Do you think I'd tell him! Or little squits of subalterns? Or any man! You understand now why I wouldn't take Derry's beastly pill. How do I know what it mightn't do to . . . '

Again he passed his hand under his armpit, his eyes taking on a yearning and calculating expression. He added:

'I thought it a duty to tell you as I was asking you for a loan. You might not get repaid. I suppose your offer still holds good?'

Drops of moisture had hitherto made

beads on his forehead; it now shone, uniformly wet.

'If you haven't consulted anybody,' Tietjens said, 'you mayn't have got it. I should have myself seen to right away. My offer still holds good!'

'Oh, I've got it, all right,' the Colonel answered with an air of infinite sapience. 'My old man — my governor — had it. Just like that. And he never told a soul till three days before his death. Neither shall I.'

'I should get it seen to,' Tietjens maintained. 'It's a duty to your children. And the King. You're too damn good a soldier for the Army to lose.'

'Nice of you to say so,' the Colonel said. 'But I've stood too much. I couldn't face waiting for the verdict.'

. . . It was no good saying he had faced worse things. He very likely hadn't, being the man he was.

The Colonel said:

'Now if I could be any good!'

Tietjens said:

'I suppose I may go along the trenches now. There's a wet place . . . '

He was determined to go along the trenches. He had to . . . what was it . . . 'find a place to be alone with Heaven.' He maintained also his conviction that he must show the men his mealsack of a body, mooning along; but attentive.

A problem worried him. He did not like putting it since it might seem to question the Colonel's military efficiency. He wrapped it up: Had the Colonel any special advice as to keeping in touch with units on the right and left? And as to passing messages?

That was a mania with Tietjens. If he had had his way he would keep the battalion day and night at communication drill. He had not been able to discover that any precautions of that sort were taken in that unit at all. Or in the others alongside . . .

He had hit on the Colonel's heel of Achilles.

★   ★   ★

In the open it became evident: more and more and more and always more evident! The news that General Campion was taking over that command had changed Tietjens' whole view of the world.

The trenches were much as he had expected. They conformed indeed exactly to the image he had had in the cellar. They resembled heaps of reddish gravel laid out ready to distribute over the roads of parks. Getting out of the dug-out had been like climbing into a trolley that had just been inverted for the purpose of discharging its load. It was a nasty job for the men, cleaving a passage and keeping under cover. Naturally the German sharp-shooters were on the lookout. Our problem was to get as much of the trench as you could set up by daylight. The German problem was to get as many of our men as possible. Tietjens would see that our men stayed under cover until nightfall; the commander of the unit opposite would attend to the sniping of as many men as he could. Tietjens himself had three first-class snipers left; they would attempt to get as many of the German snipers as they could. That was self-defence.

In addition a great many Enemy attentions would direct themselves to Tietjens' stretch of the line. The artillery would continue to plunk in a shell or so from time to time. They would not do this very often because it would invite the attention of our artillery and that might prove too costly. More or less heavy masses of high explosives would be thrown on to the line; what the Germans called *Minenwerfer* might project what our people called sausages. These being visible coming through the air, you posted lookouts who gave you warning in time to get under cover. So the Germans had rather abandoned the use of these, probably as being costly in explosives and not so very effective. They made, that is to say, good holes, but accounted for few men.

Airplanes with their beastly bullet-distributing hoppers — that is what they seemed like — would now and then duck along the trench, but not very often. The proceeding was, again, too costly: they would limit themselves as a rule to circling leisurely overhead and dropping things whilst the shrapnel burst round them — and spattered bullets over the trench. Flying pigs, aerial torpedoes, and other floating missiles, pretty, shining, silvery things with fins, would come through the air and would explode on striking the ground or after burying themselves. There was practically no end to their devices and the Huns had a new one every other week or so. They perhaps wasted themselves on new devices. A good many of them turned out to be duds. And a good many of their usually successful missiles turned out to be duds. They were undoubtedly beginning to feel the strain — mental and in their materials. So that if you had to be in these beastly places it was probably better to be in our trenches than theirs. Our war material was pretty good!

This was the war of attrition . . . A mug's game! A mug's game as far as killing men was concerned, but not an uninteresting occupation if you considered it as a struggle of various minds spread all over the broad landscape in the sunlight. They did not kill many men and they expended an infinite number of missiles and a vast amount of thought. If you took six million men armed with loaded canes and stockings containing bricks or knives and set them against another six million men similarly armed, at the end of three hours four million on the one side and the entire six million on the other would be dead. So, as far as killing went, it really was a mug's game. That was what happened if you let yourself get into the hands of the applied scientist. For all these things were the products not of the soldier but of hirsute, bespectacled creatures who peered through magnifying glasses. Or of course, on our side, they would be shaven-cheeked and less abstracted. They were efficient as slaughterers in that they enabled the millions of men to be moved. When you had only knives you could not move very fast. On the other hand, your knife killed at every stroke: you would set a million men firing at each other with rifles from eighteen hundred yards. But few rifles ever registered a hit. So the invention was relatively inefficient. And it dragged things out!

And suddenly it had become boring.

They were probably going to spend a whole day during which the Germans would strain themselves, their intelligences flickering across the world, to kill a couple of Tietjens' men, and Tietjens would exercise all his care in the effort not to have even one casualty. And at the end of the day they would all be very tired and the poor b—y men would have to set to work to repair the trenches in earnest. That was the ordinary day's work.

He was going about it . . . He had got 'A' Company Commander to come up and talk to him about his fatigues. To the right of Headquarters the trenches appeared to have suffered less than to the left and it was possible to move quite a number of men without risk. 'A' Company Commander was an astonishingly thin, bald man of fifty. He was so bald that his tin hat slid about all over his skull. He had been a small shipowner and must have married very late in life, for he spoke of having two children, one of five, one of seven. A pigeon pair. His business was now making fifty thousand a year for him. It pleased Tietjens to think that his children would be well provided for if he were killed. A nice, silent, capable man who usually looked into the distance rather abstractedly when he

233

talked. He was killed two months' later, cleanly, by a bullet.

He was impatient that things had not got a move on. What had become of the big Hun *strafe?*

Tietjens said:

'You remember the Hun company-sergeant-major that surrendered to your crowd the night before last? The fellow who said he was going to open a little sweet-stuff shop in the Tottenham Court Road with the company money he had stolen? . . . Or perhaps you did not hear?'

The remembrance of that shifty looking N.C.O. in blue-grey that was rather smart for a man coming in during a big fight stirred up intensely disagreeable feelings from the bottom of Tietjens' mind. It was detestable to him to be in control of the person of another human being — as detestable as it would have been to be himself a prisoner . . . that thing that he dreaded most in the world. It was indeed almost more detestable, since to be taken prisoner was at least a thing outside your own volition, whereas to control a prisoner, even under the compulsion of discipline on yourself, implies a certain free-will of your own. And this had been an especially loathsome affair. Even normally, though it was irrational enough, prisoners affected him with the sense that they were unclean. As if they were maggots. It was not sensible, but he knew that if he had had to touch a prisoner he would have felt nausea. It was no doubt the product of his passionate Tory sense of freedom. What distinguished man from the brutes was his freedom. When, then, a man was deprived of freedom he became like a brute. To exist in his society was to live with brutes, like Gulliver amongst the Houyhnhnms!

And this unclean fellow had been a deserter in addition!

He had been brought in the H.Q. dug-out at three in the morning after the *strafe* had completely died out. It appeared that he had come over, ostensibly in the ordinary course of the attack. But he had lain all night in a shell hole, creeping in to our lines only when things were quiet. Previously to starting he had crammed his pockets with all the company money and even the papers that he could lay his hands on. He had been brought to H.Q. at that disagreeable hour because of the money and the papers, 'A' Company judging that such things ought to be put in the hands at least of the Adjutant as quickly as possible.

The C.O., McKechnie, the Intelligence Officer, and the doctor had all, in addition to

Tietjens himself, just settled in there, and the air of the smallish place was already fetid and reeking with service rum and whisky. The appearance of the German had caused Tietjens almost to vomit, and he was already in a state of enervation from having had to bring the battalion in. His temples were racked with a sort of neuralgia that he believed to be caused by eyestrain.

Normally, the questioning of prisoners before they reached Division was strongly discountenanced, but a deserter excites more interest than an ordinary prisoner, and the C.O. who was by then in a state of hilarious mutiny absolutely ordered Tietjens to get all he could out of the prisoner. Tietjens knew a little German: the Intelligence Officer who knew that language well had been killed. Dunne, replacing him, had no German.

The shifty, thin, dark fellow with even, unusually uneasy eyes, had answered questions readily enough: Yes, the Huns were fed up with the war; discipline had become so difficult to maintain that one of his reasons for deserting had been sheer weariness over the effort to keep the men under him in order. They had no food. It was impossible to get the men, in an advance, past any kind of food dumps. He was continually being unjustly reprimanded for his want of success,

236

and standing there he cursed his late officers! Nevertheless, when the C.O. made Tietjens ask him some questions about an Austrian gun that the Germans had lately introduced to that front and that threw a self-burying shell containing an incredible quantity of H.E., the fellow had clicked his heels together and had answered: '*Nein, Herr Offizier, das waere Landesverratung!*' . . . to answer that would be to betray one's country. His psychology had been difficult to grasp. He had explained as well as he could, using a few words of English, the papers that he had brought over. They were mostly exhortations to the German soldiers, circulars containing news of disasters to and the demoralisation of the Allied troops; there were also a few returns of no great interest — mostly statistics of influenza cases. But when Tietjens had held before the fellow's eyes a type-written page with a heading that he had now forgotten, the Sergeant had exclaimed: '*Ach, nicht das!*' . . . and had made as if to snatch the paper from Tietjens' fingers. Then he had desisted, realising that he was risking his life, no doubt. But he had become as pale as death, and had refused to translate the phrases that Tietjens did not understand; and indeed Tietjens understood practically none of the words, which were all technical.

He knew the paper contained some sort of movement orders; but he was by that time heartily sick of the affair and he knew that that was just the sort of paper that the staff did not wish men in the line to meddle with. So he dropped the matter, and the Colonel and the Pals being by that time tired of listening and not grasping what was happening, Tietjens had sent the fellow at the double back to Brigade under the charge of the Intelligence Officer and a heavier escort than was usual.

What remained to Tietjens of the affair was the expression that the fellow had used when asked what he was going to do with the Company money he had stolen. He was going to open a little sweet shop in the Tottenham Court Road. He had, of course, been a waiter, in old Compton Street. Tietjens wondered vaguely what would become of him. What did they do with deserters? Perhaps they interned them: perhaps they made them N.C.O.'s in prisoners' units. He could never go back to Germany . . . That remained to him — and the horror and loathing he had felt at the episode, as if it had caused him personal deterioration. He had put the matter out of his mind.

It occurred to him now that, very likely, the urgent announcements from Staff of all sorts

238

had been inspired by that very paper! The paper that loathsome fellow had tried to grab at. He remembered that he had been feeling so sick that he hadn't bothered to have the man handcuffed . . . It raised a number of questions: Does a man desert and at the same time refuse to betray his country? Well, he might. There was no end to the contradictions in men's characters. Look at the C.O. An efficient officer and a muddled ass in one, even in soldiering matters!

On the other hand, the whole thing might be a plant of the Huns. The paper — the movement order — might have been meant to reach our Army Headquarters. On the face of it, important movement orders do not lie about in Company offices. Not usually. The Huns might be trying to call our attention to this part of the line whilst their real attack might be coming somewhere else. That again was unlikely because that particular part of the line was so weak owing to poor General Puffles' unpopularity with the great ones at home that the Huns would be mad if they attacked anywhere else. And the French were hurrying up straight to that spot in terrific force. He might, then, be a hero! . . . But he didn't look like a hero!

This sort of complication was wearisome nowadays, though once it would have delighted him to dwell on it and work it out with nice figures and calculations of stresses. Now his only emotion about the matter was that, thank God, it was none of his job. The Huns didn't appear to be coming.

He found himself regretting that the *strafe* was not coming after all. That was incredible. How could he regret not being put into immediate danger of death?

Long, thin, scrawny and mournful, with his tin hat now tilted forwards over his nose, the O.C. 'A' Company gazed into futurity and remarked:

'I'm sorry the Huns aren't coming!'

He was sorry the Huns were not coming. Because if they came they might as well come according to the information supplied by that prisoner. He had captured that fellow. He might as well therefore get the credit. It might get him remembered if he put in for leave. He wanted leave. He wanted to see his children. He had not seen them for two years now. Children of five and seven change a good deal in two years. He grumbled on. Without any shame at the revelation of his intimate motives. The quite ordinary man! But he was perfectly to be respected. He had a rather grating chest voice. It occurred to Tietjens that that man would never see his children.

He wished these intimations would not

come to him. He found himself at times looking at the faces of several men and thinking that this or that man would shortly be killed. He wished he could get rid of the habit. It seemed indecent. As a rule he was right. But then, almost every man you looked at there was certain to get killed . . . Himself excepted. He himself was going to be wounded in the soft place behind the right collar-bone.

He regretted that the *strafe* was not that morning coming! Because if they came they might as well come according to the information supplied by the prisoner he had examined in the stinking dug-out. His unit had captured the fellow. He would now be signing its H.Q. chits as Acting O.C. Ninth Glamorganshires. So he, Tietjens, had captured that fellow. And his perspicacity in having him sent immediately back to Brigade with his precious paper might get him, Tietjens, remembered favourably at Brigade H.Q. Then they would leave him in temporary command of his battalion. And if they did that he might do well enough to get a battalion of his own!

He astounded himself . . . His mentality was that of O.C. 'A' Company!

He said:

'It was damn smart of you to see that

fellow was of importance and have him sent at the double to me.' O.C. 'A' Coy. grew red over all his grim face. So, one day, he, Tietjens, might flush with pleasure at the words of some squit with a red band round his hat!

He said:

'Even if the Germans don't come it might have been helpful. It might have been even more helpful. It might have been the means of keeping them back.' Because of course if the Germans knew that we had got hold of their Movement Order they might change their plans. That would inconvenience them. It was not likely. There was perhaps not time for the news that we knew to have got through to their Important Ones. But it was possible. Such things had happened.

Aranjuez and the lance-corporal stood still and so silent in the sunlight that they resembled fragments of the reddish trench. The red gravel of the trenches began here, however, to be smirched with more agricultural marl. Later the trenches became pure alluvial soil and then ran down more smartly into stuff so wet that it was like a quicksand. A bog. It was there he had tried revetting with a siphon-drain. The thought of that extreme of his line reminded him. He said:

'You know all about keeping in communication with immediately neighbouring units?'

The grim fellow said:

'Only what they taught in the training camps at the beginning of the war, sir. When I joined up. It was fairly thorough, but it's all forgotten now.'

Tietjens said to Aranjuez:

'You're Signalling officer. What do you know about keeping in communication with units on your right and left?'

Aranjuez, blushing and stammering, knew all about buzzers and signals. Tietjens said:

'That's only for trenches, all that. But, in motion. At your O.T.C. Didn't they practice you in keeping communication between troops in motion?'

They hadn't at the O.T.C . . . At first it had been in the programme. But it had always been crowded out by some stunt. Rifle-grenade drill. Bomb-throwing. Stokes-gun drill. Any sort of machine drill as long as it was not moving bodies of men over difficult country — sand-hills, say — and hammering into them that they must keep in touch unit with unit or drop connecting files if a unit itself divided up.

It was perhaps the dominant idea of Tietjens, perhaps the main idea that he got out of warfare — that at all costs you must keep in touch with your neighbouring troops. When, later, he had to command the escorts over immense bodies of German prisoners on the march it several times occurred to him to drop so many connecting files for the benefit of the men or N.C.O.s — or even the officers, of his escort who had fallen out through sheer fatigue or disease, that he would arrive in a new camp at the day's end with hardly any escort left at all — say thirty for three thousand prisoners. The business of an escort being to prevent the escape of prisoners it might have been thought better to retain the connecting files for that purpose. But, on the other hand, he never lost a prisoner except by German bombs, and he never lost any of his stragglers at all.

He said to O.C. 'A' Company:

'Please look after this matter in your Company. I shall arrange as soon as I can to transfer you to the outside right of the unit. If the men are doing nothing lecture them, please, yourself on this subject and talk very seriously to all lance-corporals, section leaders and oldest privates of platoons. And be good enough to get into communication at once with the Company Commander of the Wiltshires immediately on our right. In one of two ways the war is over. The war of trenches. Either the Germans will immediately drive us into the North Sea or we shall drive them back. They will then be in a state of demoralisation and we shall need to move fast. Lieutenant Aranjuez, you will arrange to be present when Captain Gibbs talks to his Company and you will repeat what he says in the other Companies.'

He was talking quickly and distinctly, as he did when he was well, and he was talking stiltedly on purpose. He could not obviously call an officers' conference with a German attack possibly impending; but he was pretty certain that something of what he said would penetrate to nearly every ear of the Battalion if he said it before a Company Commander, a Signalling lieutenant and an Orderly Room lance-corporal. It would go through that the Old Man was dotty on this joke, and sergeants would see that some attention was paid to the matter. So would the officers. It was all that could be done at the moment.

He walked behind Gibbs along the trench which at this point was perfectly intact and satisfactory, the red gravel gradually giving place to marl. He remarked to the good fellow that in that way they would do something to checkmate the blasted civilians whose meddling with the processes of war had put them where they were. Gibbs agreed gloomily that civilian interference had lost the war. They so hated the regular army that whenever a civilian saw a trace of regular training remaining in this mud-fighting that they liked us to indulge in, he wrote a hundred letters under different names to the papers, and the War Secretary at once took steps to retain that hundred votes; Gibbs had been reading a home-newspaper that morning.

Tietjens surprised himself by saying:

'Oh, we'll beat them yet!' It was an expression of impracticable optimism. He sought to justify his words by saying that their Army Commander's having put up such a damn good fight in spite of the most criminal form of civilian interference had begun to put a stopper on their games. Campion's coming was a proof that soldiers were going to be allowed to have some say in the conduct of the war. It meant the single command . . . Gibbs expressed a muted satisfaction. If the French took over those lines as they certainly would if they had the Single Command he would no doubt be able to go home and see his children. All their divisions would have to be taken out of the lines to be reorganised and brought up to strength.

Tietjens said:

'As to what we were talking about . . . Supposing you detailed outside section leaders and another file to keep in touch with the Wiltshires and they did the same. Supposing that for purposes of recognition they wore handkerchiefs round their right and left arms respectively . . . It has been done . . . '

'The Huns,' Captain Gibbs said grimly, 'would probably pick them off specially. They'd probably pick off specially any one who had any sort of badge. So you would be worse off.'

They were going at his request to look at a section of his trench. Orderly Room had ordered him to make arrangements for machine-gun performances there. He couldn't. It didn't exist. Nothing existed. He supposed that to have been the new Austrian gun. New probably, but why Austrian? The Austrians did not usually interest themselves much in high explosives. This one, whatever it was, threw something that buried itself and then blew up half the universe with astonishingly little noise and commotion; just lifted up, like a hippopotamus. He, Gibbs, had hardly noticed anything as you would have if it had been, say, a mine. When they came and told him that a mine had gone off there he would not believe them . . . But you could see for yourself that it looked exactly as if a mine had been chucking things about. A small mine. But still a mine . . .

In the shelter of the broken end of the trench a fatigue of six men worked with pick and shovel, patiently, two at a time. They threw up mud and stones and patted them and, stepping down into the thus created vacancy, threw up more mud and stones. Water oozed about, uncertain where to go. There must be a spring there. That hillside was honeycombed with springs . . .

You would certainly have said there had been a mine there. If we had been advancing it would have been a small mine left by the Huns to cheer us up. But we had retreated on to ground we had always held. So it couldn't have been a mine.

Also it kicked the ground forward and backward and relatively little laterally, so that the deep hole it had created more resembled the entry into a rudimentary shaft than the usually circular shell-hole. A mound existed between Tietjens and 'B' Company trench, considerably higher than you could see over. A vast mound; a miniature Primrose Hill. But much bigger than anything they had seen created by flying pigs or other aerial missiles as yet. Anyhow the mound was high enough to give Tietjens a chance to get round it in cover and shuffle down into 'B' Company's line. He said to Gibbs:

'We shall have to see about that machine

248

gun place. Don't come any further with me. Make those fellows keep their heads down and send them back if the Huns seem like sending over any more dirt.'

6

Tietjens reclined on the reverse slope of the considerable mound in the sunlight. He had to be alone, to reflect on his sentimental situation and his machine guns. He had been kept so out of the affairs of the unit that he had suddenly remembered that he knew nothing whatever about his machine guns, or even about the fellow who had to look after him. A new fellow called Cobbe, who looked rather vacant, with an immense sunburnt nose and an open mouth. Not, on the face of him, alert enough for his job. But you never knew.

He was hungry. He had eaten practically nothing since seven the night before, and had been on his feet the greater part of the time.

He sent Lance-Corporal Duckett to 'A' Company dug-out, to ask if they could favour him with a sandwich and some coffee with rum in it. He sent Second-Lieutenant Aranjuez to 'B' Company to tell them that he was coming to take a look round on their men and quarters. 'B' Company Commander for the moment was a very young boy just out from an O.T.C. It was annoying that he had an outside Company. But Constantine, the former Commander, had been killed the night before last. He was, in fact, said to be the gentleman whose remains hung in the barbed wire which was what made Tietjens doubtful whether it could be he. He should not have been so far to the left if he had been bringing his Company in. Anyhow, there had been no one to replace him but this boy — Bennett. A good boy. So shy that he could hardly give a word of command on parade, but yet with all his wits about him. And blessed with an uncommonly experienced Company sergeant-major. One of the original old Glamorganshires. Well, beggars could not be choosers. The Company had reported that morning five cases of the influenza that was said to be ravaging the outside world. Here then was another thing for which they had to thank the outside world — this band of rag-time solitaries! They let the outside world severely alone; they were, truly, hermits. Then the outside world did this to them. Why not leave them to their monastic engrossedness?

Even the rotten and detestable Huns had it! They were said by the Divisional news-sheets to have it so badly that whole Divisions were incapable of effective action. That might be a lie, invented for the purpose of heartening us; but it was probably true.

The German men were apparently beastly underfed, and, at that, only on substitute-foods of relatively small percentage of nutritive value. The papers brought over by that N.C.O. had certainly spoken urgently of the necessity of taking every precaution against the spread of this flail. Another circular violently and lachrymosely assured the troops that they were as well fed as the civilian populations and the Corps of Officers. Apparently there had been some sort of scandal. A circular of which he had not had time to read the whole ended up with an assertion something like: 'Thus the honour of the Corps of Officers has been triumphantly vindicated.'

It was a ghastly thought, that of that whole vast territory that confronted them, filled with millions of half-empty stomachs that bred disorders in the miserable brains. Those fellows must be the most miserable human beings that had ever existed. God knows, the life of our own Tommies must be Hell. But those fellows . . . It would not bear thinking of.

And it was curious to consider how the hatred that one felt for the inhabitants of those regions seemed to skip in a wide trajectory over the embattled ground. It was the civilian populations and their rulers that one hated with real hatred. Now the swine were starving the poor devils in the trenches.

They were detestable. The German fighters and their Intelligence and staffs were merely boring and grotesque. Unending nuisances. For he was confoundedly irritated to think of the mess they had made of his nice clean trenches. It was like when you go out for an hour and leave your dog in the drawing-room. You come back and find that it has torn to pieces all your sofa-cushions. You would like to knock its head off . . . So you would like to knock the German soldiers' heads off. But you did not wish them much real harm. Nothing like having to live in that hell on perpetually half-empty, windy stomachs with the nightmares they set up! Naturally influenza was decimating them.

Anyhow, Germans were the sort of people that influenza *would* bowl over. They were bores because they came for ever true to type. You read their confounded circulars and they made you grin whilst a little puking. They were like continual caricatures of themselves and they were continually hysterical . . . Hypochondriacal . . . Corps of Officers . . . Proud German Army . . . His Glorious Majesty . . . Mighty Deeds . . . Not much of the Rag-time Army about that, and that was welling out continuously all the time

. . . Hypochondria!

A rag-time army was not likely to have influenza so badly. It felt neither its moral nor its physical pulse . . . Still, here was influenza in 'B' Company. They must have got it from the Huns the night before last. 'B' Company had had them jump in on top of them; then and there had been hand-to-hand fighting. It was a nuisance. 'B' Company was a nuisance. It had naturally been stuck into the dampest and lowest part of their line. Their company dugout was reported to be like a well with a dripping roof. It would take 'B' Company to be afflicted with such quarters . . . It was difficult to see what to do — not to drain their quarters, but to exorcise their ill-luck. Still, it would have to be done. He was going into their quarters to make a *strafe*, but he sent Aranjuez to announce his coming so as to give the decent young Company Commander a chance to redd up his house . . .

The beastly Huns! They stood between him and Valentine Wannop. If they would go home he could be sitting talking to her for whole afternoons. That was what a young woman was for. You seduced a young woman in order to be able to finish your talks with her. You could not do that without living with her. You could not live with her without seducing her; but that was the by-product. The point is that

254

you can't otherwise talk. You can't finish talks at street corners; in museums; even in drawing-rooms. You mayn't be in the mood when she is in the mood — for the intimate conversation that means the final communion of your souls. You have to wait together — for a week, for a year, for a lifetime, before the final intimate conversation may be attained . . . and exhausted. So that . . .

That in effect was love. It struck him as astonishing. The word was so little in his vocabulary . . . Love, ambition, the desire for wealth. They were things he had never known of as existing — as capable of existing within him. He had been the Younger Son, loafing, contemptuous, capable, idly contemplating life, but ready to take up the position of the Head of the Family if Death so arranged matters. He had been a sort of eternal Second-in-Command.

Now what the Hell was he? A sort of Hamlet of the Trenches! No, by God he was not . . . He was perfectly ready for action. Ready to command a battalion. He was presumably a lover. They did things like commanding battalions. And worse!

He ought to write her a letter. What in the world would she think of this gentleman who had once made improper proposals to her; balked; said 'So long!' or perhaps not even

'So long!' And then walked off. With never a letter! Not even a picture postcard! For two years! A sort of a Hamlet all right! Or a swine!

Well, then, he ought to write her a letter. He ought to say: 'This is to tell you that I propose to live with you as soon as this show is over. You will be prepared immediately on cessation of active hostilities to put yourself at my disposal; please. Signed, 'Xtopher Tietjens, Acting O.C. 9th Glams.' A proper military communication. She would be pleased to see that he was commanding a battalion. Or perhaps she would not be pleased. She was a Pro-German. She loved these tiresome fellows who tore his, Tietjens', sofa-cushions to pieces.

That was not fair. She was a Pacifist. She thought these proceedings pestilential and purposeless. Well, there were times when they appeared purposeless enough. Look at what had happened to his neat gravel walks. And to the marl too. Though that served the purpose of letting him sit sheltered. In the sunlight! With any number of larks. Someone once wrote:

A myriad larks in unison sang o'er her,
soaring out of sight!

That was imbecile really. Larks cannot sing in unison. They make a heartless noise like that produced by the rubbing of two corks one on the other . . . There came into his mind an image. Years ago; years and years ago, probably after having watched that gunner torment the fat Hun, because it had been below Max Redoubt . . . The sun was now for certain shining on Bemerton! Well, he could never be a country parson. He was going to live with Valentine Wannop! . . . he had been coming down the reverse side of the range, feeling good. Probably because he had got out of that O.P. which the German guns had been trying to find. He went down with long strides, the tops of thistles brushing his hips. Obviously the thistles contained things that attracted flies. They are apt to after a famous victory. So myriads of swallows pursued him, swirling round and round him, their wings touching; for a matter of twenty yards all round and their wings brushing him and the tops of the thistles. And as the blue sky was reflected in the blue of their backs — for their backs were below his eyes — he had felt like a Greek God striding through the sea . . .

The larks were less inspiring. Really, they were abusing the German guns. Imbecilely and continuously, they were screaming imprecations and threats. They had been relatively sparse until just now. Now that the shells were coming back from a mile or so off, the sky was thick with larks. A myriad — two myriad — corks at once. Not in unison. Sang o'er him, soaring out of sight! . . . You might almost say that it was a sign that the Germans were going to shell you again. Wonderful 'hinstinct' set by the Almighty in their little bosoms! It was perhaps also accurate. No doubt the shells as they approached more and more shook the earth and disturbed the little bosoms on their nests. So they got up and shouted; perhaps warning each other; perhaps mere defiance of the artillery.

He was going to write to Valentine Wannop. It was a clumsy swine's trick not to have written to her before. He had proposed to seduce her; hadn't done it, and had gone off without a word . . . Considering himself rather a swell, too!

He said:

'Did you get a bit to eat, Corporal?'

The Corporal balanced himself before Tietjens on the slope of the mound. He blushed, rubbing his right sole on his left instep, holding in his right hand a small tin can and a cup, in his left an immaculate towel containing a small cube.

Tietjens debated whether he should first

drink of the coffee and army rum to increase his zest for the sandwiches, or whether he should first eat the sandwiches and so acquire more thirst for the coffee ... It would be reprehensible to write to Valentine Wannop. The act of the cold-blooded seducer. Reprehensible! ... It depended on what was in the sandwiches. It would be agreeable to fill the void below and inwards from his breast-bone. But whether do it first with a solid or warm moisture?

The lance-corporal was deft ... He set the coffee tin, cup, and towel on a flat stone that stuck out of that heap; the towel unfolded, served as a table-cloth; there appeared three heaps of ethereal sandwiches. He said he had eaten half a tin of warm mutton and haricot beans, whilst he was cutting the sandwiches. The meat in the sandwiches consisted of *foie gras*, that pile: bully beef reduced to a paste with butter that was margarine, anchovy paste out of a tin and minced onion out of pickles; the third pile was bully beef *nature*-seasoned with Worcester sauce ... All the materials he had at disposal!

Tietjens smiled on the boy at his work. He said this must be a regular *chef*. The boy said:

'Not a *chef*, yet, sir!' He had a camp stool hung on his trenching tool behind his hip. He had been chief assistant to one of the chief cooks in the Savoy. He had been going to go to Paris. 'What you call a *marmiton*, sir!' he said. With his trenching tool he was scooping out a level place in front of the flat rock. He set the camp stool on the flattened platform.

Tietjens said:

'You used to wear a white cap and white overalls?'

He liked to think of the blond boy resembling Valentine Wannop dressed all in slim white. The lance-corporal said:

'It's different now, sir!' He stood at Tietjens' side, always caressing his instep. He regarded cooking as an Art. He would have preferred to be a painter, but Mother hadn't enough money. The source of supply dried up during the War . . . If the C.O. would say a word for him after the War . . . He understood it was going to be difficult to get jobs after the War. All the blighters who had got out of serving, all the R.A.S.C., all the Lines of Communication men would get first chance. As the saying was, the further from the Line the better the pay. And the chance, too!

Tietjens said:

'Certainly I shall recommend you. You'll get a job all right. I shall never forget your sandwiches.' He would never forget the keen, clean flavour of the sandwiches or the warm generosity of the sweet, be-rummed coffee! In the blue air of that April hillside. All the objects on that white towel were defined, with iridescent edges. The boy's face, too! Perhaps not physically iridescent. His breath, too, was very easy. Pure air! He was going to write to Valentine Wannop: 'Hold yourself at my disposal. Please. Signed . . . ' Reprehensible! Worse than reprehensible! You do not seduce the child of your father's oldest friend. He said.

'I shall find it difficult enough to get a job after the War!'

Not only to seduce the young woman, but to invite her to live a remarkably precarious life with him. It isn't done!

The lance-corporal said:

'Oh, sir; no, sir! . . . You're Mr. Tietjens, of Groby!'

He had often been to Groby of a Sunday afternoon. His mother was a Middlesbrough woman. Southbank, rather. He had been to the Grammar School and was going to Durham University when . . . Supplies stopped. On the eight nine fourteen . . .

They oughtn't to put North Riding, Yorkshire, boys in Welsh-traditioned units. It was wrong. But for that he would not have to run against this boy of disagreeable reminiscences.

'They say,' the boy said, 'that the well at Groby is three hundred and twenty feet deep, and the cedar at the corner of the house a hundred and sixty. The depth of the well twice the height of the tree!' He had often dropped stones down the well and listened: they made an astonishingly loud noise. Long: like echoes gone mad! His mother knew the cook at Groby. Mrs. Harmsworth. He had often seen . . . he rubbed his ankles more furiously, in a paroxysm . . . Mr. Tietjens, the father, and him, and Mr. Mark and Mr. John and Miss Eleanor. He once handed Miss Eleanor her riding crop when she dropped it . . .

Tietjens was never going to live at Groby. No more feudal atmosphere! He was going to live, he figured, in a four-room attic flat, on the top of one of the Inns of Court. With Valentine Wannop. *Because* of Valentine Wannop!

He said to the boy:

'Those German shells seem to be coming back. Go and request Captain Gibbs as soon as they get near to take his fatigues under cover until they have passed.'

He wanted to be alone with Heaven . . . He drank his last cup of warm, sweetened coffee, laced with rum . . . He drew a deep breath. Fancy drawing a deep breath of satisfaction after a deep draft of warm coffee, sweetened with condensed milk and laced with rum! ... Reprehensible! Gastronomically reprehensible! ... What would they say at the Club? ... Well, he was never going to be at the Club! The Club claret was to be regretted! Admirable claret. And the cold side-board!

But, for the matter of that, fancy drawing deep breaths of satisfaction over the mere fact of lying in command of a battalion! — on a slope, in the clear air, with twenty thousand — two myriad! — corks making noises overhead and the German guns directing their projectiles so that they were slowly approaching! Fancy!

They were, presumably, trying out their new Austrian gun. Methodically, with an infinite thoroughness. If, that is to say, there really was a new Austrian gun. Perhaps there wasn't. Division had been in a great state of excitement over such a weapon. It stood in Orders that everyone was to try to obtain every kind of information about it, and it was said to throw a projectile of a remarkable, high explosive efficiency. So Gibbs had jumped to the conclusion that the thing that had knocked to pieces his projected machine-gun emplacement had been the new gun.

In that case they were trying it out very thoroughly.

The actual report of the gun or guns — they fired every three minutes, so that might mean that there was only one and that it took about three minutes to re-load — was very loud and rather high in tone. He had not yet heard the actual noise made by the projectile, but the reports from a distance had been singularly dulled. When, presumably, the projectile had effected its landing, it bored extraordinarily into the ground and then exploded with a time-fuse. Very likely it would not be very dangerous to life, but, if they had enough of the guns and the H.E. to plaster the things all along the Line, and if the projectiles worked as efficiently as they had done on poor Gibbs' trench, there would be an end of trench-warfare on the Allied side. But, of course, they probably had not either enough guns or enough high explosive and the thing would very likely act less efficiently in other sorts of soils. They were very likely trying that out. Or, if they were firing with only one gun they might be trying how many rounds could be fired before the gun became ineffective. Or they might be trying only the attrition game: smashing up the trenches, which was always useful, and then sniping the men who tried to repair them. You could bag a few men in that way, now and then. Or, naturally, with planes . . . There was no end to these tiresome alternatives! Presumably, again, our planes might stop that gun or battery. Then it would stop!

Reprehensible! . . . He snorted! If you don't obey the rules of your club you get hoofed out, and that's that! If you retire from the post or Second-in-Command of Groby, you don't have to . . . oh, attend battalion parades! He had refused to take any money from Brother Mark on the ground of a fantastic quarrel. But he had not any quarrel with Brother Mark. The sardonic pair of them were just matching obstinacies. On the other hand you had to set to the tenantry an example of chastity, sobriety, probity, or you could not take their beastly money. You provided them with the best Canadian seed corn; with agricultural experiments suited to their soils; you sat on the head of your agent; you kept their buildings in repair; you apprenticed their sons; you looked after their daughters, when they got into trouble and after their bastards, your own or another man's. But you must reside on the estate. *You must reside on the estate.* The money that comes out of those poor devils' pockets must go back into the land so that the estate and all on it, down to the licensed beggars,

265

may grow richer and richer and richer. So he had invented his fantastic quarrel with Brother Mark; because he was going to take Valentine to live with him. You could not have a Valentine Wannop having with you in a Groby the infinite and necessary communings. You could have a painted doxy from the servants' hall, quarrelling with the other maids, who would want her job, and scandalising the parsons for miles round. In their sardonic way the tenants appreciated that: it was in the tradition and all over the Riding they did it themselves. But not a lady, the daughter of your father's best friend! They wanted Quality women to *be* Quality and they themselves would go to ruin, spend their dung 'and seed' money on whores and wreck the fortunes of the Estate, sooner than that you should indulge in infinite conversation . . . So he hadn't taken a penny of their money from his brother, and he wouldn't take a penny when he in turn became Groby. Fortunately, there was the heir . . . Otherwise he could not have gone with that girl!

Two pangs went through him. His son had never written to him; the girl might have married a War Office clerk! On the re-bound! That was what it would be: a civilian War Office clerk would be the most exact contrast to himself! . . . But the son's letters would have been stopped by the mother. That was what they did to people who were where *he* was. As the C.O. had said! And Valentine Wannop, who had listened to his conversation, would never want to mingle intimately in another's! Their communion was immutable and not to be shaken!

So he was going to write to her: freckled, downright, standing square on feet rather widely planted apart, just ready to say: 'Oh, *chuck* it, Edith Ethel!' She made the sunlight!

Or no, by Heavens, he could not write to her! If he stopped one or went dotty . . . Wouldn't it make it infinitely worse for her to know that his love for her had been profound and immutable? It would make it far worse, for by now the edges of passion had probably worn less painful. Or there was the chance of it! . . . But impenitently he would go on willing her to submit to his will; through mounds thrown up by Austrian projectiles and across the seas. They would do what they wanted and take what they got for it!

He reclined, on his right shoulder, feeling like some immense and absurd statue: a collection of meal-sacks done in mud, with grotesque shorts revealing his muddy knees . . . The figure on one of Michael Angelo's Medici tombs. Or perhaps his *Adam* . . . He felt the earth move a little beneath him. The

267

last projectile must have been pretty near. He would not have noticed the sound, it had become such a regular sequence. But he noticed the quiver in the earth . . .

Reprehensible! He said. For God's sake *let* us be reprensible! And have done with it! We aren't Hun strategists for ever balancing pros and cons of militant morality!

He took, with his left hand, the cup from the rock. Little Aranjuez came round the mound. Tietjens threw the cup downhill at a large bit of rock. He said to Aranjuez's wistful, enquiring eyes:

'So that no toast more ignoble may ever be drunk out of it!'

The boy gasped and flushed:

'Then you've got someone that you love, sir!' he said in his tone of hero-worship. 'Is she like Nancy, in Bailleul?'

Tietjens said:

'No, not like Nancy . . . Or, perhaps, yes, a little like Nancy!' He did not want to hurt the boy's feelings by the suggestion that anyone unlike Nancy could be loved. He felt a premonition that that child was going to be hurt. Or, perhaps, it was only that he was already so suffering.

The boy said:

'Then you'll get her, sir. You'll certainly get her!'

'Yes, I shall probably get her!' Tietjens said.

The lance-corporal came, too, round the mound. He said that 'A' Company were all under cover. They went all together round the heap in the direction of 'B' Company's trench down into which they slid. It descended sharply. It was certainly wet. It ended practically in a little swamp. The next battalion had even some yards of sand-bag parapet before entering the slope again with its trench. This was Flanders. Duck country. The bit of swamp would make personal keeping in communication difficult. Where Tietjens had put in his tile-siphons a great deal of water had exuded. The young O.C. Company said that they had had to bale the trench out, until they had made a little drain down into the bog. They baled out with shovels. Two of the shovels still stood against the brushwood revetments of the parapet.

'Well, you should not leave your shovels about!' Tietjens shouted. He was feeling considerable satisfaction at the working of his siphon. In the meantime we had begun a considerable artillery demonstration. It became overwhelming. There was some sort of Bloody Mary somewhere a few yards off, or so it seemed. She pooped off. The planes had perhaps reported the position of the Austrian gun. Or we might be *strafing* their trenches to make them shut up that weapon. It was like being a dwarf at a conversation, a conflict — of mastodons. There was so much noise it seemed to grow dark. It was a mental darkness. You could not think. A Dark Age! The earth moved.

He was looking at Aranjuez from a considerable height. He was enjoying a considerable view. Aranjuez's face had a rapt expression — like that of a man composing poetry. Long dollops of liquid mud surrounded them in the air. Like black pancakes being tossed. He thought: 'Thank God I did not write to her. We are being blown up!' The earth turned like a weary hippopotamus. It settled down slowly over the face of Lance-Corporal Duckett who lay on his side, and went on in a slow wave.

It was slow, slow, slow ... like a slowed-down movie. The earth manœuvred for an infinite time. He remained suspended in space. As if he were suspended as he had wanted to be in front of that cockscomb in whitewash. Coincidence!

The earth sucked slowly and composedly at his feet.

It assimilated his calves, his thighs. It imprisoned him above the waist. His arms being free, he resembled a man in a life-buoy. The earth moved him slowly. It was solidish.

Below him, down a mound, the face of little Aranjuez, brown, with immense black eyes in bluish whites, looked at him. Out of viscous mud. A head on a charger! He could see the imploring lips form the words: 'Save me, Captain!' He said: 'I've got to save myself first!' He could not hear his own words. The noise was incredible.

A man stood over him. He appeared immensely tall because Tietjens' face was on a level with his belt. But he was a small Cockney Tommy really. Name of Cockshott. He pulled at Tietjens' two arms. Tietjens tried to kick with his feet. Then he realised it was better not to kick with his feet. He was pulled out. Satisfactorily. There had been two men at it. A second, a corporal had come. They were all three of them grinning. He slid down with the sliding earth towards Aranjuez. He smiled at the pallid face. He slipped a lot. He felt a frightful burning on his neck, below and behind the ear. His hand came down from feeling the place. The finger tips had no end of mud and a little pinkishness on them. A pimple had perhaps burst. He had at least two men not killed. He signed agitatedly to the Tommies. He made gestures of digging. They were to get shovels.

He stood over Aranjuez, on the edge of liquid mud. Perhaps he would sink in. He did not sink in. Not above his boot tops. He felt his feet to be enormous and sustaining. He knew what had happened. Aranjuez was sunk in the issuing hole of the spring that made that bog. It was like being on Exmoor. He bent down over an ineffable, small face. He bent down lower and his hands entered the slime. He had to get on his hands and knees.

Fury entered his mind. He had been sniped at. Before he had had that pain he had heard, he realised, an intimate drone under the hellish tumult. There was reason for furious haste. Or, no . . . They were low. In a wide hole. There was no reason for furious haste. Especially on your hands and knees.

His hands were under the slime, and his forearms. He battled his hands down greasy cloth; under greasy cloth. *Slimy*, not greasy! He pushed outwards. The boy's hands and arms appeared. It was going to be easier. His face was now quite close to the boy's, but it was impossible to hear what he said. Possibly he was unconscious. Tietjens said: 'Thank God for my enormous physical strength!' It was the first time that he had ever had to be thankful for great physical strength. He lifted the boy's arms over his own shoulders so that his hands might clasp themselves behind his neck. They were slimy and disagreeable. He was short in the wind. He heaved back. The boy came up a little. He was certainly fainting. He gave no assistance. The slime was filthy. It was a condemnation of a civilisation that he, Tietjens, possessed of enormous physical strength, should never have needed to use it before. He looked like a collection of meal-sacks; but at least he could tear a pack of cards in half. If only his lungs weren't . . .

Cockshott, the Tommie, and the corporal were beside him, grinning. With the two shovels that ought not to have stood against the parapet of their trench. He was intensely irritated. He had tried to indicate with his signs that it was Lance-Corporal Duckett that they were to dig out. It was probably no longer Lance-Corporal Duckett. It was probably by now 'it.' The body! He had probably lost a man, after all!

Cockshott and the corporal pulled Aranjuez out of the slime. He came out reluctantly, like a lugworm out of sand. He could not stand. His legs gave way. He drooped like a flower done in slime. His lips moved, but you could not hear him. Tietjens took him from the two men who supported him between the arms and laid him a little way up the mound. He shouted in the ear of the Corporal:

'Duckett! Go and dig out Duckett! At the double!'

He knelt and felt the boy's back. His spine might have been damaged. The boy did not wince. His spine might be damaged all the same. He could not be left there. Bearers could be sent with a stretcher if one was to be found. But they might be sniped coming. Probably, he, Tietjens, could carry that boy, if his lungs held out. If not, he could drag him. He felt tender, like a mother, and enormous. It might be better to leave the boy there. There was no knowing. He said: 'Are you wounded?' The guns had mostly stopped. Tietjens could not see any blood flowing. The boy whispered: 'No, sir!' He was, then, probably just faint. Shell shock, very likely. There was no knowing what shell shock was or what it did to you. Or the mere vapour of the projectile.

He could not stop there.

He took the boy under his arm as you might do a roll of blankets. If he took him on his shoulders he might get high enough to be sniped. He did not go very fast, his legs were so heavy. He bundled down several steps in the direction of the spring in which the boy had been. There was more water. The spring was filling up that hollow. He could not have left the boy there. You could only imagine that his body had corked up the springhole before. This had been like being at home where they had springs like that. On the moors, digging out badgers. Digging earth drains, rather. Badgers have dry lairs. On the moors above Groby. April sunlight. Lots of sunlight and skylarks.

He was mounting the mound. For some feet there was no other way. They had been in the shaft made by that projectile. He inclined to the left. To the right would take them quicker to the trench, but he wanted to get the mound between them and the sniper. His breathing was tremendous. There was more light falling on them.

Exactly! . . . Snap! Snap! Snap! . . . Clear sounds from a quarter of a mile away . . . Bullets whined overhead. Long sounds, going away. Not snipers. The men of a battalion. A chance! Snap! Snap! Snap! Bullets whined overhead. Men of a battalion get excited when shooting at anything running. They fire high. Trigger pressure. He was now a fat, running object. Did they fire with a sense of hatred or fun! Hatred probably. Huns have not much sense of fun.

His breathing was unbearable. Both his legs were like painful bolsters. He would be on the relatively level in two steps if he made them . . . Well, make them! . . . He was on the level. He had been climbing, up clods. He *had* to take an immense breath. The ground under his left foot gave way. He had been holding Aranjuez in front of his own body as much as he could, under his right arm. As his left foot sank in, the boy's body came right on top of him. Naturally this stiffish earth in huge clods had fissures in it. Apertures. It was not like regular digging.

The boy kicked, screamed, tore himself loose . . . Well, if he wanted to go! The scream was like a horse's in a stable on fire. Bullets had gone overhead. The boy rushed off, his hands to his face. He disappeared round the mound. It was a conical mound. He, Tietjens, could now crawl on his belly. It was satisfactory.

He crawled. Shuffling himself along with his hips and elbows. There was probably a text-book way of crawling. He did not know it. The clods of earth appeared friendly. For bottom soil thrown to the top they did not feel or smell so very sour. Still, it would take a long time to get them into cultivation or under grass. Probably, agriculturally speaking, that country would be in pretty poor condition for a long time . . .

He felt pleased with his body. It had had no exercise to speak of for two months — as second-in-command. He could not have expected to be in even the condition he was in. But the mind had probably had a good deal to do with that! He had, no doubt, been in a devil of a funk. It was only reasonable. It was disagreeable to think of those Hun devils hunting down the unfortunate. A disagreeable business. Still, we did the same . . . That boy must have been in a devil of a funk. Suddenly. He had held his hands in front of his face. Afraid to see. Well, you couldn't blame him. They ought not to send out schoolgirls. He was like a girl. Still, he ought to have stayed to see that he, Tietjens, was not pipped. He might have thought he was hit from the way his left leg had gone down. He would have to be *strafed*. Gently.

Cockshott and the corporal were on their hands and knees digging with the short-handled shovels that are known as trenching-tools. They were on the rear side of the mound.

'We've found im, sir,' the corporal said. 'Regular buried. Just seed is foot. Dursen't use a shovel. Might cut im in arf!'

Tietjens said:

'You're probably right. Give me the shovel!' Cockshott was a draper's assistant, the corporal a milkman. Very likely they were not good with shovels.

He had had the advantage of a boyhood crowded with digging of all sorts. Duckett was buried horizontally, running into the side of the conical mound. His feet at least stuck out like that, but you could not tell how the body was disposed. It might turn to either side or upwards. He said:

'Go on with your tools above! But give me room.'

The toes being to the sky, the trunk could hardly bend downwards. He stood below the feet and aimed terrific blows with the shovel eighteen inches below. He liked digging. This earth was luckily dryish. It ran down the hill conveniently. This man had been buried probably ten minutes. It seemed longer, but was probably less. He ought to have a chance. Probably earth was less suffocating than water. He said to the corporal:

'Do you know how to apply artificial respiration? To the drowned?'

Cockshott said:

'I do, sir. I was swimming champion of Islington baths!' A rather remarkable man, Cockshott. His father had knocked up the arm of a man who tried to shoot Mr. Gladstone in 1866 or thereabouts.

A lot of earth falling away, obligingly, after one withdrawal of the shovel Lance-Corporal Duckett's thin legs appeared to the fork, the knees drooping.

Cockshott said:

' 'E aint rubbin' 'is ankles this journey!'

The corporal said:

'Company C'mander is killed, sir. Bullet clean thru the ed!'

It annoyed Tietjens that here was another head wound. He could not apparently get away from them. It was silly to be annoyed, because in trenches a majority of wounds had to be head wounds. But Providence might just as well be a little more imaginative. To oblige one. It annoyed him, too, to think that he had *strafed* that boy just before he was killed. For leaving his shovels about. A *strafe* leaves a disagreeable impression on young boys for quite half an hour. It was probably the last incident in his life. So he died depressed . . . Might God be making it up to him!

He said to the corporal:

'Let me come.' Duckett's left hand and wrist had appeared, the hand drooping and improbably clean, level with the thigh. It gave the line of the body; you could clear away beside him.

' 'E wasn't on'y twenty-two,' the corporal said. Cockshott said: 'Same age as me. Very particular 'e was about your rifle pull-throughs.'

A minute later they pulled Duckett out, by the legs. A stone might have been resting on his face, in that case his face would have been damaged. It wasn't, though you had had to chance it. It was black, but asleep . . . As if Valentine Wannop had been reposing in an ash-bin. Tietjens left Cockshott applying artificial respiration very methodically and efficiently to the prostrate form.

It was to him a certain satisfaction that, at any rate, in that minute affair he hadn't lost one of the men but only an officer. As satisfaction it was not military correct, though as it harmed no one there was no harm in it. But for his men he always felt a certain greater responsibility; they seemed to him to be there infinitely less of their own volition. It was akin to the feeling that made him regard cruelty to an animal as a more loathsome crime than cruelty to a human being, other than a child. It was no doubt irrational.

Leaning, in the communication trench, against the corrugated iron that boasted a great whitewashed A, in a very clean thin Burberry boasting half a bushel of badges of rank — worsted crowns and things! — and in a small tin hat that looked elegant, was a slight figure. How the *devil* can you make a tin hat look elegant! It carried a hunting switch and wore spurs. An Inspecting General. The General said benevolently:

'Who are you?' and then with irritation: 'Where the devil is the officer commanding this Battalion? Why can't he be found?' He added: 'You're disgustingly dirty. Like a blackamoor. I suppose you've an explanation.'

Tietjens was being spoken to by General Campion. In a hell of a temper. He stood to attention like a scarecrow.

He said:

'I am in command of this Battalion, sir. I am Tietjens, second-in-command. Now in command temporarily. I could not be found because I was buried. Temporarily.'

The General said:

'You . . . Good God!' and fell back a step, his jaw dropping. He said: 'I've just come from London!' And then: 'By God, you don't stop in command of a Battalion of mine a second after I take over!' He said: 'They said this was the smartest battalion in my unit!' and snorted with passion. He added: 'Neither my galloper nor Levin can find you or get you found. And there you come strolling along with your hands in your pockets!'

In the complete stillness, for, the guns having stopped, the skylarks, too, were taking a spell, Tietjens could hear his heart beat out of little dry scraping sounds from his lungs. The heavy beats were very accelerated. It gave an effect of terror. He said to himself:

'What the devil has his having been in

London to do with it?' And then: 'He wants to marry Sylvia! I'll bet he went to marry Sylvia!' That was what his having been to London had to do with it. It was an obsession with him: the first thing he said when surprised and passionate.

They always arranged these periods of complete silence for the visits of Inspecting Generals. Perhaps the Great General Staffs of both sides arrange that for each other. More probably our guns had split themselves in the successful attempt to let the Huns know that we wanted them to shut up — that we were firing with what Papists call a special intention. That would be as effective as a telephone message. The Huns would know there was something up. Never put the other side in a temper when you can help it.

He said:

'I've just had a scratch, sir. I was feeling in my pockets for my field-dressing.'

The General said:

'A fellow like you has no right to be where he can be wounded. Your place is the lines of communication. I was mad when I sent you here. I shall send you back.'

He added:

'You can fall out. I want neither your assistance nor your information. They said there was a damn smart officer in command

here. I wanted to see him . . . Of the name of
. . . Of the name of . . . It does not matter.
Fall out . . . '

Tietjens went heavily along the trench. It
came into his head to say to himself:

'It *is* a land of Hope and Glory!' Then he
exclaimed: 'By God! I'll take the thing before
the Commander-in-Chief. I'll take the thing
before the King in Council if necessary. By
God I will!' The old fellow had no business to
speak to him like that. It was importing
personal enmity into service matters. He
stood still reflecting on the terms of his letter
to Brigade. The Adjutant Notting came along
the trench. He said:

'General Campion wants to see you, sir. He
takes over this Army on Monday.' He added:
'You've been in a nasty place, sir. Not hurt, I
trust!' It was a most unusual piece of
loquacity for Notting.

Tietjens said to himself:

'Then I've got five days in command of this
unit. He can't kick me out before he's in
command.' The Huns would be through them
before then. Five days' fighting! Thank God!

He said:

'Thanks. I've seen him. No, I'm all right.
Beastly dirty!'

Notting's beady eyes had a tinge of agony
in them. He said:

'When they said you had stopped one, sir, I thought I should go mad. We *can't* get through the work!'

Tietjens was wondering whether he should write his letter to Brigade before or after the old fellow took over. Notting was saying:

'The doctor says Aranjuez will get through all right.'

It would be better, if he were going to base his appeal on the grounds of personal prejudice. Notting was saying:

'Of course he will lose his eye. In fact it . . . it is not practically there. But he'll get through.'

Part Three

1

Coming into the square was like being suddenly dead, it was so silent and so still to one so lately jostled by the innumerable crowd and deafened by unceasing shouts. The shouting had continued for so long that it had assumed the appearance of being a solid and unvarying thing, like life. So the silence appeared like Death; and now she had death in her heart. She was going to confront a madman in a stripped house. And the empty house stood in an empty square all of whose houses were so eighteenth-century and silver grey and rigid and serene that they ought all to be empty too and contain dead, mad men. And was this the errand? For to-day when all the world was mad with joy? To become bear-ward to a man who had got rid of all his furniture and did not know the porter — mad without joy!

It turned out to be worse than she expected. She had expected to turn the handle of a door of a tall, empty room; in a space made dim with shutters she would see him, looking suspiciously round over his shoulder, a grey badger or a bear taken at its dim occupations. And in uniform. But she was not given time even to be ready. In the last moment she was to steel herself incredibly. She was to become the cold nurse of a shell-shock case.

But there was not any last moment. He charged upon her. There in the open. More like a lion. He came, grey all over, his grey hair — or the grey patches of his hair — shining, charging down the steps, having slammed the hall door. And lopsided. He was carrying under his arm a diminutive piece of furniture. A cabinet.

It was so quick. It was like having a fit. The houses tottered. He regarded her. He had presumably checked violently in his clumsy stride. She hadn't seen because of the tottering of the houses. His stone-blue eyes came fishily into place in his wooden countenance — pink and white. *Too* pink where it was pink and too white where it was white. Too much so for health. He was in grey homespuns. He should not wear homespuns or grey. It increased his bulk. He could be made to look . . . Oh, a fine figure of a man, let us say!

What was he doing? Fumbling in the pocket of his clumsy trousers. He exclaimed — she shook at the sound of his slightly grating, slightly gasping voice — :

'I'm going to sell this thing . . . Stay here.' He had produced a latchkey. He was panting fiercely beside her. Up the steps. He was beside her. Beside her. Beside her. It was infinitely sad to be beside this madman. It was infinitely glad. Because if he had been sane she would not have been beside him. She could be beside him for long spaces of time if he were mad. Perhaps he did not recognise her! She might be beside him for long spaces of time with him not recognising her. Like tending your baby!

He was stabbing furiously at the latchhole with his little key. He *would*: that was normal. He was a stab-the-keyhole sort of clumsy man. She would not want that altered. But she would see about his clothes. She said: 'I am deliberately preparing to live with him for a long time!' Think of that! She said to him:

'Did you send for me?'

He had the door open; he said, panting — his *poor* lungs!

'No.' Then: 'Go in!' and then: 'I was just going . . .'

She was in his house. Like a child . . . He had not sent for her . . . Like a child faltering on the sill of a vast black cave.

It *was* black. Stone flags. Pompeian-red

walls scarred pale-pink where fixed hall-furniture had been removed. Was it *here* she was going to live?

He said, panting, from behind her back:

'Wait here!' A little more light fell into the hall. That was because he was gone from the doorway.

He was charging down the steps. His boots were immense. He lolloped all over on one side because of the piece of furniture he had under his arm. He was grotesque, really. But joy radiated from his homespuns when you walked beside him. It welled out; it enveloped you . . . Like the warmth from an electric heater, only that did not make you want to cry and say your prayers — the haughty oaf.

No, but he was not haughty. Gauche, then! No, but he was not gauche . . . She could not run after him. He was a bright patch, with his pink ears and silver hair. Gallumphing along the rails in front of the eighteenth-century houses. *He* was eighteenth-century all right . . . But then the eighteenth century never went mad. The only century that never went mad. Until the French Revolution; and that was either not mad or not eighteenth-century.

She stepped irresolutely into the shadows; she returned irresolutely to the light . . . A long hollow sound existed: the sea saying: Ow, Ow, Ow along miles and miles. It was the armistice. It was Armistice Day. She had forgotten it. She was to be cloistered on Armistice Day! Ah, not cloistered! Not cloistered there. My beloved is mine and I am his! But she might as well close the door!

She closed the door as delicately as if she were kissing him on the lips. It was a symbol. It was Armistice Day. She ought to go away; instead she had shut the door on . . . Not on Armistice Day! What was it like to be . . . changed!

No! She ought not to go away! She ought not to go away! She ought *not*! He had told her to wait. She was not cloistered. This was the most exciting spot on the earth. It was not her fate to live nun-like. She was going to pass her day beside a madman; her night, too . . . Armistice Night! That night would be remembered down unnumbered generations. Whilst one lived that had seen it the question would be asked: What did you do on Armistice Night? My beloved is mine and I am his!

The great stone stairs were carpetless: to mount them would be like taking part in a procession. The hall came in straight from the front door. You had to turn a corner to the right before you came to the entrance of a room. A queer arrangement. Perhaps the eighteenth century was afraid of draughts and did not like the dining-room door near the front entrance . . . My beloved is . . . Why does one go repeating that ridiculous thing. Besides it's from the *Song of Solomon*, isn't it? *The Canticle of Canticles!* Then to quote it is blasphemy when one is . . . No, the essence of prayer is volition, so the essence of blasphemy is volition. She did not want to quote the thing. It was jumped out of her by sheer nerves. She was afraid. She was waiting for a madman in an empty house. Noises whispered up the empty stairway!

She was like Fatima. Pushing open the door of the empty room. He might come back to murder her. A madness caused by sex obsessions is not infrequently homicidal . . . What did you do on Armistice Night? 'I was murdered in an empty house!' For, no doubt he would let her live till midnight.

But perhaps he had not got sex obsessions. She had not the shadow of a proof that he had; rather that he hadn't! Certainly, rather that he hadn't. Always the gentleman.

They had left the telephone! The windows were duly shuttered, but in the dim light from between cracks the nickel gleamed on white marble. The mantel-shelf. Pure Parian marble, the shelf supported by rams' heads. Singularly chaste. The ceilings and rectilinear mouldings in an intricate symmetry. Chaste, too. Eighteenth-century. But the eighteenth century was not chaste . . . *He* was eighteenth-century.

She ought to telephone to her mother to inform that Eminence in untidy black with violet tabs here and there of the grave step that her daughter was . . .

What was her daughter going to do?

She ought to rush out of the empty house. She ought to be trembling with fear at the thought that he was coming home very likely to murder her. But she wasn't. What was she? Trembling with ecstasy? Probably. At the thought that he was coming. If he murdered her . . . Can't be helped! She was trembling with ecstasy all the same. She must telephone to her mother. Her mother might want to know where she was. But her mother never *did* want to know where she was. She had her head too screwed on to get into mischief! . . . Think of *that*!

Still, on such a day her mother might like to. They ought to exchange gladnesses that her brother was safe for good, now. And others, too. Normally her mother was irritated when she rang up. She would be at her work. It was amazing to see her at work. Perhaps she never would again. Such untidiness of papers. In a little room. Quite a little room. She never would work in a big room because a big room tempted her to walk about and she could not afford the time to walk about.

She was writing at two books at once now. A novel . . . Valentine did not know what it was about. Her mother never let them know what her novels were about till they were finished. And a woman's history of the War. A history by a woman for women. And there she would be sitting at a large table that hardly left room for more than getting round it. Grey, large, generous-featured and tired, she would be poking over one set of papers on one side of the table or just getting up from over the novel, her loose pince-nez falling off; pushing round the table between its edge and the wall to peer at the sheets of the woman's history that were spread all over that region. She would work for ten minutes or twenty-five or an hour at the one and then for an hour and a half or half an hour or three-quarters at the other. What a muddle her dear old head must be in!

With a little trepidation she took the telephone. It had got to be done. She could not live with Christopher Tietjens without first telling her mother. Her mother ought to be given the chance of dissuading. They say you ought to give a lover a chance of a final scene before leaving him or her for good. Still more your mother. That was jannock.

It broke the word of promise to the ear, the telephone! . . . Was it blasphemy to quote Shakespeare when one was going to . . . Perhaps bad taste. Shakespeare, however, was not spotless. So they said . . . Waiting! Waiting! How much of one's life wasn't spent waiting, with one's weight boring one's heels into the ground . . . But *this* thing was dead. No roar came from its mouth and when you jabbed the little gadget at the side up and down no bell tinked . . . It had probably been disconnected. They had perhaps cut him off for not paying. Or he had cut it off so that she might not scream for the police through it whilst he was strangling her. Anyhow they were cut off. They would be cut off from the world on Armistice Night . . . Well, they would probably be cut off for good!

What nonsense. He had not known that she was coming. He had not asked her to come.

So, slowly, slowly she went up the great stone staircase, the noises all a-whispering up before her . . . 'So, slowly, slowly she went up and slowly looked about her. Henceforth take warning by the fall . . . ' Well, she did not need to take warning: she was not going to fall in the way Barbara Allen did. Contrariwise!

He had not sent for her. He had not asked Edith Ethel to ring her up. Then presumably she felt humiliated. But she did not feel humiliated! It was in effect fairly natural. He *was* quite noticeably mad, rushing out, lopsided, with bits of furniture under his arm and no hat on his noticeable hair. Noticeable! That was what he was. He would never pass in a crowd! . . . He *had* got rid of all his furniture as Edith Ethel had alleged. Very likely he had not recognised the porter, too. She, Valentine Wannop, had seen him going to sell his furniture. Madly! Running to do it. You do not run when you are selling furniture if you are sane. Perhaps Edith Ethel had seen him running along with a table on his head. And she was by no means certain that he had recognised her, Valentine Wannop!

So Edith Ethel might have been almost justified in ringing her up. Normally it would have been an offence, considering the terms on which they had parted. Considering that Edith Ethel had accused her of having a child by this very man! It was pretty strong, even if she had seen him running about the Square with furniture, and even if there had been no one else who could help . . . But she ought to have sent her miserable rat of a husband. There was no excuse!

Still, there had been nothing else for her,

Valentine, to do. So there was no call for her to feel humiliated. Even if she had not felt for this man as she did she would have come, and, if he had been very bad, would have stayed.

He had not sent for her! this man who had once proposed love to her and then had gone away without a word and who had never so much as sent her a picture-postcard! Gauche! Haughty! Was there any other word for him? There could not be. Then she ought to feel humiliated. But she did not.

She felt frightened, creeping up the great staircase, and entering a great room. A very great room. All white, again with stains on the walls from which things had been removed. From over the way the houses confronted her, eighteen-centuryishly. But with a touch of gaiety from their red chimney-pots . . . And now she was spying, with her heart in her mouth. She was terribly frightened. This room was inhabited. As if set down in a field, the room being so large, there camped . . . A camp-bed for the use of officers, G.S. one, as the saying is. And implements of green canvas, supported on crossed white wood staves: a chair, a bucket with a rope handle, a washing-basin, a table. The bed was covered over with a flea-bag of brown wool. She was terribly frightened. The further she penetrated the house the more she was at his mercy. She ought to have stayed downstairs. She was spying on him.

These things looked terribly sordid and forlorn. Why did he place them in the centre of the room? Why not against a wall? It is usual to stand the head of a bed against a wall when there is no support for the pillows. Then the pillows do not slip off. She would change . . . No, she would not. He had put the bed in the centre of the room because he did not want it to touch walls that had been brushed by the dress of . . . You must not think bad things about that woman!

They did not look sordid and forlorn. They looked frugal. And glorious! She bent down and drawing down the flea bag at the top, kissed the pillows. She would get him linen pillows. You would be able to get linen now. The war was over. All along that immense line men could stand up!

At the head of the room was a dais. A box of square boarding, like the model-throne artists have in studios. Surely she did not receive her guests on a dais; like Royalty. She was capable . . . *You must not* . . . . It was perhaps for a piano. Perhaps she gave concerts. It was used as a library now. A row of calf-bound books stood against the wall on the back edge of the platform. She approached them to see what books he had selected. They must be the books he had read in France. If she could know what books he had read in France she would know what some of his thoughts there had been. She knew he slept between very cheap cotton sheets.

Frugal and glorious. That was he! And he had designed this room to love her in. It was the room she would have asked . . . The furnishing . . . Alcestis never had . . . For she, Valentine Wannop, was of frugal mind, too. And his worshipper. Having reflected glory . . . Damn it, she was getting soppy. But it was curious how their tastes marched together. He had been neither haughty nor gauche. He had paid her the real compliment. He had said: 'Her mind so marches with mine that she will understand.'

The books were indeed a job lot. Their tops ran along against the wall like an ill-arranged range of hills; one was a great folio in calf, the title indented deep and very dim. The others were French novels and little red military text-books. She leaned over the dais to read the title of the tall book. She expected it to be Herbert's Poems or his *Country Parson* . . . . *He* ought to be a Country Parson. He never would be now. She was depriving the church of . . . Of a Higher Mathematician, really.

The title of the book was *Vir. Obscur.*

Why did she take it that they were going to live together? She had no official knowledge that he wanted to. But *they* wanted to TALK. You can't talk unless you live together. Her eye, travelling downwards along the dais caught words on paper. They threw themselves up at her from among a disorder of half a dozen typed pages; they were in big, firm, pencilled letters. They stood out because they were pencilled; they were:

A man could stand up on a bleedin' 'ill!

Her heart stopped. She must be out of condition. She could not stand very well, but there was nothing to lean on to. She had — she didn't know she had — read also the typed words:

'*Mrs. Tietjens is leaving the model cabinet by Barker of Bath which she believes you claim . . . '*

She looked desperately away from the letter. She did not want to read the letter. She could not move away. She believed she was dying. Joy never kills . . . But it . . . '*fait peur.*' 'Makes afraid.' Afraid! Afraid! Afraid! There was nothing now between them. It was as if they were already in each other's arms. For surely the rest of the letter must say that Mrs. Tietjens had removed the furniture. And his comment — amazingly echoing the words she had just thought — was that he could stand up. But it wasn't in the least amazing. My beloved is mine . . . Their thoughts marched together; not in the least amazing. They could now stand on a hill together. Or get into a little hole. For good. And talk. For ever. She must not read the rest of the letter. She must not be certain. If she were certain she would have no hope of preserving her . . . Of remaining . . . Afraid and unable to move. She would be forced to read the letter because she was unable to move. Then she would be lost. She looked beseechingly out of the window at the house-fronts over the way. They were friendly. They would help her. Eighteenth-century. Cynical, but not malignant. She sprang right off her feet. She could move then. She hadn't had a fit.

Idiot. It was only the telephone. It went on and on. Drrinn; drinnnn; drRinn. It came from just under her feet. No, from under the dais. The receiver was on the dais. She hadn't consciously noticed it because she had believed the telephone was dead. Who notices a dead telephone?

She said — it was as if she was talking into his ear, he so pervaded her — she said:

'Who are you?'

One ought not to answer all telephone calls, but one does so mechanically. She ought not to have answered this. She was in a compromising position. Her voice might be recognised. Let it be recognised. She desired to be known to be in a compromising position! What did you do on Armistice Day!

A voice, heavy and old, said:

'You *are* there, Valentine . . . '

She cried out:

'Oh, poor *mother* . . . . But he's not here.' She added: 'He's not been here with me. I'm still only waiting.' She added again: 'The house is empty!' She seemed to be stealthy, the house whispering round her. She seemed to be whispering to her mother to save her and not wanting the house to hear her. The house was eighteenth-century. Cynical. But not malignant. It wanted her undoing, but knew that women liked being . . . ruined.

Her mother said, after a long time:

'Have you *got* to do this thing? . . . My little Valentine . . . My little Valentine!' She wasn't sobbing.

Valentine said:

'Yes, I've got to do it!' She sobbed. Suddenly she stopped sobbing.

She said quickly:

'Listen mother. I've had no conversation with him. I don't know even whether he's sane. He appears to be mad.' She wanted to give her mother hope. Quickly. She had been speaking quickly to get hope to her mother as quickly as possible. But she added: 'I believe that I shall die if I cannot live with him.'

She said that slowly. She wanted to be like a little child trying to get truth home to its mother.

She said:

'I have waited too long. All these years.' She did not know that she had such desolate tones in her voice. She could see her mother looking into the distance with every statement that came to her, thinking. Old and grey. And majestic and kind . . . Her mother's voice came:

'I have sometimes suspected . . . My poor child . . . It has been for a long time?' They were both silent. Thinking. Her mother said:

'There isn't any practical way out?' She pondered for a long time. 'I take it you have thought it all out. I know you have a good head and you are good.' A rustling sound. 'But I am not level with these times. I should be glad if there were a way out. I should be glad if you could wait for each other. Or perhaps find a legal . . . '

Valentine said:

'Oh, mother, don't cry!' . . . 'Oh, mother, I can't . . . ' . . . 'Oh, I will come . . . Mother, I will come back to you if you order it.' With each phrase her body was thrown about as if by a wave. She thought they only did that on the stage. Her eyes said to her:

... 'Dear sir,

'*Our Client, Mrs. Christopher Tietjens of Groby-in-Cleveland* ... '

They said:

'*After the occurrence at the Base-Camp at* ... '

They said:

'*Thinks it useless* ... '

She was agonised for her mother's voice. The telephone hummed in E-flat. It tried B. Then it went back to E-flat. Her eyes said:

'*Proposes when occasion offers to remove to Groby* ... ' in fat, blue typescript. She cried agonisedly:

'Mother. Order me to come back or it will be too late ... '

She had looked down, unthinkingly ... as one does when standing at the telephone. If she looked down again and read to the end of the sentence that contained the words 'It is useless,' it would be too late! She would know that his wife had given him up!

Her mother's voice came, turned by the means of its conveyance into the voice of a machine of Destiny.

'No I can't. I am thinking.'

Valentine placed her foot on the dais at which she stood. When she looked down it covered the letter. She thanked God. Her mother's voice said:

'I cannot order you to come back if it would kill you not to be with him.' Valentine could feel her late-Victorian advanced mind, desperately seeking for the right plea — for any plea that would let her do without seeming to employ maternal authority. She began to talk like a book, an august Victorian book; Morley's *Life of Gladstone*. That was reasonable: she wrote books like that.

She said they were both good creatures of good stock. If their consciences let them commit themselves to a certain course of action they were probably in the right. But she begged them, in God's name to assure themselves that their consciences *did* urge that course. She *had* to talk like a book!

Valentine said:

'It is nothing to do with conscience.' That seemed harsh. Her mind was troubled with a quotation. She could not find it. Quotations ease strain; she said: 'One is urged by blind destiny!' A Greek quotation, then! 'Like a victim upon an altar. I am afraid; but I consent!' . . . Probably Euripides; the *Alcestis* very likely! If it had been a Latin author the phrases would have occurred to her in Latin. Being with her mother made her talk like a book. Her mother talked like a book: then *she* did. They *must*; if they did not they would scream . . . But they were English ladies. Of scholarly habits of mind. It was horrible. Her mother said:

'That is probably the same as conscience — race conscience!' She could not urge on them the folly and disastrousness of the course they appeared to propose. She had, she said, known too many irregular unions that had been worthy of emulation and too many regular ones that were miserable and a cause of demoralisation by their examples . . . She was a gallant soul. She could not in conscience go back on the teachings of her whole life. She wanted to. Desperately! Valentine could feel the almost physical strainings of her poor, tired brain. But she could not recant. She was not Cranmer! She was not even Joan of Arc. So she went on repeating:

'I can only beg and pray you to assure yourself that not to live with that man will cause you to die or to be seriously mentally injured. If you think you can live without him or wait for him, if you think there is any hope of later union without serious mental injury I beg and pray . . . '

She could not finish the sentence . . . It was fine to behave with dignity at the crucial moment of your life! It was fitting, it was proper. It justified your former philosophic life. And it was cunning. Cunning!

For now she said:

'My child! my little child! You have sacrificed all your life to me and my teaching. How can I ask you now to deprive yourself of the benefit of them?'

She said:

'I *can't* persuade you to a course that might mean your eternal unhappiness!' . . . The *can't* was like a flame of agony!

Valentine shivered. That was cruel pressure. Her mother was no doubt doing her duty; but it was cruel pressure. It was very cold. November is a cold month. There were footsteps on the stairs. She shook.

'Oh, he is coming. He is coming!' she cried out. She wanted to say: 'Save me!' She said: 'Don't go away! Don't . . . Don't go away!' What do men do to you, men you love? Mad men. He was carrying a sack. The sack was the first she saw as he opened the door. Pushed it open; it was already half-open. A sack was a dreadful thing for a madman to carry. In an empty house. He dumped the sack down on the hearthstone. He had coal-dust on his right forehead. It was a heavy sack. Bluebeard would have had in it the corpse of his first wife. Borrow says that the gipsies say: 'Never trust a young man with grey hair!' He had only half-grey hair and he was only half young. He was panting. He must be stopped carrying heavy sacks. Panting like a fish. A great motionless carp, hung in a tank.

He said:

'I suppose you would want to go out. If you don't we will have a fire. You can't stop here without a fire.'

At the same moment her mother said:

'If that is Christopher I will speak to him.'

She said away from the mouthpiece:

'Yes, let's go out. Oh, oh, oh. Let's go out . . . Armistice . . . My mother wants to speak to you.' She felt herself to be suddenly a little Cockney shop-girl. A midinette in an imitation Girl Guide's uniform. 'Afride of the gentleman, my dear.' Surely one could protect oneself against a great carp! She could throw him over her shoulder. She had enough Ju Jitsu for that. Of course a little person trained to Ju Jitsu can't overcome an untrained giant if he expects it. But if he doesn't expect it she can.

His right hand closed over her left wrist. He had swum towards her and had taken the telephone in his left. One of the window-panes was so old it was bulging and purplish. There was another. There were several. But the first one was the purplishest. He said:

'Christopher Tietjens speaking!' He could not think of anything more recherché to say than that — the great inarticulate fellow! His hand was cool on her wrist. She was calm, but streaming with bliss. There was no other word for it. As if you had come out of a bath of warm nectar and bliss streamed off you. His touch had calmed her and covered her with bliss.

He let her wrist go very slowly. To show that the grasp was meant for a caress! It was their first caress!

Before she had surrendered the telephone she had said to her mother:

'He doesn't know . . . Oh, realise that he doesn't know!'

She went to the other end of the room and stood watching him.

He heard the telephone from its black depths say:

'How are you, my dear boy? My dear, dear boy; you're safe for good.' It gave him a disagreeable feeling. This was the mother of the young girl he intended to seduce. He intended to. He said:

'I'm pretty well. Weakish. I've just come out of hospital. Four days ago.' He was never going back to that bloody show. He had his application for demobilisation in his pocket. The voice said:

'Valentine thinks you are very ill. Very ill, indeed. She came to you because she thinks that.' She hadn't come, then, because . . . But, of course, she would not have. But she might have wanted them to spend Armistice Day together! She might have! A sense of disappointment went over him. Discouragement. He was very raw. That old devil, Campion! Still, one ought not to be as raw as that. He was saying, deferentially:

'Oh, it was mental rather than physical. Though I had pneumonia all right.' He went on saying that General Campion had put him in command over the escorts of German prisoners all through the lines of several armies. That really nearly had driven him mad. He couldn't bear being a beastly gaoler.

Still — Still! — he saw those grey spectral shapes that had surrounded and interpenetrated all his later days. The image came over him with the mood of repulsion at odd moments — at the very oddest; without suggestion there floated before his eyes the image, the landscape of greyish forms. In thousands, seated on upturned buckets, with tins of fat from which they ate at their sides on the ground, holding up newspapers that were not really newspapers; on grey days. They were all round him. And he was their gaoler. He said: 'A filthy job!'

Mrs. Wannop's voice said:

'Still, it's kept you alive for us!'

He said:

'I sometimes wish it hadn't!' He was astonished that he had said it; he was astonished at the bitterness of his voice. He added: 'I don't mean that in cold blood of course,' and he was again astonished at the deference in his voice. He was leaning down, positively, as if over a very distinguished, elderly, seated lady. He straightened himself. It struck him as distasteful hypocrisy to bow before an elderly lady when you entertained designs upon her daughter. Her voice said:

'My dear boy . . . my dear, almost son . . . '

Panic overcame him. There was no mistaking those tones. He looked round at Valentine. She had her hands together as if she were wringing them. She said, exploring his face painfully with her eyes:

'Oh, be kind to her. Be kind to her . . . '

Then there had been revelation of their . . . you couldn't call it intimacy!

He never liked her Girl Guides' uniform. He liked her best in a white sweater and a fawn-coloured short skirt. She had taken off her hat — her cowboyish hat. She had had her hair cut. Her fair hair.

Mrs. Wannop said:

'I've got to think that you have saved us.

311

To-day I have to think that you have saved us . . . And of all you have suffered.' Her voice was melancholy, slow, and lofty.

Intense, hollow reverberations filled the house. He said:

'That's nothing. That's over. You don't have to think of it.'

The reverberations apparently reached her ear. She said:

'I can't hear you. There seems to be thunder.'

External silence came back. He said:

'I was telling you not to think of my sufferings.'

She said:

'Can't you wait? You and she? Is there no . . . ' The reverberations began again. When he could again hear she was saying:

' . . . Has had to contemplate such contingencies arising for one's child. It is useless to contend with the tendency of one's age. But I had hoped . . . '

The knocker below gave three isolated raps, but the echoes prolonged them. He said to Valentine:

'That's the knocking of a drunken man. But then half the population might well be drunk. If they knock again, go down and send them away.'

She said:

'I'll go in any case before they can knock again.'

* * *

She heard him say as she left the room — she could not help waiting for the end of the sentence; she *must* gather all that she could as to that agonising interview between her mother and her lover. Equally, she must go or she would go mad. It was no good saying that her head was screwed on straight. It wasn't. It was as if it contained two balls of string with two ends. On the one her mother pulled, on the other, he . . . She heard him say:

'I don't know. One has desperate need. Of talk. I have not really spoken to a soul for two years!' Oh, blessed, adorable man! She heard him going on, getting into a stride of talk:

'It's that that's desperate. I'll tell you. I'll give you an instance. I was carrying a boy. Under rifle-fire. His eye got knocked out. If I had left him where he was his eye would not have been knocked out. I thought at the time that he might have been drowned, but I ascertained afterwards that the water never rose high enough. So I am responsible for the loss of his eye. It's a sort of monomania. You see, I am talking of it now. It recurs. Continuously. And to have to bear it in

313

complete solitude . . . '

She was not frightened going now down the great stairs. They whispered, but she was like a calm Fatima. *He* was Sister Anne, and a brother, too. The enemy was fear. She must not fear. He rescued her from fear. It is to a woman that you must come for refuge from regrets about a boy's eyes.

Her physical interior turned within her. He had been under fire! He might never have been there, a grey badger, a tender, tender grey badger leaning down and holding a telephone. Explaining things with tender care. It was lovely how he spoke to her mother; it was lovely that they were all three together. But her mother would keep them apart. She was taking the only way to keep them apart if she was talking to him as she had talked to her.

There was no knowing. She had heard him say:

He was pretty well . . . 'Thank God!' . . . Weakish . . . 'Ah, give *me* the chance to cherish him!' He had just come out of hospital. Four days ago. He had had pneumonia all right, but it had been mental rather than physical . . .

Ah, the dreadful thing about the whole war was that it had been — the suffering had been — mental rather than physical. And they had not thought of it . . . He had been under fire. She had pictured him always as being in a Base, thinking. If he had been killed it would not have been so dreadful for him. But now he had come back with his obsessions and mental troubles . . . And he needed his woman. And her mother was forcing him to abstain from his woman! That was what was terrible. He had suffered mental torture and now his pity was being worked on to make him abstain from the woman that could atone.

Hitherto, she had thought of the War as physical suffering only; now she saw it only as mental torture. Immense miles and miles of anguish in darkened minds. That remained. Men might stand up on hills, but the mental torture could not be expelled.

She ran suddenly down the steps that remained to her and was fumbling at the bolts of the front door. She was not skilful at that. She was thinking about the conversation that dreadfully she felt to be continuing. She must stop the knocking. The knocker had stayed for just long enough for the abstention of an impatient man knocking on a great door. Her mother was too cunning for them. With the cunning that makes the mother wild-duck tumble apparently broken-winged just under your feet to decoy you away from her little things. STORGE, Gilbert White calls it! For, of course, she could never have his lips upon hers when she thought of that crafty, beloved, grey Eminence sitting at home and shuddering . . . But she *would*!

She found the gadget that opened the door — the third she had tried amongst incomprehensible, painted century-old fixings. The door came open exactly upon a frustrated sound. A man was being propelled towards her by the knocker to which he held . . . She had saved *his* thoughts. Without the interruption of the knocker he might be able to see that mother's device was just cunning. They were cunning, the great Victorians . . . Oh, poor mother!

A horrible man in uniform looked at her hatefully, with piercing, hollow, black eyes in a fallen-away face. He said:

'I must see that fellow Tietjens; you're not Tietjens!' As if she were defrauding him. 'It's urgent,' he said. 'About a sonnet. I was dismissed the Army yesterday. *His* doing. And Campion's. His wife's lover!'

She said fiercely:

'He's engaged. You can't see him. If you want to see him you must wait!' She felt horror that Tietjens should ever have had to do with such a brute beast. He was unshaven;

black. And filled with hatred. He raised his voice to say:

'I'm McKechnie. Captain McKechnie of the Ninth. Vice-Chancellor's Latin Prizeman! One of the Old Pals!' He added: 'Tietjens forced himself in on the Old Pals!'

She felt the contempt of the scholar's daughter for the Prize-man; she felt that Apollo with Admetus was as nothing for sheer disgust compared with Tietjens buried in a band of such beings.

She said:

'It is not necessary to shout. You can come in and wait.'

At all costs Tietjens must finish his conversation with her mother undisturbed. She led this fellow round the corner of the hall. A sort of wireless emanation seemed to connect her with the upper conversation. She was aware of it going on, through the wall above, diagonally; then through the ceiling in perpendicular waves. It seemed to work inside her head, her end of it, like waves, churning her mind.

She opened the shutters of the empty room round the corner, on the right. She did not wish to be alone in the dark with this hating man. She did not dare to go up and warn Tietjens. At all costs he must not be disturbed. It was not fair to call what her mother was doing, cunning. It was instinct, set in her breast by the Almighty, as the saying is . . . Still, it was Early Victorian instinct! Tremendously cunning in itself.

The hateful man was grumbling:

'He's been sold up, I see. That's what comes of selling your wife to Generals. To get promotion. They're a cunning lot. But he overreached himself. Campion went back on him. But Campion, too, overreached *himself* . . . '

She was looking out of the window, across the green square. Light was an agreeable thing. You could breathe more deeply when it was light . . . Early Victorian instinct! . . . The Mid-Victorians had had to loosen the bonds. Her mother, to be in the van of Mid-Victorian thought, had had to allow virtue to 'irregular unions.' As long as they were high-minded. But the high-minded do not consummate irregular unions. So all her books had showed you high-minded creatures contracting irregular unions of the mind or of sympathy; but never carrying them to the necessary conclusion. They would have been ethically at liberty to, but they didn't. They ran with the ethical hare, but hunted with the ecclesiastical hounds . . . Still, of course, she could not go back on her premises just because it was her own daughter!

She said:

'I beg your pardon!' to that fellow. He had been saying:

'They're too damn cunning. They over-reach themselves!' Her mind spun. She did not know what he had been talking about. Her mind retained his words, but she did not understand what they meant. She had been sunk in the contemplation of Early Victorian Thought. She remembered the long — call it 'liaison' of Edith Ethel Duchemin and little Vincent Macmaster. Edith Ethel, swathed in opaque crêpe, creeping widow-like along the very palings she could see across the square, to her high-minded adulteries, amidst the whispered applause of Mid-Victorian England. So circumspect and right! . . . She had her thoughts to keep, all right. Well under control! . . . Well, she had been patient.

The man said agonisedly:

'My filthy, bloody, swinish uncle, Vincent Macmaster. *Sir* Vincent Macmaster! And this fellow Tietjens. All in a league against me . . . Campion too . . . But he overreached himself . . . A man got into Tietjens' wife's bedroom. At the Base. And Campion sent him to the front. To get him killed. Her other lover, you see?'

She listened. She listened with all her attention straining. She wanted to be able to

319

. . . She did not know what she wanted to be able to do! The man said:

'Major-General Lord Edward Campion, V.C., K.C.M.G., tantivy turn, turn, etcetera. Too cunning. Too b—y cunning by half. Sent Tietjens to the front too to get him killed. Me too. We all three went up to Division in a box-car — Tietjens, his wife's lover, and me. Tietjens confessed that bleedin' swab. Like a beastly monk. Told him that when you die — *in articulo mortis*, but you won't understand what that means! — your faculties are so numbed that you feel neither pain nor fear. He said death was no more than an anæsthetic. And that trembling, whining pup drank it in . . . I can see them now. In a box-car. In a cutting.'

She said:

'You've had shell-shock? You've got shell-shock now!'

He said, like a badger snapping:

'I haven't. I've got a bad wife. Like Tietjens. At least she isn't a bad wife. She's a woman with appetites. She satisfies her appetites. That's why they're hoofing me out of the Army. But at least, I don't sell her to Generals. To Major-General Lord Edward Campion, VC., K.C.M.G., etc. I got divorce leave and didn't divorce her. Then I got second divorce leave. And didn't divorce her.

It's against my principles. She lives with a British Museum Palæontologist and he'd lose his job. I owe that fellow Tietjens a hundred and seventy quid. Over my second divorce leave. I can't pay him. I didn't divorce, but I've spent the money. Going about with my wife and her friend. On principle!'

He spoke so inexhaustibly and fast, and his topics changed so quickly that she could do no more than let the words go into her ears. She listened to the words and stored them up. One main line of topic held her; otherwise she could not think. She only let her eyes run over the friezes of the opposite houses. She gathered that Tietjens had been unjustly dismissed by Campion, whilst saving two lives under fire. McKechnie grudgingly admitted heroism to Tietjens, in order to blacken the General. The General wanted Sylvia Tietjens. So as to get her he had sent Tietjens into the hottest part of the line. But Tietjens had refused to get killed. He had a charmed life. That was Provvy spiting the General. All the same, Providence could not like Tietjens, a cully who comforted his wife's lover. A dirty thing to do. When Tietjens would not be killed the General came down into the Line and *strafed* him to Hell. Didn't she, Valentine, understand why? He wanted Tietjens cashiered so that he, Campion,

321

might be less disgustingly disgraced for taking up with the wife. But he had overreached himself. You can't be cashiered for not being on the spot to lick a General's boots when you are saving life under rifle-fire. So the General had to withdraw his words and find Tietjens a dirty scavenger's job. Made a bleedin' gaoler of him!

She was standing in the doorway so that this fellow should not run upstairs to where the conversation was going on. The windows consoled her. She only gathered that Tietjens had had great mental trouble. He must have. She knew nothing of either Sylvia Tietjens or the General except for their beautiful looks. But Tietjens must have had great mental trouble. Dreadful!

It was hateful. How could she stand it! But she must, to keep this fellow from Tietjens, who was talking to her mother.

And . . . if his wife was a bad wife, didn't it . . .

The windows were consoling. A little dark boy of an officer passed the railings of the house, looking up at the windows.

McKechnie had talked himself hoarse. He was coughing. He began to complain that his uncle, Sir Vincent Macmaster, had refused him an introduction to the Foreign Office. He had made a scene at the Macmasters' already

322

that morning. Lady Macmaster — a haggard wanton, if there ever was one — had refused him access to his uncle, who was suffering from nervous collapse. He said suddenly:

'Now about this sonnet: I'm at least going to show this fellow . . . ' Two more officers, one short, the other tall, passed the window. They were laughing and calling out. ' . . . that I'm a better Latinist than he . . . '

She sprang into the hall. Thunder again had come from the door.

In the light outside a little officer with his half profile towards her seemed to be listening. Beside him was a thin lady, very tall. At the bottom of the steps were the two laughing officers. The boy, his eye turned towards her, with a shrinking timidity you would have said, exclaimed in a soft voice:

'We've come for Major Tietjens . . . This is Nancy. Of Bailleul, you know!' He had turned his face still more towards the lady. She was unreasonably thin and tall, the face of her skin drawn. She was much the older. Much. And hostile. She must have put on a good deal of colour. Purplish. Dressed in black. She ducked a little.

Valentine said:

'I'm afraid . . . He's engaged . . . '

The boy said:

'Oh, but he'll see us. This is Nancy, you know!'

One of the officers said:

'We said we'd look old Tietjens up . . . ' He had only one arm. She was losing her head. The boy had a blue band round his hat. She said:

'But he's dreadfully urgently engaged . . . '

The boy turned his face full on her with a gesture of entreaty.

'Oh, but . . . ' he said. She nearly fell, stepping back. His eye-socket contained nothing; a disorderly reddish scar. It made him appear to be peering blindly; the absence of the one eye blotted out the existence of the other. He said in Oriental pleading tones:

'The Major saved my life; I must see him!' The sleeveless officer called out:

'We said we'd look old Tietjens up . . . IT's armi . . . hick . . . At Rouen in the pub . . . ' The boy continued:

'I'm Aranjuez, you know! Aranjuez . . . ' They had only been married last week. He was going to the Indian Army to-morrow. They *must* spend Armistice Day with the Major. Nothing would be anything without the Major. They had a table at the Holborn.

The third officer — he was a very dark, silky-voiced, young Major — crept slowly up the steps, leaning on a stick, his dark eyes on her face.

'It *is* an engagement, you know!' he said. He had a voice like silk and bold eyes. 'We really did make an engagement to come to Tietjens' house to-day . . . Whenever it happened . . . a lot of us. In Rouen. Those who were in Number Two.'

Aranjuez said:

'The C.O.'s to be there. He's dying, you know. And it would be nothing without the Major . . . '

She turned her back on him. She was crying because of the pleading tones of his voice and his small hands. Tietjens was coming down the stairs, mooning slowly.

2

Standing at the telephone, Tietjens had recognised at once that this was a mother, pleading with infinite statesmanship for her daughter. There was no doubt about that. How could he continue to . . . to entertain designs on the daughter of this voice? . . . But he *did*. He couldn't. He did. He *couldn't*. He did . . . You may expel Nature by pleading . . . *tamen usque recur* . . . . She must recline in his arms before midnight. Having cut her hair had made her face look longer. Infinitely attracting. Less downright: with a refinement. Melancholy! Longing! One must comfort.

There was nothing to answer to the mother on sentimental lines. He wanted Valentine Wannop enough to take her away. That was the overwhelming answer to Mrs. Wannop's sophistications of the advanced writer of a past generation. It answered her then; still more it answered her now, to-day, when a man could stand up. Still, he could not overwhelm an elderly, distinguished, and inaccurate lady! It is not done.

He took refuge in the recital of facts. Mrs. Wannop, weakening her ground, asked:

'*Isn't* there any legal way out? Miss Wanostrocht tells me your wife . . . '

Tietjens answered:

'I can't divorce my wife. She's the mother of my child. I can't live with her, but I can't divorce her.'

Mrs. Wannop took it lying down again, resuming her proper line. She said that he knew the circumstances and that if his conscience . . . And so on and so on. She believed, however, in arranging things quietly if it could be done. He was looking down mechanically, listening. He read that our client Mrs. Tietjens of Groby-in-Cleveland requests us to inform you that after the late occurrences at a Base Camp in France she thinks it useless that you and she should contemplate a common life for the future . . . He had contemplated that set of facts enough already. Campion during his leave had taken up his quarters at Groby. He did not suppose that Sylvia had become his mistress. It was improbable in the extreme. Unthinkable! He had gone to Groby with Tietjens' sanction in order to sound his prospects as candidate for the Division. That is to say that, ten months ago, Tietjens had told the General that he might make Groby his headquarters as it had been for years. But, in that communication trench he had not told Tietjens that he had been at Groby. He had said 'London,' specifically.

That *might* be an adulterer's guilty conscience but it was more likely that he did not want Tietjens to know that he had been under Sylvia's influence. He had gone for Tietjens bald-headed, beyond all reason for a Commander-in-Chief speaking to a Battalion Commander. Of course he might have the wind up at being in the trenches and being kept waiting so near the area of a real *strafe* as he might well have taken that artillery lark to be. He might have let fly just to relieve his nerves. But it was more likely that Sylvia had bewildered his old brains into thinking that he, Tietjens, was such a villain that he ought not to be allowed to defile the face of the earth. Still less a trench under General Campion's control.

Campion had afterwards taken back his words very handsomely — with a sort of distant and lofty deprecation. He had even said that Tietjens had deserved a decoration, but that there were only a certain number of decorations now to be given and that he imagined that Tietjens would prefer it to be given to a man to whom it would be of more advantage. And he did not like to recommend for decoration an officer so closely connected with himself. He said this before members of his staff . . . Levin and some others. And he went on rather pompously, that he was going to employ Tietjens on a very responsible and delicate duty. He had been asked by H.M. Government to put the charge over all enemy prisoners between Army H.Q. and the sea in charge of an officer of an exceptionally trustworthy nature, of high social position and weight; in view of the enemy's complaints to The Hague of ill-treatment of prisoners.

So Tietjens had lost all chance of distinction, command pay, cheerfulness, or even equanimity. And all tangible proof that he had saved life under fire — if the clumsy mud-bath of his incompetence could be called saving life under fire. He could go on being discredited by Sylvia till kingdom come, with nothing to show on the other side but the uncreditable fact that he had been a gaoler. Clever old General! Admirable old godfather-in-law!

Tietjens astonished himself by saying to himself that if he had had any proof that Campion had committed adultery with Sylvia he would kill him! Call him out and kill him . . . That of course was absurd. You do not kill a General Officer commanding in chief an Army. And a good General, too. His reorganisation of that Army had been everything that was shipshape and soldierly;

his handling it in the subsequent fighting had been impeccably admirable. It was in fact the apotheosis of the Regular Soldier. That alone was a benefit to have conferred on the country. He had also contributed by his political action to forcing the single command on the Government. When he had gone to Groby he had let it be quite widely known that he was prepared to fight that Division of Cleveland on the political issue of single command or no single command — and to fight it in his absence in France. Sylvia no doubt would have run the campaign for him!

Well, that, and the arrival of the American troops in large quantities, had no doubt forced the hand of Downing Street. There could no longer have been any question of evacuating the Western Front. Those swine in their corridors were scotched. Campion was a good man. He was good — impeccable! — in his profession; he had deserved well of his country. Yet, if Tietjens had had proof that he had committed adultery with his, Tietjens', wife he would call him out. Quite properly. In the eighteenth-century traditions for soldiers. The old fellow could not refuse. He was of eighteenth-century traditions, too.

Mrs. Wannop was informing him that she had had the news of Valentine's having gone to him from a Miss Wanostrocht. She had she said, at first agreed that it was proper that Valentine should look after him if he were mad and destitute. But this Miss Wanostrocht had gone on to say that she had heard from Lady Macmaster that Tietjens and her daughter had had a liaison lasting for years. And . . . Mrs. Wannop's voice hesitated . . . Valentine seemed to have announced to Miss Wanostrocht that she intended to live with Tietjens. 'Maritally,' Miss Wanostrocht had expressed it.

It was the last word alone of Mrs. Wannop's talk that came home to him. People would talk. About him. It was his fate. And hers. Their identities interested Mrs. Wannop, as novelist. Novelists live on gossip. But it was all one to him.

The word 'Maritally!' burst out of the telephone like a blue light! That girl with the refined face, the hair cut longish, but revealing its thinner refinement . . . That girl longed for him as he for her! The longing had refined her face. He must comfort . . .

He was aware that for a long time, from below his feet a voice had been murmuring on and on. Always one voice. Who could Valentine find to talk to or to listen to for so long? Old Macmaster was almost the only name that came to his mind. Macmaster would not harm her. He felt her being united

331

to his by a current. He had always felt that her being was united to his by a current. This then was the day!

The war had made a man of him! It had coarsened him and hardened him. There was no other way to look at it. It had made him reach a point at which he would no longer stand unbearable things. At any rate from his equals! He counted Campion as his equal; few other people, of course. And what he wanted he was prepared to take . . . What he had been before, God alone knew. A Younger Son? A Perpetual Second-in-Command? Who knew. But to-day the world changed. Feudalism was finished; its last vestiges were gone. It held no place for him. He was going — he was damn well going! — to make a place in it for . . . A man could now stand up on a hill, so he and she could surely get into some hole together!

He said:

'Oh, I'm not destitute, but I was penniless this morning. So I ran out and sold a cabinet to Sir John Robertson. The old fellow had offered me a hundred and forty pounds for it before the war. He would only pay forty to-day — because of the immorality of my character.' Sylvia had completely got hold of the old collector. He went on: 'The Armistice came too suddenly. I was determined to spend it with Valentine. I expected a cheque to-morrow. For some books I've sold. And Sir John was going down to the country. I had got into an old suit of *mufti* and I hadn't a civilian hat.' Reverberations came from the front door. He said earnestly:

'Mrs. Wannop . . . If Valentine and I can, we will . . . But to-day's to-day! . . . If we can't we can find a hole to get into . . . I've heard of an antiquity shop near Bath. No special regularity of life is demanded of old furniture dealers. We should be quite happy! I have also been recommended to apply for a vice-consulate. In Toulon, I believe. I'm quite capable of taking a practical hold of life!'

All the Government Departments, staffed of course by non-combatants, were aching to transfer those who had served to any other old Department. The Department of Statistics would transfer him . . .

A great many voices came from below stairs. He could not leave Valentine to battle with a great number of voices. He said:

'I've got to go!' Mrs. Wannop's voice answered:

'Yes; do. I'm very tired.'

★ ★ ★

He came mooning slowly down the stairs. He smiled. He exclaimed:

'Come up, you fellows. There's some hooch for you!' He had a royal aspect. An all-powerfulness. They pushed past her and then past him on the stairs. They all ran up the stairs, even the man with the stick. The armless man shook hands with his left hand as he ran. They exclaimed enthusiasms . . . On all celebrations it is proper for His Majesty's officers to exclaim and to run upstairs when whiskey is mentioned. How much the more so to-day!

They were alone now in the hall, he on a level with her. He looked into her eyes. He smiled. He had never smiled at her before. They had always been such serious people. He said:

'We shall have to celebrate! But I'm not mad. I'm not destitute!' He had run out to get money to celebrate with her. He had meant to go and fetch her. To celebrate that day together.

She wanted to say: 'I am falling at your feet. My arms are embracing your knees!'

Actually she said:

'I suppose it is proper to celebrate together to-day!'

Her mother had made their union. For they looked at each other for a long time.

What had happened to their eyes? It was as if they had been bathed in soothing fluid: they could look the one at the other. It was no longer the one looking and the other averting the eyes, in alternation. Her mother had spoken between them. They might never have spoken of themselves! In one heart-beat a-piece whilst she had been speaking they had been made certain that their union had already lasted many years . . . It was warm; their hearts beat quietly. They had already lived side by side for many years. They were quiet in a cavern. The Pompeian red bowed over them; the stairways whispered up and up. They would be alone together now. For ever!

She knew that he desired to say 'I hold you in my arms. My lips are on your forehead. Your breasts are being hurt by my chest!'

He said:

'Who have you got in the dining-room? It used to be the dining-room!'

Dreadful fear went through her. She said:

'A man called McKechnie. Don't go in!'

He went toward danger, mooning along. She would have caught at his sleeve, but Caesar's wife must be as brave as Cæsar. Nevertheless she slipped in first. She had slipped past him before at a hangingstile. A Kentish kissing gate. She said:

'Captain Tietjens is here!' She did not know whether he was a Captain or a Major. Some called him one, some another.

McKechnie looked merely grumbling: not homicidal. He grumbled:

'Look here, my bloody swine of an uncle, your pal, has had me dismissed from the army!'

Tietjens said:

'Chuck it. You know you've been demobilised to go to Asia Minor for the Government. Come and celebrate.' McKechnie had a dirty envelope. Tietjens said: 'Oh, yes. The sonnet. You can translate it under Valentine's inspection. She's the best Latinist in England!' He said: 'Captain McKechnie: Miss Wannop!'

McKechnie took her hand:

'It isn't fair. If you're such a damn good Latinist as that . . . ' he grumbled.

'You'll have to have a shave before you come with us!' Tietjens said.

They three went up the stairs together, but they two were alone. They were going on their honeymoon journey . . . The bride's going away! . . . She ought not to think such things. It was perhaps blasphemy. You go away in a neatly shining coupé with cockaded footmen!

He had re-arranged the room. He had positively re-arranged the room. He had removed the toilet-furnishings in green canvas: the camp-bed — three officers on it — was against the wall. That was his thoughtfulness. He did not want these people to have it suggested that she slept with him there . . . Why not? Aranjuez and the hostile thin lady sat on green canvas pillows on the dais. Bottles leaned against each other on the green canvas table. They all held glasses. They were in all five of H.M. Officers. Where had they come from? There were also three mahogany chairs with green rep, sprung seats. Fat seats. Glasses were on the mantelshelf. The thin, hostile lady held a glass of dark red in an unaccustomed manner.

They all stood up and shouted:

'McKechnie! Good old McKechnie!' 'Hurray McKechnie!' 'McKechnie!' opening their mouths to the full extent and shouting with all their lungs. You could see that!

A swift pang of jealousy went through her.

McKechnie turned his face away. He said:

'The Pals! The old pals!' He had tears in his eyes.

A shouting officer sprang from the camp-bed — her nuptial couch! Did she *like* to see three officers bouncing about on her nuptial couch? What an Alcestis! She sipped sweet port! It had been put into her hand by the soft, dark, armless major! — The shouting

337

officer slapped Tietjens violently on the back. The officer shouted:

'I've picked up a skirt . . . A proper little bit of fluff, sir!'

Her jealousy was assuaged. Her lids felt cold. They had been wet for an instant or so: the moisture had cooled! It's salt of course! . . . She belonged to this unit! She was attached to him . . . for rations and discipline. So she was attached to it. Oh, happy day! Happy, happy day! . . . There was a song with words like that. She had never expected to see it. She had never expected . . .

Little Aranjuez came up to her. His eyes were soft, like a deer's, his voice and little hands caressing . . . No he had only one eye! Oh dreadful! He said:

'You are the Major's dear friend . . . He made a sonnet in two and a half minutes!' He meant to say that Tietjens had saved his life.

She said:

'Isn't he wonderful!' Why?

He said:

'He can do anything! Anything! . . . He ought to have been . . . '

A gentlemanly officer with an eye-glass wandered in . . . Of course they had left the front door open. He said with an exquisite's voice:

'Hullo, Major! Hullo, Monty! . . . Hullo,

the Pals!' and strolled to the mantelpiece to take a glass. They all yelled, 'Hullo, Duck-foot ... Hullo, Brassface!' He took his glass delicately and said: 'Here's to hoping! ... The mess!'

Aranjuez said:

'Our only V.C ... ' Swift jealousy went through her.

Aranjuez said:

'*I* say ... that *he* ... ' Good boy! Dear boy! Dear little brother! ... Where was her own brother? Perhaps they were not going to be on terms any more! All around them the world was roaring. They were doing their best to make a little roaring unit there, the tide creeping into silent places!

The thin woman in black on the dais was looking at them. She drew her skirts together. Aranjuez had his little hands up as if he were going to lay them pleadingly on her breast. Why pleadingly? ... Begging her to forget his hideous eye-socket. He said:

'Wasn't it splendid ... wasn't it ripping of Nancy to marry me like this? ... We shall all be such friends.'

The thin woman caught her eye. She seemed more than ever to draw her skirts away though she never moved ... That was because she, Valentine, was Tietjens' mistress ... There's a picture in the National Gallery called *Titian's Mistress* . . . . She passed perhaps with them all for having . . . The woman smiled at her, a painfully forced smile. For Armistice . . . She, Valentine, was outside the pale. Except for holidays and days of National rejoicing . . .

She felt . . . nakedish, at her left side. Sure enough Tietjens was gone. He had taken McKechnie to shave. The man with the eyeglass looked critically round the shouting room. He fixed her and bore towards her. He stood over, his legs wide apart. He said:

'Hey! Hullo! Who'd have thought of seeing *you* here? Met you at the Prinseps'. Friend of friend Hun's, aren't you?' He said:

'Hullo, Aranjuez! Better?'

It was like a whale speaking to a shrimp: but still more like an uncle speaking to a favourite nephew! Aranjuez blushed with sheer pleasure. He faded away as if in awe before tremendous eminences. For him she too was an eminence. His life-hero's . . . woman!

The V.C. was in the mood to argue about politics. He always was. She had met him twice during evenings at friends' called Prinsep. She had not known him because of his eye-glasses; he must have put that up along with his ribbon. It took your breath away: like a drop of blood illuminated by a light that never was.

He said:

'They say you're receiving for Tietjens! Who'd have thought it? You're a pro-German — he's such a sound Tory. Squire of Groby and all, eh what?'

He said:

'Know Groby?' He squinted through his glasses round the room. 'Looks like a mess this . . . Only needs the *Vie Parisienne* and the *Pink Un* . . . Suppose he has moved his stuff to Groby. He'll be going to live at Groby, now. The war's over!'

He said:

'But you and old Tory Tietjens in the same room . . . By Jove the war's over . . . The lion lying down with the lamb's nothing . . . ' He exclaimed 'Oh damn! Oh, damn, damn, damn . . . I say . . . I didn't mean it . . . Don't cry. My dear little girl. My dear Miss Wannop. One of the best I always thought you. You don't suppose . . . '

She said:

'I'm crying because of Groby really . . . It's a day to cry on anyhow . . . You're quite a good sort, really!'

He said:

'Thank you! Thank you! Drink some more port! He's a good fat old beggar, old Tietjens. A good officer!' He added: 'Drink a *lot* more port!'

He had been the most asinine, creaking, 'what about your king and country,' shocked, outraged and speechless creature of all the many who for years had objected to her objecting to men being unable to stand up . . . Now he was a rather kind brother!

They were all yelling.

'Good old Tietjens! Good old Fat Man! Pre-war hooch! He'd be the one to get it!' No one like Fat Man Tietjens. He lounged at the door; easy; benevolent. In uniform now. That was better. An officer, yelling like an enraged Redskin, dealt him an immense blow behind the shoulder blades. He staggered, smiling into the centre of the room. An officer gently pushed her into the centre of the room. She was against him. Khaki encircled them. They began to yell and to prance, most joining hands. Others waved the bottles and smashed underfoot the glasses. Gipsies break glasses at their weddings. The bed was against the wall. She did not like the bed to be against the wall. It had been brushed by . . .

They were going round them: yelling in unison:

'Over here! Pom Pom Over here! Pom
    Pom!
That's the word, that's the word; Over
    here . . . '

At least they weren't over there! They were prancing. The whole world round them was yelling and prancing round. They were the centre of unending roaring circles. The man with the eye-glass had stuck a half-crown in his other eye. He was well-meaning. A brother. She had a brother with the V.C. All in the family.

Tietjens was stretching out his two hands from the waist. It was incomprehensible. His right hand was behind her back, his left in her right hand. She was frightened. She was amazed. Did you ever! He was swaying slowly. The elephant! They were dancing! Aranjuez was hanging on to the tall woman like a kid on a telegraph pole. The officer who had said he had picked up a little bit of fluff . . . well, he had! He had run out and fetched it. It wore white cotton gloves and a flowered hat. It said: 'Ow! Now!' . . . There was a fellow with a most beautiful voice. He led: better than a gramophone. Better . . .

Les petites marionettes, font! font! font . . .

On an elephant. A dear, meal-sack elephant. She was setting out on . . .

We do hope that you have enjoyed reading this large print book.

Did you know that all of our titles are available for purchase?

We publish a wide range of high quality large print books including:
Romances, Mysteries, Classics
General Fiction
Non Fiction and Westerns

Special interest titles available in large print are:
The Little Oxford Dictionary
Music Book
Song Book
Hymn Book
Service Book

Also available from us courtesy of Oxford University Press:
Young Readers' Dictionary
(large print edition)
Young Readers' Thesaurus
(large print edition)

For further information or a free brochure, please contact us at:
Ulverscroft Large Print Books Ltd.,
The Green, Bradgate Road, Anstey,
Leicester, LE7 7FU, England.
Tel: (00 44) 0116 236 4325
Fax: (00 44) 0116 234 0205

Other titles published by
The House of Ulverscroft:

SOME DO NOT . . .

Ford Madox Ford

Christopher Tietjens, quietly preoccupied with his disastrous marriage to the beautiful, faithless Sylvia, takes a diverting golfing weekend in the country at the suggestion of his friend Macmaster. This is to change the course of the brilliant mathematician's life, for it is here he meets suffragette Valentine Wannop. Despite their mutual attraction and affection however, Tietjens refuses to betray Sylvia as she has betrayed him. With the coming of the War, the world of sureties and moral codes that Tietjens has known, believed in and upheld is shattered — as is he . . .

NO MORE PARADES

Ford Madox Ford

Captain Christopher Tietjens endures cold, mud and air-raids in a French base camp, preoccupied with his crumbling marriage, and battling not the German forces but the nightmare bureaucracy of the British Army. Abandoned — so he supposes — by the heartless Sylvia, he is bombarded by insistent thoughts of Valentine Wannop, though his sense of honour forbids him from furthering their association beyond anything but chaste friendship. Then all is altered by the sudden appearance of Sylvia in France, for her machinations will throw everything into chaos . . .